Also by Jeannette Walls

The Glass Castle

Half Broke Horses

The Silver Star

JEANNETTE WALLS

**SIMON &
SCHUSTER**

London · New York · Sydney · Toronto · New Delhi

A CBS COMPANY

First published in Great Britain by Simon & Schuster UK Ltd, 2013
This paperback edition first published by Simon & Schuster UK Ltd, 2014
A CBS COMPANY

Designed by Maura Fadden Rosenthal

1 3 5 7 9 10 8 6 4 2

Simon & Schuster UK Ltd
1st Floor
222 Gray's Inn Road
London
WC1X 8HB

www.simonandschuster.co.uk
www.simonandschuster.com.au

Simon & Schuster Australia, Sydney
Simon & Schuster India, New Delhi

A CIP catalogue record for this book
is available from the British Library

Paperback ISBN: 978-1-47112-909-4
Ebook ISBN: 978-1-47112-910-0

Printed and bound by CPI Group (UK) Ltd, Croydon, CR0 4YY

To John,
For helping me figure out Bean,
And for loving her

*The pure and simple truth
is rarely pure
and never simple.*

—Oscar Wilde

The Silver Star

CHAPTER ONE

My sister saved my life when I was just a baby. Here's what happened. After a fight with her family, Mom decided to leave home in the middle of the night, taking us with her. I was only a few months old, so Mom put me in the infant carrier. She set it on the roof of the car while she stashed some things in the trunk, then she settled Liz, who was three, in the backseat. Mom was going through a rough period at the time and had a lot on her mind—craziness, craziness, craziness, she'd say later. Completely forgetting that she'd left me on the roof, Mom drove off.

Liz started shrieking my name and pointing up. At first Mom didn't understand what Liz was saying, then she realized what she'd done and slammed on the brakes. The carrier slid forward onto the hood, but since I was strapped in, I was all right. In fact, I wasn't even crying. In the years afterward, whenever Mom told the story, which she found hilarious and acted out in dramatic detail, she liked to say thank goodness Liz had her wits about her, otherwise that carrier would have flown right off and I'd have been a goner.

Liz remembered the whole thing vividly, but she never thought it was funny. She had saved me. That was the kind of sister Liz was. And that was why, the night the whole mess started, I wasn't worried that Mom had been gone for four days. I was more worried about the chicken potpies.

I really hated it when the crust on our chicken potpies got burned, but the timer on the toaster oven was broken, and so that night I was staring into the oven's little glass window because, once those pies began turning brown, you had to watch them the entire time.

Liz was setting the table. Mom was off in Los Angeles, at some recording studio auditioning for a role as a backup singer.

"Do you think she'll get the job?" I asked Liz.

"I have no idea," Liz said.

"I do. I have a good feeling about this one."

Mom had been going into the city a lot ever since we had moved to Lost Lake, a little town in the Colorado Desert of Southern California. Usually she was gone for only a night or two, never this long. We didn't know exactly when she'd be back, and since the telephone had been turned off—Mom was arguing with the phone company about some long-distance calls she said she didn't make—she had no way of calling us.

Still, it didn't seem like a big deal. Mom's career had always taken up a sizeable chunk of her time. Even when we were younger, she'd have a sitter or a friend watch us while she flew off to some place like Nashville—so Liz and I were used to being on our own. Liz was in charge, since she was fifteen and I'd just turned twelve, but I wasn't the kind of kid who needed to be babied.

When Mom was away, all we ate were chicken potpies. I loved them and could eat them every night. Liz said that if you had a glass of milk with your chicken potpie, you were getting a dinner that included all four food groups—meat, vegetables, grain, and dairy—so it was the perfect diet.

Plus, they were fun to eat. You each got your very own pie in the nifty little tinfoil pie plate, and you could do whatever you wanted with it. I liked to break up the crust and mush it together with the bits of carrots and peas and the yellow gunk. Liz thought mushing it all together was uncouth. It also made the crust soggy, and what she found so appealing about chicken potpies was the contrast between the crispy crust and the goopy filling. She preferred to leave the crust intact, cutting dainty wedges with each bite.

Once the piecrusts had turned that wonderful golden brown, with the little ridged edges almost but not quite burned, I told Liz they were ready. She pulled them out of the toaster oven, and we sat down at the red Formica table.

At dinnertime, when Mom was away, we liked to play games Liz made up. One she called Chew-and-Spew, where you waited until the other person had a mouthful of food or milk, then you tried to make her laugh. Liz pretty much always won, because it was sort of easy to make me laugh. In fact, sometimes I laughed so hard the milk came shooting out of my nose.

Another game she made up was called the Lying Game. One person gave two statements, one true, the second a lie, and the other person got to ask five questions about the statements, then had to guess which one was the lie. Liz usually won the Lying Game, too, but as with Chew-and-Spew, it didn't matter who won. What was fun was playing the game. That night I was excited because I had what I thought was an unbelievable stumper: A frog's eyeballs go into its mouth when it's swallowing or a frog's blood is green.

"That's easy," Liz said. "Green blood is the lie."

"I can't believe you guessed it right away!"

"We dissected frogs in biology."

I was still talking about how hilarious and bizarre it was that a frog used its eyeballs to swallow when Mom walked through the door carrying a white box tied with red string. "Key lime pie for my girls!" she announced, holding up the box. Her face was glowing and she had a giddy smile. "It's a special occasion, because our lives are about to change."

As Mom cut the pie and passed the slices around, she told us that while she'd been at that recording studio, she'd met a man. He was a record producer named Mark Parker, and he'd told her that the reason she wasn't landing gigs as a backup singer was that her voice was too distinctive and she was upstaging the lead singers.

"Mark said I wasn't cut out to play second fiddle to anyone," Mom explained. He told her she had star quality, and that night he took her out to dinner and they talked about how to jump-start her career. "He's so smart and funny," Mom said. "You girls will adore him."

"Is he serious, or is he just a tire-kicker?" I asked.

"Watch it, Bean," Mom said.

Bean's not my real name, of course, but that's what everyone calls me. Bean.

It wasn't my idea. When I was born, Mom named me Jean, but the first time Liz laid eyes on me, she called me Jean the Bean because I was teeny like a bean and because it rhymed—Liz was always rhyming—and then simply Bean because it was shorter. But sometimes she would go and make it longer, calling me the Beaner or Bean Head, maybe Clean Bean when I'd taken a bath, Lean Bean because I was so skinny, Queen Bean just to make me feel good, or Mean Bean if I was in a bad mood. Once, when I got food poisoning after eating a bowl of bad chili, she called me Green Bean, and then later, when I was hugging the toilet and feeling even worse, she called me Greener Beaner.

Liz couldn't resist playing with words. That was why she loved the name of our new town, Lost Lake. "Let's go look for it," she'd say, or "I wonder who lost it," or "Maybe the lake should ask for directions."

We'd moved to Lost Lake from Pasadena four months ago, on New Year's Day of 1970, because Mom said a change of scenery would give us a fresh start for the new decade. Lost Lake was a pretty neat place, in my opinion. Most of the people who lived there were Mexicans who kept chickens and goats in their yards, which was where they practically lived themselves, cooking on grills and dancing to the Mexican music that blared from their radios. Dogs and cats roamed the dusty streets, and irrigation canals at the edge of town carried water to the crop fields. No one looked sideways at you if you wore your big sister's hand-me-downs or your mom drove an old brown Dart. Our neighbors lived in little adobe houses, but we rented a cinder-block bungalow. It was Mom's idea to paint the cinder blocks turquoise blue and the door and windowsills tangerine orange. "Let's not even pretend we want to blend in," she said.

Mom was a singer, songwriter, and actress. She had never actually been in a movie or made a record, but she hated to be called "aspiring," and truth be told, she was a little older than the people described that way in the movie magazines she was always buying. Mom's thirty-sixth birthday was coming up, and she complained that the singers who were getting all the attention, like Janis Joplin and Joni Mitchell, were at least ten years younger than her.

Even so, Mom always said her big break was right around the corner. Sometimes she got callbacks after auditions, but she usually came home shaking her head and saying the guys at the studio were just tire-kickers who wanted a second look at her cleavage. So while Mom had her career, it wasn't one that produced much in the way of income—yet. Mostly we lived on Mom's inheritance. It hadn't been a ton of money to begin with, and by the time we moved to Lost Lake, we were on a fairly tight budget.

When Mom wasn't taking trips into L.A.—which were drain-
ing because the drive was nearly four hours in each direction—
she tended to sleep late and spend the day writing songs, playing
them on one of her four guitars. Her favorite, a 1961 Zemaitis,
cost about a year's rent. She also had a Gibson Southern Jumbo,
a honey-colored Martin, and a Spanish guitar made from Brazil-
ian rosewood. If she wasn't practicing her songs, she was working on a musical play based on her life, about breaking away from
her stifling Old South family, jettisoning her jerk of a husband and
string of deadbeat boyfriends—together with all the tire-kickers
who didn't reach the boyfriend stage—and discovering her true
voice in music. She called the play "Finding the Magic."

Mom always talked about how the secret to the creative process
was finding the magic. That, she said, was what you needed to do in
life as well. Find the magic. In musical harmony, in the rain on your
face and the sun on your bare shoulders, in the morning dew that
soaked your sneakers and the wildflowers you picked for free in the
roadside ditch, in love at first sight and those sad memories of the
one who got away. "Find the magic," Mom always said. "And if you
can't find the magic," she added, "then make the magic."

The three of us were magic, Mom liked to say. She assured us that
no matter how famous she became, nothing would ever be more
important to her than her two girls. We were a tribe of three, she
said. Three was a perfect number, she'd go on. Think of it. The holy
trinity, three musketeers, three kings of Orient, three little pigs, three
stooges, three blind mice, three wishes, three strikes, three cheers,
three's a charm. The three of us were all we needed, Mom said.

But that didn't keep her from going out on dates with tire-kickers.

CHAPTER TWO

Over the next few weeks, Mom kept talking about how Mark Parker had "discovered" her. She said it as a joke, but you could tell it actually had a sort of fairy-tale quality that appealed to her. It was a magic moment.

Mom began taking more trips into Los Angeles—sometimes for a day, sometimes for two or three—and when she came back, she was gushy with Mark Parker stories. He was an extraordinary guy, she said. He was working with her on the score for "Finding the Magic," tightening the lyrics, pushing her on the phrasing, and polishing the arrangement. Mark ghosted a lot of lyrics, she told us. One day she brought home an album and pulled out the liner notes. Mark had circled the lyrics of a love song and had scrawled next to them, "I wrote this about you before I met you."

Arrangement was Mark's specialty. On another day Mom brought back a second album, this one by the Tokens, with their hit recording of "The Lion Sleeps Tonight." Mark had done the arrangement for the song, she explained, which had been recorded a couple of times without taking off. At first the Tokens didn't want to do Mark's version, but he talked them into it and even sang some of the backup vocals. You could hear his baritone on the harmonies if you listened closely.

. . .

Mom was still pretty for a mom. She had been homecoming queen at her high school in Virginia, where she'd grown up, and you could see why. She had large hazel eyes and sun-streaked blond hair that she kept in a ponytail when she was at home but combed out and teased up when she went to Los Angeles. She'd put on a few pounds or so since her high school days, she admitted, but she said the weight gave her a little extra cleavage, and a singer could never have too much in that department. If nothing else, it got you callbacks.

Mark liked her curves, Mom told us, and after she began seeing him, she started looking and acting younger. Her eyes were animated when she came home, describing how Mark had taken her sailing or made her poached scallops, and how she had taught him to dance the Carolina shag. Mom's name was Charlotte, and Mark had invented a cocktail for her with peach schnapps, bourbon, grenadine, and Tab that he called the Shakin' Charlotte.

Not everything about Mark was perfect, however. He had a dark side, Mom explained. He was moody, like all true artists, but then so was she, and their collaboration had its share of stormy moments. Sometimes late at night Mom called Mark—she had paid up the disputed charges, so we had phone service again—and Liz and I could hear her yelling into the receiver, saying things like "That song needs to end on a chord, not a fade-out!" or "Mark, you expect too much of me!" These were creative differences, Mom said. Mark was ready to produce a demo tape of her best songs to play for the big labels, and it was natural for artistic types to have passionate disagreements as a deadline approached.

I kept asking Mom when Liz and I were going to meet Mark Parker. Mom said that Mark was very busy, always jetting off to New York or London, and didn't have the time to come all the way out to

Lost Lake. I suggested that we drive into Los Angeles some weekend to meet him, but Mom shook her head. "Bean, the truth of it is, he's jealous of you and Liz," she said. "He told me he thinks I talk about you girls too much. I'm afraid Mark can be a little possessive."

After Mom had been seeing Mark for a couple of months, she came home to tell us that, despite his hectic schedule and his possessiveness, Mark had agreed to come out to Lost Lake to meet Liz and me the following Wednesday after school. The three of us spent Tuesday evening furiously cleaning the bungalow, stuffing junk in the closet, scrubbing the rings of grime off the kitchen sink and the toilet, moving Mom's purple butterfly chair to cover the spot where she'd spilled tea on the rug, wiping around the doorknobs and the windowsills, untangling Mom's wind chimes, and scraping the odd dried bit of Chew-and-Spew from the floor. As we worked, we sang "The Lion Sleeps Tonight." We joined in on the lyrics together, "In the jungle, the mighty jungle . . ." Then Liz did the "o-wim-o-weh o-wim-o-weh o-wim-o-weh" chorus, Mom hit the "a-wooo-wooo-wooo" high notes, and I chimed in with the bass: "ee-dum-bum-buway."

The next day, as soon as school was out, I hurried back to the bungalow. I was in sixth grade, in the elementary school, and Liz was a freshman in the high school, so I always got home first. Mom had told us Mark drove a yellow Triumph TR3 with wire wheels but the only car parked in front of the bungalow that afternoon was our old brown Dart, and when I got inside, I found Mom sitting on the floor, surrounded by a mess of books, records, and sheet music that had been pulled from the shelves. She looked like she'd been crying.

"What happened?" I asked.

"He's gone," Mom said.

"But what happened?"

"We got into a fight. I told you he's moody." To lure Mark to Lost Lake, Mom explained, she had told him that Liz and I would be spending the night with friends. Once he'd arrived, she'd told him there had been a slight change of plans, and Liz and I were coming home after school. Mark exploded. He said he felt tricked and entrapped, and he stormed out.

"What a jerk," I said.

"He's not a jerk. He's passionate. He's Byronic. And he's obsessed with me."

"Then he'll be back."

"I don't know," Mom said. "It's pretty serious. He said he was leaving for his villa in Italy."

"Mark has a villa in Italy?"

"It's not really his. A movie-producer friend owns it, but he lets Mark use it."

"Wow," I said. Mom had always wanted to spend time in Italy, and here was a guy who could jet over there whenever he felt like it. Except for the fact that he didn't want to meet me and Liz, Mark Parker was everything Mom had ever wanted in a man. "I wish he liked us," I said, "because other than that, he's too good to be true."

"What's that supposed to mean?" Mom pulled up her shoulders and stared at me. "Do you think I'm making it all up?"

"Oh, not for a second," I said. "Making up a boyfriend would be just too kooky." But as soon as the words came out of my mouth, it occurred to me that Mom was, in fact, making it all up. My face suddenly felt hot, like I was seeing Mom naked. Mom and I were looking at each other, and I realized she could tell that I knew she had made it up.

"Screw you!" Mom shouted. She was on her feet and started yelling about everything she'd done for me and Liz, how hard she'd struggled, how much she'd sacrificed, what an ungrateful couple of parasites we were. I tried to calm Mom down, but that made her angrier. She never should have had kids, she went on, especially me. I was a mistake. She'd thrown away her life and her career for us, run through her inheritance for us, and we didn't even appreciate it.

"I can't stand being here!" she screamed. "I've got to get away."

I was wondering what I could say to smooth things over when Mom grabbed her big handbag off the couch and stormed out, slamming the door behind her. I heard her gun the Dart, then she drove away, and except for the gentle clinking of the wind chimes, the bungalow was silent.

I fed Fido, the little turtle Mom had bought me at Woolworth's when she wouldn't let me get a dog. Then I curled up in Mom's purple butterfly chair—the one she liked to sit in when she was writing music—staring out the picture window with my feet tucked up beside me, stroking Fido's little head with my forefinger and waiting for Liz to get home from school.

Truth be told, Mom had a temper and was given to her share of tantrums and meltdowns when things got overwhelming. The fits usually passed quickly, and then we all moved on as if nothing had happened. This one was different. Mom had said things that she'd never said before, like about me being a mistake. And the whole business about Mark Parker was epically weird. I needed Liz to help sort it all out.

Liz could make sense of anything. Her brain worked that way. Liz was talented and beautiful and funny and, most of all, incredibly smart. I'm not saying all that just because she was my sister. If you met her, you'd agree. She was tall and slender with pale skin and long, wavy reddish-gold hair. Mom was always calling her a pre-

Raphaelite beauty, which made Liz roll her eyes and say it was too bad she didn't live over one hundred years ago, in pre-Raphaelite days.

Liz was one of those people who always made grown-ups, particularly teachers, go slack-jawed and use words like "prodigy" and "precocious" and "gifted." Liz knew all these things that other people didn't know—like who the pre-Raphaelites were—because she was always reading, usually more than one book at a time. She also figured out a lot on her own. She could do complicated math calculations without pencil and paper. She could answer really tricky brainteaser-type riddles and loved saying words backward—like calling Mark Parker "Kram Rekrap." She loved anagrams, where you rearranged the letters of words to make different words, turning "deliver" into "reviled" and "funeral" into "real fun." And she loved spoonerisms, like when you mean to say "dear old queen" but instead say "queer old dean," or when "bad money" comes out as "mad bunny" and "smart feller" turns into "fart smeller." She was also a killer Scrabble player.

Liz's school let out only an hour after mine, but that afternoon it felt like forever. When she finally arrived at the bungalow, I didn't even let her set her books down before I started pouring out every detail of Mom's blowup.

"I just don't understand why she would make up all this Mark Parker stuff," I said.

Liz sighed. "Mom's always been a bit of a fibber," she said. Mom was all the time telling us things that Liz suspected weren't true, like how she used to go foxhunting with Jackie Kennedy in Virginia when they were both girls, or how she'd been the dancing banana in a cereal commercial. Mom had a red velvet jacket and liked to tell the story of how, when June Carter Cash had heard her play in a Nashville bar, she joined Mom onstage and they sang a duet together that brought the crowd to its feet. June Carter Cash had been wearing the red velvet jacket, and right there onstage she gave it to Mom.

"It didn't happen," Liz said. "I saw Mom buy that jacket at a church tag sale. She didn't know I was watching, and I never said anything." Liz looked out the window. "Mark Parker is just another dancing banana."

"I really blew it, didn't I?"

"Don't beat yourself up, Bean."

"I should have kept my big mouth shut. But I never really said anything, either."

"She knew you knew," Liz said, "and she couldn't handle it."

"Mom wasn't just making up a little story about some guy she met," I said. "There were the phone calls. And those liner notes."

"I know," Liz said. "It's kind of scary. I think she's gone through about all of her money, and it's giving her some sort of a nervous breakdown."

Liz said we should clean up the place so that when Mom came back, we could pretend the whole Mark Parker mess had never happened. We put the books back on the shelves, stacked the sheet music, and slid the records into their jackets. I came across the liner notes where Mark Parker had supposedly written to Mom: "I wrote this about you before I met you." It was flat-out creepy.

CHAPTER THREE

We expected Mom to come back that night or the next day, but by the weekend, we still hadn't heard from her. Whenever I started to fret, Liz told me not to worry, Mom always came back. Then we got the letter.

Liz read it first, then handed it to me and went to sit in the butterfly chair at the picture window.

My Darling Liz and Sweet Bean,

It's 3 a.m. and I'm writing from a hotel in San Diego. I know I have not been at the top of my game recently, and to finish my songs—and be the mother I want to be—I need to make some time and space for myself. I need to find the magic again. I also pray for balance.

You both should know that nothing in the world is more important to me than my girls and that we will be together again soon and life will be better than ever!

The $200 I'm sending will keep you in chicken potpies until I get back. Chins up and don't forget to floss!

Love,

Mom

I joined Liz at the window and she squeezed my hand.

"Is she coming back?" I asked.

"Of course," Liz said.

"But when? She didn't say when."

"I don't think she knows."

Two hundred dollars buys you a lot of chicken potpies. We got them at Spinelli's grocery, over on Balsam Street, an air-conditioned place with a wood floor and a big freezer in the back where the pies were stored. Mr. Spinelli, a dark-eyed man with hairy forearms who was always flirting with Mom, sometimes put them on sale. When he did, we could get eight for a dollar, and then we really stocked up.

We ate our pies in the evening at the red Formica table, but we didn't much feel like playing Chew-and-Spew—or the Lying Game— so after dinner, we just cleaned up, did our homework, and went to bed. We'd looked after ourselves before when Mom was away, but thinking she might be away for days and days somehow made us take our responsibilities more seriously. When Mom was home, she sometimes let us stay up late, but without her around, we always went to bed on time. Since she wasn't there to write excuses, we were never late to school and never skipped a day, which she sometimes let us do. We never left dirty dishes in the sink, and we flossed our teeth.

Liz had been doing some babysitting, but after Mom had been gone a week, she decided to take on extra work, and I got a job delivering *Grit*, a newspaper with useful stories about, say, keeping squirrels from eating the wires in your car's engine by putting mothballs in an old pair of panty hose and hanging them under the hood. For the time being, money wasn't a problem, and while the bills were piling up, Mom was always late paying them anyway. Still, we knew we couldn't live this way forever, and every day, turning down the block on the way home from school, I looked up the driveway, hoping to see the brown Dart parked beside the bungalow.

One day after Mom had been gone almost two weeks, I went to Spinelli's after school to stock up on chicken potpies. I thought I'd never get tired of chicken potpies, but I had to admit they were sort of wearing on me, particularly because we'd been eating them for breakfast, too. A couple of times, we bought beef potpies, but they were hardly ever on sale, and Liz said you needed a magnifying glass to see the meat.

Mr. Spinelli had a grill behind the counter where he made hamburgers and hot dogs, wrapping them in tinfoil and keeping them under the red warming light, which steamed the buns until they were nice and soggy. They sure smelled good, but they were beyond our budget. I loaded up on more chicken potpies.

"Haven't seen your mom in a while, Miss Bean," Mr. Spinelli said. "What's she been up to?"

I froze up, then said, "She broke her leg."

"That's a shame," he said. "Tell you what. Get yourself an ice-cream sandwich. On me."

That night Liz and I were doing our homework at the Formica table when there was a knock at the door. Liz opened it, and Mr. Spinelli stood outside, holding a brown paper bag with a loaf of bread sticking out the top.

"This is for your mother," he said. "I came to see how she's doing."

"She's not here," Liz said. "She's in Los Angeles."

"Bean said she broke her leg."

Liz and Mr. Spinelli looked over at me, and I started glancing around, avoiding their eyes, acting, I knew, about as guilty as the hound dog who stole the hambone.

"She broke her leg in Los Angeles," Liz said smoothly. She was always quick on her feet. "But it's not serious. A friend's bringing her back in a few days."

"Good," Mr. Spinelli said. "I'll come see her then." He held out the groceries to Liz. "Here, you take these."

"What are we going to do now?" I asked Liz once Mr. Spinelli had left.

"I'm thinking," Liz said.

"Is Mr. Spinelli going to send the bandersnatches after us?"

"He might."

"Bandersnatches" was the word Liz took from *Through the Looking Glass*—her favorite book—for the do-gooding government busybodies who snooped around making sure that kids had the sort of families the busybodies thought they should have. Last year in Pasadena, a few months before we moved to Lost Lake, a bandersnatch had come poking around when the school principal got the idea that Mom was negligent in her parenting after I told a teacher our electricity got turned off because Mom forgot to pay the bill. Mom hit the ceiling. She said the principal was just another meddling do-gooder, and she warned us never to discuss our home life at school.

If the bandersnatches did come after us, Liz said, they might put the two of us in a foster home or juvenile delinquent center. They might separate us. They might throw Mom in jail for abandoning her kids. Mom hadn't abandoned us, she just needed a little break. We could handle the situation fine if the bandersnatches would only leave us alone. It was their meddling that would create the problems.

"But I've been thinking," Liz said. "If we have to, we can go to Virginia."

Mom had come from a small town in Virginia called Byler, where her father had owned a cotton mill that made stuff like towels, socks, and underwear. Mom's brother, our Uncle Tinsley, had sold the mill a few years ago, but he still lived in Byler with his wife, Martha, in a big old house called Mayfield. Mom had grown up in the house but had left twelve years ago, when she was twenty-three, driving off that night with me on the roof. She hadn't had much to do with her family since she left, not returning even when her parents died, but we knew Uncle Tinsley still lived at Mayfield because from time to time Mom complained it was unfair that he'd inherited it just because he was older and a guy. It would be hers if anything ever happened to Uncle Tinsley, and she'd sell it in a heartbeat, because the place had nothing but bad memories for her.

Since I was only a few months old when we left, I didn't remember either Mayfield or Mom's family. Liz had some memories, and they weren't bad at all. In fact, they were sort of magical. She remembered a white house on a hill surrounded by huge trees and bright flowers. She remembered Aunt Martha and Uncle Tinsley playing duets on a grand piano in a room with French doors that were opened to the sun. Uncle Tinsley was a tall, laughing man who held her hands while he swung her around and lifted her up to pick peaches from a tree.

"How are we going to get there?" I asked.

"We'll take the bus." Liz had called the depot to find out about the fares to Virginia. They weren't cheap, she said, but we had enough money for two cross-country tickets. "If it comes to that," she added.

The next day, when I turned down the block on my way home from school, I saw a squad car parked outside the bungalow. A policeman in a blue uniform was cupping his hands around his eyes and peering through the picture window. That Mr. Spinelli had ratted us out after all. Trying to think what Liz would do in the same situation,

I slapped my head to show anyone who happened to be watching that I had forgotten something. "I left my homework in my desk!" I cried out for good measure, turned around, and headed back up the block.

I was waiting outside the high school when Liz came down the steps. "What are you so bug-eyed about?" she asked.

"Cops," I whispered.

Liz pulled me away from the other students streaming past, and I told her about the policeman peering through the window.

"That's it," Liz said. "Beaner, we're going to Virginia."

Liz always carried our money under the lining in her shoe, so we went straight to the bus depot. Since the school year was almost over, Liz said, none of our teachers would miss us. After all, we'd shown up in the middle of the year. Also, it was high picking season for strawberries, apricots, and peaches, and the teachers were used to the way the migrant families were always coming and going at harvest time.

I stayed outside the depot, studying the silver sign of the running greyhound on the roof, while Liz bought the tickets. It was early June, the streets were quiet, and the sky was pure California blue. After a couple of minutes, Liz came back out. We'd been afraid that the clerk might raise questions about a kid buying tickets, but Liz said the woman had slid them across the counter without batting an eye. Some grown-ups, at least, knew how to mind their own business.

The bus left at six forty-five the following morning. "Shouldn't we call Uncle Tinsley?" I asked.

"I think it's better if we just show up," Liz said. "That way, he can't say no."

• • •

That night, after finishing off our chicken potpies, Liz and I got out the suitcases left from what Mom called her deb days. They were a matching set in a sort of tweedy tan with dark brown crocodile trim and straps, and brass hinges and locks. They were monogrammed with Mom's initials: CAH, for Charlotte Anne Holladay.

"What should we take?" I asked.

"Clothes but no stuff," Liz said.

"What about Fido?"

"Leave him here," Liz said, "with extra food and water. He'll be fine until Mom comes back."

"What if Mom doesn't come back?"

"She'll be back. She's not abandoning us."

"And I don't want to abandon Fido."

What could Liz say to that? She sighed and shook her head. Fido was coming to Virginia.

Packing those deb-days suitcases got me to thinking about all the other times we'd picked up and moved on short notice. That was what Mom did whenever she got fed up with the way things were going. "We're in a rut," she'd announce, or "This town is full of losers," or "The air has gone stale here," or "We've hit a dead end." Sometimes it was arguments with neighbors, sometimes it was boyfriends who took a powder. Sometimes the place we'd moved to didn't meet her expectations, and sometimes she simply seemed to get bored with her own life. Whatever the case, she would announce that it was time for a fresh start.

Over the years, we'd moved to Venice Beach, Taos, San Jose, Tucson, plus these smaller places most folks had never heard of, like Bisbee and Lost Lake. Before moving to Pasadena, we'd moved to Seattle because Mom thought that living on a houseboat on the

Sound would get her creative juices flowing. Once we got there, we discovered that houseboats were more expensive than you'd think, and we ended up in a moldy apartment with Mom constantly complaining about the rain. Three months later we were gone.

While Liz and I had been on our own plenty of times, we'd never taken a trip without Mom. That didn't seem like such a big deal, but I kept wondering what to expect once we got to Virginia. Mom never had anything good to say about the place. She was always going on about the backward-thinking lintheads who drove cars with duct-taped fenders, and also about the mint-julep set who lived in the big old houses, selling off ancestor portraits to pay their taxes and feed their foxhounds, all the while reminiscing about the days when the coloreds knew their place. That was a long time ago, when Mom was growing up. Things had changed a lot since then, and I figured Byler must have, too.

After turning off the lights, Liz and I lay side by side. I'd been sharing a bed with Liz for as long as I could remember. It started after we left Virginia when I was a baby, and Mom found that putting me in with Liz made me stop crying. Later on, we sometimes lived for pretty long stretches in motels with only two beds or in furnished apartments with a pull-down Murphy bed. In Lost Lake, we shared a bed so small we had to face the same direction, the person behind wrapping her arms around the person in front, because otherwise we'd end up pulling the covers off each other. If my arm was going numb, I'd gently nudge Liz, even asleep, and we'd both roll over simultaneously. Most kids had their own beds, and some people might have thought sleeping with your sister was peculiar—not to mention crowded—but I loved it. You never felt lonely at night, and you always had someone to talk to. In fact, that was when you had your best conversations, lying spoon-style in the dark, talking just above a whisper.

"Do you think we'll like Virginia?" I asked.

"You'll like it, Bean."

"Mom hated it."

"Mom has found something wrong with every place we've ever lived."

I fell asleep quickly, like I usually did, but even though it was still dark when my eyes popped open, I felt completely awake and charged up, the way you do when you've got to jump out of bed and get cracking because you have a big day ahead with no time to waste.

Liz was up, too. She turned on the light and sat down at the kitchen table. "We have to write Mom a letter," she said.

While I heated up our chicken potpies and poured out the last of the orange juice, Liz worked on the letter. She said she had to write it in such a way that Mom would understand it but no one else would.

The letter was classic Liz.

Dear Queen of Hearts,

Due to the sudden presence of bandersnatches in the vicinity, we decided it was prudent to vacate the premises and pay a visit to the Mad Hatter Tinsley and Martha, the Dormouse. We'll be waiting for you on the other side of the Looking Glass, in your old haunted haunts, that Land of the Lintheads, where Bean was born and the borogoves are mimsy.

Love,

Tweedledee and Tweedledum

We left the letter on the kitchen table, held down by the glazed iris-blue mug Mom had made when she was in her ceramic-pottery phase.

CHAPTER FOUR

Two people got off the bus when it pulled into the depot, so we were able to snag their primo seats up front on the right side, which had better views than the left side, behind the driver. Liz let me have the window, and I held Fido in his Tupperware bowl with a little water in the bottom, an upside-down saucer for him to sit on, and holes punched in the lid so he could breathe.

As we pulled away, I looked out the window, hoping Mom had returned and would come running up the street before we left for parts unknown. But the street was empty.

The bus was crowded, and since everyone on it was making a journey with a purpose, we played What's Their Story?—another game Liz had made up—trying to guess where the passengers were going and why, whether they were happy or scared, whether they were heading toward something wonderful and exciting or fleeing from danger or failure, whether they were going off on a visit or leaving their home forever. Some were easy. The young military guy snoozing with his head on his duffel bag was on home leave to visit his family and girlfriend in ranchland. A frail woman with a small daughter had a strained look in her eyes and one hand wrapped in a splint. Liz guessed that she was on the run from a man who beat her. A thin guy in a plaid jacket with lank hair pushed behind his jug ears was sitting across from us. As I looked at him, trying to figure out if he was an absentminded mathematical genius or just a schlub, he caught my eye and winked.

I quickly looked away—it was always so embarrassing to be caught staring at people—but when I glanced back at him a little bit later, he was still eyeballing me. He winked again. I had that uh-oh feeling, and sure enough, when Liz got up to go to the bathroom, the schlub came over and sat down next to me, draping his arm across the back of my seat. He pressed his finger down on Fido's Tupperware bowl.

"What you got in there?" he asked.

"My pet turtle."

"You got a ticket for him?" He looked at me intently, then gave another wink. "Just funning you," he said. "You girls going far?"

"Virginia," I said.

"All on your own?"

"We've got our mother's permission." And then I added, "And our father's."

"I see," he said. "You're sisters." He leaned in on me. "You've got incredibly beautiful eyes, you know."

"Thank you," I said, and looked down. All of a sudden, I felt very uncomfortable.

Just then Liz came back from the bathroom. "You're in my seat, mister," she said.

"Simply getting to know your sister, miss." He rose up out of the seat. "She says you're going all the way to Virginia? Heck of a long journey for two pretty young gals to be making on their own."

"None of your business," Liz told him. She sat down. "A total perv," she whispered to me. "I can't believe you told that odiosity where we were going. That's such a Bean-headed thing to do."

The Perv took his seat but kept staring over at us, so Liz decided we needed to move. The only two free seats were at the very back, next to the bathroom. You could smell the chemicals and the other gross stuff in the toilet, and every time folks squeezed past us to use it, you could hear them running the water, blowing their noses, and hawking, not to mention doing number one or number two.

The Perv came back to use the bathroom a couple of times, but we stared straight ahead, pretending not to see him.

The bus went only as far as New Orleans. Since we were sitting in the back, we were the last ones off. When we went to pick up our luggage, the Perv was gone. Our next bus didn't leave for two hours, so we put the luggage in a locker with Fido and went for a walk. Liz and I both had a serious case of what she called rigor buttis.

It was a hot, hazy day, and the air was so thick and humid that you could barely breathe. Outside the depot, a long-haired guy in an American-flag vest was playing "House of the Rising Sun" on a saxophone. There were people everywhere, wearing either crazy clothes—tuxedo jackets but no shirts, top hats with feathers—or hardly anything, and they were all eating, drinking, laughing, and dancing to the music that street performers were playing on just about every corner.

"You can really feel the voodoo," Liz said.

A trolley car came down the street, and we got on for a quick tour of the city. It was less than half full, and we took a seat in the middle. Just before the doors closed, a man shoved his hand between them, and they opened again. It was the Perv. He took the seat right behind us.

Liz grabbed my hand, and we moved up to a seat at the front. The Perv followed. We moved to the back. He followed. The other passengers were watching us, but no one said a thing. It was one of those situations where people knew something wasn't right, but at the same time, there was no law against a man changing seats.

At the next stop, Liz and I got off, still holding hands. So did the Perv. Liz led me into the crowd on the sidewalk, the Perv behind us. Then Liz quickly pulled me around, and we jumped back on the trolley. This time, the doors closed before the Perv could get his hand in. The other passengers all started hooting and cheering, pointing and clapping, shouting things like "Dusted him!" and "Ditched his ass!" As we pulled away, we could see the Perv through the window. He actually stomped his foot.

Once we were safely on the bus heading east—the Perv didn't get on—we had a lot of fun rehashing the whole encounter, the way we not only tricked the Perv but humiliated him in front of a trolley full of people. It made me feel like we could handle just about anything the world might throw at us. When it got dark, I fell asleep with my head resting on Liz's shoulder but I woke up a short while later and could hear her very quietly crying.

In Atlanta, we changed for the bus to Richmond, and in Richmond, we changed buses for the ride to Byler. For the first time since coming east, we left the freeway for the smaller back roads. The Virginia countryside rolled and dipped, so we were always either swinging through a curve or climbing up or dropping down a hill. It was all so green. There were shiny green cornfields, dark green mountains, and golden-green hay fields lined with deep green hedgerows and soft green trees.

After heading west for three hours, we reached Byler late in the afternoon. It was a small, low-lying town on a bending river with layers of blue mountains rising up behind it. The bridge across the river clanked under the wheels of the bus. The streets of the town, lined with two-story brick buildings painted in fading colors, were quiet and had plenty of empty parking spaces. The bus stopped at a brick depot with a black metal roof. I had never seen a metal roof on anything except a shack.

We were the only passengers who got off. As the bus pulled away, a middle-aged woman came through the door of the depot. She wore a red sweatshirt with a bulldog on it and was carrying a ring of keys. "You all waiting for someone?" she asked.

"Not really," Liz said. "You don't happen to know how to get to Tinsley Holladay's house, do you?"

The woman studied Liz with sudden interest. "Mayfield?" she asked. "The Holladay house? You all know Tinsley Holladay?"

"He's our uncle," I said.

Liz gave me a glance that said I should let her do the talking.

"Well, knock me over with a feather. You all are Charlotte's girls?"

"That's right," Liz said.

"Where's your momma?"

"We're visiting on our own," Liz said.

The woman locked the depot door. "It's quite a hike to Mayfield," she said. "I'll give you all a ride."

The woman obviously wasn't a perv, so we put the suitcases in the back of her battered pickup and climbed into the front. "Charlotte Holladay," the woman said. "She was a year ahead of me at Byler High."

We drove out of the town and into the countryside. The woman kept fishing for details about Mom, but Liz was evasive, so the woman started talking about Mayfield, how twenty years ago there was always something going on there—oyster roasts, Christmas parties, cotillions, moonlight horseback rides, Civil War costume balls. "In those days everyone was hankering for an invitation there," she said. "All us girls would have given our left arm to be Charlotte Holladay. She had everything." The woman gave a little nod.

A couple of miles outside town, we came to a small white church surrounded by tall trees and a group of old houses—some big and fancy, some fairly run-down. We continued past the church to a low stone wall with a set of wrought-iron gates held up by thick stone pillars. Carved into one of the pillars was MAYFIELD.

The woman stopped. "Charlotte Holladay," she said once more. "When you all see your momma, tell her Tammy Elbert says hello."

The gates were locked, so we climbed over the low stone wall and followed the gravel driveway up a slope and around a thick stand of trees. There at the top of the hill stood the house, three stories high, painted white, with a dark green metal roof and what looked to be about twenty brick chimneys sprouting up all over the place. There were six fat white columns holding up the roof of the long front porch and, off to one side, a wing with a row of French doors.

"Oh my gosh," I told Liz. "It's the house I've been dreaming about all my life."

Ever since I could remember, I'd been having this dream at least once a month about a big white house at the top of a knoll. In the dream, Liz and I open the front door and run through the halls, exploring room after room after room of beautiful paintings and fine furniture and flowing curtains. There are fireplaces and tall windows, French doors with lots of panes of glass that let in long shafts of sunlight, and wonderful views of gardens, trees, and hills. I always thought it was just a dream, but this was the exact house.

As we got closer, we realized the house was in pretty sorry shape. The paint was peeling, the dark green roof had brown rust stains, and brambly vines crawled up the walls. At one corner of the house, where a piece of gutter had broken off, the siding was dark and rotting. We climbed the wide steps to the porch, and a blackbird flew out of a broken window.

Liz rapped the brass knocker and then, after several seconds, rapped it again. At first I thought no one was home, but then, through the small glass panes on the sides of the door, I saw some shadowy movement. We heard the scraping and sliding of bolts, and the door opened. A man appeared holding a shotgun across his chest. He had rumpled graying hair, his hazel eyes were bloodshot, and he was wearing only a bathrobe and a pair of argyle socks.

"Get off my property," he said.

"Uncle Tinsley?" Liz asked.

"Who are you?"

"It's me. Liz."

He stared at her

"Your niece."

"And I'm Bean. Or Jean."

"We're Charlotte's daughters," Liz said.

"Charlotte's girls?" He stared at us. "Jesus Christ. What are you doing here?"

"We came for a visit," I said.

"Where's Charlotte?"

"We're not exactly sure," Liz said. She took a deep breath and started explaining how Mom had needed some time to herself and we were fine on our own until the police got snoopy. "So we decided to come visit you."

"You decided to come all the way from California to visit me?"

"That's right," Liz said.

"And I'm supposed to just take you in?"

"It's a visit," I said.

"You can't simply show up here out of the blue." He wasn't

expecting guests, he went on. The housekeeper hadn't been around in a while. He was in the midst of several important projects and had papers and research material spread throughout the house that couldn't be disturbed. "I can't just let you all in here," he said.

"We don't mind a mess," I said. "We're used to messes." I tried to peer behind Uncle Tinsley into the house, but he blocked the doorway.

"Where's Aunt Martha?" Liz asked.

Uncle Tinsley ignored the question. "It's not that it's a mess," he said to me. "It's all highly organized, and it can't be disturbed."

"Well, what are we supposed to do?" Liz asked.

Uncle Tinsley looked at the two of us for a long moment, then leaned the shotgun against the wall. "You can sleep in the barn."

Uncle Tinsley led us along a brick path that ran beneath towering trees with peeling white bark. It was twilight by then. Fireflies floated upward like little points of light in the tall grass.

"Charlotte needed time by herself, so she just took off?" Uncle Tinsley asked.

"More or less," Liz said.

"She's going to come back," I said. "She wrote us a letter."

"So this is another one of Charlotte's debacles?" Uncle Tinsley shook his head in disgust. "Charlotte," he muttered. His sister was nothing but trouble, he went on. She was spoiled as a girl, a pampered little princess, and by the time she had grown up, she expected to get whatever she wanted. Not only that, whatever you did for her, it wasn't enough. Give her money and she thought she deserved more. Try to set up a job for her and the work was beneath her. Then, when her life got difficult, she blamed Mother and Father for everything that went wrong.

Uncle Tinsley was being pretty harsh about Mom, and I felt the urge to defend her, but this didn't seem like a good time to start arguing with him. Liz seemed to feel the same way, because she didn't say anything, either.

The barn, which stood at the end of the tree line, was huge, with peeling white paint and a green metal roof, just like the house. Inside, on a floor made of brick laid in a zigzag pattern, was a black carriage with gilt trim. Next to it was a station wagon with real wooden sides.

Uncle Tinsley led us through a room with dusty saddles and bridles and all these faded horse-show ribbons hanging on the walls, then up a narrow flight of stairs. At the top, there was this neat little room that I didn't expect at all, with a bed and table, a kitchenette, and a woodburning stove.

"This used to be the groom's quarters," Uncle Tinsley said. "Back in the day."

"Where is Aunt Martha?" Liz asked again.

"Charlotte didn't tell you?" Uncle Tinsley went over to the window and gazed at the fading light. "Martha passed away," he said. "Six years ago this September. Trucker ran a red light."

"Aunt Martha?" Liz said. "I can't believe she's gone."

Uncle Tinsley turned around and faced us. "You don't remember her. You were too small."

"I remember her really well," Liz said. She told Uncle Tinsley she remembered baking bread with her. Aunt Martha had worn a red apron, and Liz could still smell the bread. She also remembered Aunt Martha humming while she pruned roses in her white leather gloves. And she remembered Aunt Martha and Uncle Tinsley playing the grand piano together with the French doors open to the sun. "I think about her a lot."

Uncle Tinsley nodded. "Me, too," he said. Then he paused, as if he was going to say something else, but he just shook his head and walked out the door, saying as he shut it, "You'll be fine in here."

We listened to him clambering down the steps. I noticed a small refrigerator next to the sink, and that was when I realized I was starving. I opened the refrigerator, but it was empty and unplugged. We decided it probably wasn't a good idea to pester Uncle Tinsley about food. I was resigned to going to bed on an empty stomach, but a few minutes later, we heard footsteps on the stairs again. Uncle Tinsley appeared in the door, carrying a silver tray with a small pot, two bowls, a pitcher of water, and two wineglasses.

"Venison stew," he said. He unloaded the tray onto the table. "It's dark in here. You need some light." He flipped a switch on the wall, and an overhead bulb came on. "You all have a good night's sleep," he said, and closed the door again.

Liz filled the bowls, and we sat down at the table. I took a bite of the stew. "What's venison?" I asked.

"Deer."

"Oh."

I took another bite.

"It's pretty good," I said.

CHAPTER FIVE

The birds woke me early the next morning. I had never heard such noisy birds. I went to the window, and they were everywhere—in the trees right outside, on the ground, swooping in and out of the barn like they owned the place, all the different chirps and tweets and warbling making this incredible commotion.

Liz and I got dressed and walked down to the house. When we knocked on the front door, there was no answer, so we went around to the back. Through a window, we could see Uncle Tinsley moving around inside the kitchen. Liz rapped on the windowpane, and Uncle Tinsley opened the door but blocked it like he had the night before. He had shaved, his wet hair was combed, the part was straight, and instead of his bathrobe, he was wearing gray trousers and a light blue shirt with TMH monogrammed on the pocket.

"How did you girls sleep?" he asked.

"Just fine," Liz said.

"The birds sure are noisy," I said.

"I don't use pesticides, so the birds love it around here," Uncle Tinsley said.

"Did Mom call, by any chance?" Liz asked.

"Afraid not."

"She does have the number, right?" I asked.

"This number hasn't changed since we got it—two, four, six, eight," he said. "First phone number handed out in Byler, so we got to choose it. Speaking of choosing, how do you like your poached eggs?"

"Hard!" I said.

"Soft," Liz said.

"Have a seat over there." He pointed to some rusty cast-iron lawn furniture.

A few minutes later, he came out carrying that same silver tray, loaded up with a stack of toast and three plates that each had a poached egg in the center. The plates had gold curlicues around the rim, but the edges were chipped. I picked up a corner of my egg and scooted a piece of toast under it, then stabbed the yolk with my fork, chopped up the white part of the egg, and mushed it all together.

"Bean always mutilates her food," Liz told Uncle Tinsley. "It's disgusting."

"It tastes better mixed up," I said. "But that's not the only reason. First of all, you don't have to take as many bites, so it saves time. Second, you don't have to work as hard chewing, because if it's all mushed up, it's sort of prechewed. Finally, food gets all mixed up in your stomach anyway, so that's obviously the way it was meant to be."

Uncle Tinsley gave a little chuckle and turned to Liz. "Is she always like this?"

"Oh, yeah," Liz said. "She's the Beanhead."

We offered to wash the dishes, but Uncle Tinsley insisted it was easier if he did them himself, without a couple of kids underfoot. He told us to go off and do whatever girls our age did.

Liz and I walked around to the front of the house, where there were two big trees with shiny dark leaves and big white flowers.

Beyond them, on the far side of the lawn, was a row of huge green bushes with a gap in the middle. We walked through the gap and found ourselves in an area surrounded by the dark green bushes. A few tough irises pushed up through the weeds in old, overgrown flower beds. In the center was a round brick-edged pond. It was full of dead leaves, but in the water beneath, I saw a flash of brilliant orange.

"Fish!" I yelled. "Goldfish! There's goldfish in this pond!"

We knelt and studied the orange fish fluttering in and out of the shadows beneath the clumps of dead leaves. I decided this would be a great place for Fido to have a swim. The poor turtle had to be feeling cooped up after all that time in his box.

I ran back to the barn, but when I opened the Tupperware, Fido was floating in the water. He'd seemed fine when I fed him earlier. I set him down on the tabletop, scooting him along with my finger, trying to jump-start him, even though I knew it was hopeless. Fido was dead, and it was all my fault. I had thought I could protect Fido and take care of him, but that bus trip had been too much for the poor little guy. He'd have been better off if I'd left him in Lost Lake.

I put Fido back in the Tupperware dish and carried him out to the pond. Liz put an arm around me and said we needed to ask Uncle Tinsley where to bury him.

Uncle Tinsley was still puttering in the kitchen when we knocked.

"I thought the two of you were going to go off and play," he said.

"Fido died," I said.

Uncle Tinsley glanced at Liz.

"Bean's turtle," she said.

"We need to know where to bury him," I said.

Uncle Tinsley stepped out of the house and closed the door behind him. I handed him the Tupperware dish, and he looked down at Fido. "We bury all the family pets in the family cemetery," he said. He led us back to the barn, where he picked up a shovel with a long wooden handle, then we all headed up the hill behind it.

"Fido's a peculiar name for a turtle," he said as we walked along.

"Bean really wanted a dog," Liz said, explaining how Mom had told us it was always the kids who wanted the pet but the mother who ended up taking care of it, and she had no interest in walking and cleaning up after a dog. So she'd bought me a turtle.

"Fido means 'I am faithful,' " I said. "Fido was a very faithful turtle."

"I bet he was," Uncle Tinsley said.

Beyond the barn were a bunch of dilapidated wooden buildings. Uncle Tinsley pointed out the smokehouse, the milking shed and the foaling shed, the henhouse, the icehouse, and the springhouse, explaining that Mayfield used to be a real working farm, though hands did most of the work. He still had all 205 acres, including a stretch of woods, as well as the big hay field where the cemetery was. These days, a farmer up the road, Mr. Muncie, hayed the field and gave Uncle Tinsley eggs and vegetables in return.

We passed through an orchard, Uncle Tinsley showing us the apple, peach, and cherry trees, and out into a large pasture. At the top of the pasture, a cluster of trees shaded the family cemetery, which was surrounded by a rusting wrought-iron fence. The cemetery was weedy, and a number of the weathered old headstones had toppled over. Uncle Tinsley led us to one well-tended grave with a newish headstone. This was Martha's, he said, with a vacant spot next to it for him when the time came.

The pets, he explained, were buried around the perimeter, near their owners. "Let's put Fido near Martha," Uncle Tinsley said. "I think she would have liked him."

Uncle Tinsley dug a small hole, and I placed Fido in it, using the Tupperware dish as his coffin. I found a nice piece of white quartz for a headstone. Uncle Tinsley gave a short eulogy. Fido had been a brave and indeed a faithful turtle, he said, who had made the long and perilous journey from California in order to serve as a guardian for his two sister-owners. Once he'd gotten them safely to Virginia, Fido's job was over, and he felt free to leave them for that secret island in the middle of the ocean that is turtle heaven.

The eulogy made me feel a lot better about both Fido and Uncle Tinsley. On the way back down the hill, I asked about the goldfish we'd found in the pond. "The fish are koi," Uncle Tinsley said. "That was Mother's garden. One of the finest private gardens in all of Virginia, back in the day. Mother won prizes for it. She was the envy of every lady in the garden club."

We swung around the barn and the big white house came into view. I started telling Uncle Tinsley about my house dream and how, when we first arrived at Mayfield, I realized it was the actual house in the dream.

Uncle Tinsley became thoughtful. He rested the shovel against an old water trough in front of the barn. "I guess you'd better see the inside of the house, then," he said. "Just to make sure."

We followed Uncle Tinsley up the big porch steps. He took a deep breath and opened the door.

The front hall was large and dark, with a lot of wooden cabinets that had glass doors. Everything was a mess. Newspapers, magazines, books, and mail were stacked high on the tables and the floor, alongside boxes of rocks and bottles filled with dirt and sand and liquids.

"It may look a tad cluttered," he said, "but that's because I'm in the middle of reorganizing everything."

"It's not so bad," Liz said. "It just needs a little tidying up."

"We can help," I said.

"Oh, no. Everything's under control. Everything has its place, and I know where everything is."

Uncle Tinsley showed us the parlor, the dining room, and the ballroom. Oil paintings hung crooked on the walls and a few were falling out of their frames. The Persian carpets were worn and frayed, the silk curtains were faded and torn, and the stained wallpaper was peeling away from the walls. A grand piano covered with a dark green velvet cloth stood in the big ballroom with the French doors. There was all this stuff piled on every available surface—more stacks of paper and notebooks, antique binoculars, pendulum clocks, rolled-up maps, stacks of chipped china, old pistols, ships in bottles, statues of rearing horses, framed photographs, and all these little wooden boxes, one filled with coins, another with buttons, another with old medals. Everything was coated with a thick layer of dust.

"There sure is a ton of stuff in here," I said.

"Yes, but every single thing you see has value," Uncle Tinsley said. "If you have the brains to appreciate it."

He led us up a curving staircase and down a long hall. At the end of the hall, he stopped in front of a pair of doors that faced each other. Both had brass door knockers shaped like birds. "This is the bird wing," Uncle Tinsley told us. "This is where you'll stay. Until your mother comes to pick you up."

"We're not sleeping in the barn anymore?" I asked.

"Not without Fido there to protect you."

Uncle Tinsley opened the doors. We each had our own room, he told us. Both were wallpapered with bird motifs—common birds, like robins and cardinals, and exotic birds, like cockatiels and flamingos. The bird wing, he explained, had been designed for his twin aunts, who were little girls when the house was built. They had loved birds and kept a big Victorian birdhouse full of different kinds of finches.

"Where was Mom's room?" I asked.

"She never mentioned it?" he asked. "The whole bird wing was hers." He pointed through the door of one room. "When she brought you back from the hospital after you were born, she put you in that cradle in the corner there."

I looked over at the cradle. It was small and white and made of wicker, and I couldn't understand quite why, but it made me feel very safe.

CHAPTER SIX

The next morning, over our poached eggs, Liz and I tried to talk Uncle Tinsley into letting us help him clean up the house just a little bit. But he insisted that nothing in the house could be thrown out or even moved. Everything, he said, was either a family treasure or part of one of his collections or necessary for his geological research.

We spent the morning following Uncle Tinsley around the house as he explained what all the stuff meant to him. He'd pick something up, say an ivory-handled letter opener or a tricornered hat, and give us a long explanation of where it came from, who had owned it, and why it had extraordinary significance. I came to realize that everything was, in fact, organized in a way that only he fully understood.

"This place is like a museum," I said.

"And you're the curator," Liz told Uncle Tinsley.

"Well said," he replied. "But it's been a good while since I gave my last tour." We were standing in the ballroom. Uncle Tinsley looked around. "I admit the place is a tad cluttered. That was the phrase Martha liked to use. I've always loved to collect things, but when she was alive, she helped me keep the impulse in check."

Uncle Tinsley finally agreed to let us throw out some of the old newspapers and magazines and carry up to the attic and down to the basement boxes of mineral samples, spools of thread from the mill, and Confederate paper money. We washed windows, aired out rooms, scrubbed floors and counters, and vacuumed the rugs and curtains with this old Hoover from the 1950s that reminded me of a little spaceship.

By the end of the week, the house looked a lot better. Still, it didn't meet most people's definition of neat and tidy, and you had to accept the fact that you weren't living in a regular house but a place more like a junk shop crammed with all kinds of fascinating stuff— if you had the brains to see its value.

Venison stew and eggs were the staples of Uncle Tinsley's diet. He didn't shoot big bucks for trophies, he explained, but if he bagged two or three does during deer season, had the meat processed and double-wrapped, then stored it in the basement freezer, he had enough to last the entire year. So most nights we had venison stew with things like carrots, onions, tomatoes, and potatoes and barley mixed in. The meat was a lot tougher than the chicken in potpies, and sometimes you really had to work your jaws before you could swallow it, but it was also spicier and tastier.

Thanks to Mr. Muncie, the eighty-seven-year-old neighbor who hayed the big pasture, Uncle Tinsley didn't have to buy eggs and vegetables, and he made hot cereal from rolled oats he got at the feed store. But he decided growing girls needed milk and cheese, plus we were short on staples such as salt, so at the end of our first week, Uncle Tinsley declared it was time for a grocery run. We all climbed into the station wagon with the wood panels, which Uncle Tinsley called the Woody. We hadn't left Mayfield since the day we arrived, and I was itching to check out the area.

We drove past the white church and the cluster of houses, then along the winding road that led through farmland, with cornrows and grazing cattle, on the way to Byler. I was looking out the window as we passed a big fenced-in field, and I suddenly saw these two huge birdlike creatures. "Liz!" I shouted. "Look at those crazy birds!"

They reminded me of chickens, only they were the size of ponies, with long necks and legs and dark brown feathers. Their heads bobbed as they moved along with big careful steps.

"What the heck are they?" I asked.

Uncle Tinsley gave that little chuckle of his. "Scruggs's emus."

"Like ostriches, right?" Liz said.

"Near enough."

"Are they pets?" I asked.

"They weren't supposed to be. Scruggs thought he could make some money off them but never figured out how. So they're the world's ugliest lawn ornaments."

"They're not ugly," Liz said.

"Take a look at them up close sometime."

Once we got to Byler, Uncle Tinsley gave us what he called the nickel tour. The main street, lined with big green trees, was Holladay Avenue. The buildings were old-fashioned, made of brick and stone. Some had pillars and carvings, one had a big round clock with Roman numerals, and you got the feeling that Byler once was a bustling and prosperous place, though it looked like nothing new had been built in the town for fifty years. More than a few of the storefronts were vacant and had masking tape crisscrossing the glass. A sign on one door said BACK IN HALF AN HOUR, as if the shopkeeper had intended to return but never did.

Maybe it was because of the humid air, but Byler struck me as very sleepy. People seemed to move slowly, and a lot of them were hardly moving at all, just sitting in chairs under store awnings, some of the men in overalls, talking, whittling, or leaning back, chewing tobacco and reading newspapers.

"What year are we in here?" Liz joked.

"The sixties never happened in this town," Uncle Tinsley said, "and people like it that way."

He stopped the Woody at a red light. An older black man wearing a fedora started across the street in front of us. When he got to the middle of the intersection, he looked at us, smiled, and touched his hat. Uncle Tinsley waved.

"Who's he?" I asked.

"Don't know him," Uncle Tinsley said.

"But you waved at him."

"You only wave at people you know? You must be from California." He burst out laughing.

The mill stood at the end of Holladay Avenue, right on the river. It was made of dark red brick laid in patterns of arches and diamonds, and it covered an entire block. The windows were two stories high, and smoke poured out of a pair of soaring chimneys. A sign in front said HOLLADAY TEXTILES.

"Charlotte tell you much of the family history?" Uncle Tinsley asked.

"It wasn't Mom's favorite subject," Liz said.

Before the Civil War, Uncle Tinsley explained, the Holladay family had owned a cotton plantation.

"A plantation?" I asked. "Our family had slaves?"

"We certainly did."

"I wish I didn't know that," Liz said.

"Those slaves were always treated well," Uncle Tinsley said. "My great-great-grandfather Montgomery Holladay liked to say if he was down to one final crust of bread, he would, by God, have shared it with them."

I glanced at Liz, who rolled her eyes.

If you went back far enough, Uncle Tinsley went on, just about all American families who could afford them owned slaves, not only Southerners. Ben Franklin owned slaves. Anyway, he continued, the Yankees burned down the whole plantation during the war, but the family still knew the cotton business. Once the war was over, Montgomery Holladay decided there was no point in shipping cotton to the factories up north to make the Yankees rich, so he sold the land and moved to Byler, where he used the money to build the mill.

The Holladay family, Uncle Tinsley explained, had owned the cotton mill—and pretty much the town itself—for generations. The mill was good to the Holladays, and in turn, the Holladays were good to the workers. The family built them houses with indoor plumbing and gave out free toilet paper to go with the toilets. The Holladays also gave out hams on Christmas and sponsored a baseball team called the Holladay Hitters. The millworkers never made much in terms of wages, but most of them had been dirt farmers before the mill opened, and factory work was a step up. The main thing, he went on, was that everyone in Byler, rich and poor, considered themselves part of one big family.

Things started to go downhill fast about ten years ago, Uncle Tinsley continued. Foreign mills began undercutting everybody's prices at the same time those Northern agitators started going around stirring up the workers to strike for higher wages. Southern mills started losing money, and as the years went by, more and more of them shut down.

By then, Uncle Tinsley said, his father had passed, and he was running Holladay Textiles himself. It, too, was in the red. Some Chicago investors agreed to buy the mill, but it didn't bring much, only enough for him and Charlotte to get by if they watched their pennies. Meanwhile, the new owners laid off workers and did whatever they could to squeeze every last ounce of profit out of the place, not just doing away with the Christmas hams and the Holladay Hitters but cutting back bathroom breaks, turning off the air-conditioning, and using dirty cotton.

"Back in the day, Holladay Textiles made a quality product," Uncle Tinsley said. "Now they turn out towels so thin you can read a newspaper through them."

"It all sounds too depressing," Liz said.

Uncle Tinsley shrugged. "Things change, even in this town."

"Did you ever think of leaving Byler?" I asked. "Like Mom?"

"Leave Byler?" Uncle Tinsley asked. "Why would I leave Byler? I'm a Holladay. This is where I belong."

CHAPTER SEVEN

At Mayfield we slept with the windows open, and you could hear the frogs croaking at night. I conked out as soon as my head hit the pillow, but those noisy birds woke me early every day. One morning in late June, after we'd been at Mayfield for almost two weeks, I woke up and reached out for Liz and then remembered that she was in the next room. Much as I had loved sharing a bed with Liz, I'd always thought it would be neat to have a room of my very own. The truth was, it felt lonely.

I went into Liz's room to see if she was awake. She was sitting up in bed, reading a book called *Stranger in a Strange Land,* which she'd come across while we were cleaning the house. I lay down beside her.

"I wish Mom would hurry up and call," I said. I'd been expecting to hear from her any day. I constantly checked the phone to make sure it was connected, because Uncle Tinsley didn't particularly appreciate getting calls and sometimes unplugged it. "Uncle Tinsley's going to think we're a couple of moochers."

"I think he actually likes having us here," Liz said. She held up the book. "We're like friendly aliens visiting from another planet."

Truth be told, in the time we'd been there, Uncle Tinsley hadn't had a single other visitor. He had one of those big old-fashioned radios, but he didn't seem that interested in what was going on in the world, and he never turned it on. What fascinated him were genealogy and geology. He spent most of his time in his library, writing to county historical societies, requesting information on, say, the Middleburg Holladays, and going through what he called his archives, boxes of crumbling old letters, faded journals, and yellowed newspaper clippings that referred to the Holladay family in any way. And there was nothing he didn't know about the earth, its layers of rocks and soil and underground water. He studied geological charts, conducted tests on little glass jars of soil and trays of rocks, and read scientific reports to cite in the articles he wrote and occasionally published.

While Liz liked to lie in bed and read after she woke up, I always wanted to get up and get cracking and I went downstairs for breakfast. Uncle Tinsley was in the ballroom, nursing a cup of coffee and staring out the French doors. "I hadn't realized how tall the grass has gotten," he said. "I do believe it's time to mow."

After breakfast, I went with Uncle Tinsley up to the equipment shed. Inside was an old-timey red tractor with FARMALL on the side, a little side step up to the seat, and an empty paint can over the exhaust pipe that, Uncle Tinsley explained, kept out the critters. The tractor coughed when he turned the engine over, but then it fired right up, a big belch of black smoke coming out from under the paint can. Uncle Tinsley backed it up to his pull-behind mower, a big green contraption, and I helped him attach the mower to the rear of the tractor, getting grease all over my hands and under my fingernails.

While Uncle Tinsley mowed, I used a shovel and rake to clear the leaves from the koi pond. I discovered overgrown brick paths running between the old flower beds, and I started pulling the weeds off them. It was hard work—the wet leaves were heavier than you'd think, and the weeds were itchy—but by the end of the morning, I had cleared out the pond and most of the brick around it. The flower beds, however, still had a ways to go before they won any new prizes. Uncle Tinsley motioned me over. "Let's see if we can get us some peaches for lunch," he said.

He hoisted me up onto the tractor's little side step, explaining that you really weren't supposed to do this but every farm kid did it anyway, and with me standing on the step and hanging on for dear life, we drove past the barn, up the hill to the orchard, the old Farmall shaking so much it made my teeth rattle and my eyeballs jiggle.

The apples and pears were too green, Uncle Tinsley said, they'd be ripe in August and September. But he had some early peaches that were ready to eat. They were old varieties, bred centuries ago for the climate in this particular county, and they tasted nothing like the mealy Styrofoam that passed for fruit in your modern supermarkets.

There was fruit on the ground under the peach trees, and bees, wasps, and butterflies were swarming around, feasting on it. Uncle Tinsley pulled a peach down and passed it to me. It was small and red, covered with fuzz, and warm from the sun. That peach was so juicy that when I bit into it, I felt like it almost burst in my mouth. I wolfed it down, all that juice leaving my chin and fingers sticky.

"Dang," I said.

"Now, that's a peach," Uncle Tinsley said. "A Holladay peach."

We brought back a paper bag full of peaches. They were so irresistible that Liz and I ate them all that afternoon, and the next morning, I went back up to the orchard for more.

The peach trees were behind the apples, and as I approached, I saw the branches of one swaying back and forth. When I got closer, I realized that someone was behind the tree, a guy, and he was filling a bag with peaches just as fast as he could.

"Hey!" I shouted. "What are you doing?"

The guy, who was about my age, looked at me. We stared at each other for a moment. He had longish brown hair that flopped in his face and eyes as dark as coffee. He was shirtless, and his sunbaked skin was streaked with sweat and grime, like he ran around half-wild. He held a peach in one hand, and I saw that part of a finger was missing.

"What are you doing?" I shouted again. "Those are our peaches."

The boy suddenly turned and ran, the bag in one hand, arms and legs pumping like a sprinter's.

"Stop!" I shouted. "Thief!"

I ran after him for a few steps, but he was fast and had a good head start, and I knew I couldn't catch him. I was so mad at that dirty kid for stealing our delicious peaches that I picked one up and threw it after him. "Peach thief!"

I headed back to the house. Uncle Tinsley was in the library, working on his geology papers. I fully expected him to share my outrage over the low-down scoundrel stealing our peaches. Instead, he smiled and started asking me questions. What did he look like? How tall was he? Did I happen to notice if he was missing part of a finger?

"He sure was," I said. "Probably got it chopped off for stealing."

"That's Joe Wyatt," Uncle Tinsley said. "He's your father's family. His father was your father's brother. He's your cousin."

I was so stunned, I sat down on the floor.

"And I don't mind him taking a few peaches," he added.

Mom didn't talk much about either Liz's dad or my dad. All she'd told us was that she had met Liz's dad, Shelton Stewart, while in college in Richmond, and after a whirlwind romance, they got married in the most lavish wedding Byler had seen in a generation. Mom became pregnant almost immediately, and it didn't take long for her to discover that Shelton Stewart was a dishonest parasite. He'd come from an old South Carolina family, but their money was gone, and he expected Mom's family to support them while he spent his days playing golf and shooting grouse. Her father made it clear that wasn't going to happen, and so, shortly after Liz was born, Shelton Stewart walked out on Mom, and she and Liz never saw him again.

My dad, Mom had told us, was a Byler boy. He was a blast to be around, with this incredible energy, but she and he came from different worlds. Besides, he died in a mill accident before I was born. And that was all she would say.

"You knew my dad?" I asked Uncle Tinsley.

"Of course I did."

That made me so nervous, I started rubbing my hands together. Mom's account of my dad had always left me hankering for more details, but she said she didn't want to talk about him and we were both better off if we put it behind us. Mom didn't have a picture of him, and she wouldn't tell me his name. I'd always wondered what my dad had looked like. I didn't look like my mom. Did I look like my dad? Was he handsome? Funny? Smart?

"What was he like?" I asked.

"Charlie. Charlie Wyatt," Uncle Tinsley said. "He was a cocky fellow." He paused and looked at me. "He wanted to marry your mother, you know, but she never took him that seriously."

"How come?"

"Charlie was a fling, as far as she was concerned. Charlotte was pretty shaken up when that wastrel, Liz's father, decided he didn't want to be a father after all. She went through a wild-divorcée period and got involved with a number of men whom Mother and Father disapproved of. Charlie was one of them. She never considered marrying him. The way she saw it, he was just a linthead."

"What's that?" I'd heard Mom use the word, but I didn't know what it meant.

"A millworker. They come off their shifts covered in lint."

I sat there on the floor, trying to take it in. All my life I had wanted to find out more about my dad and his family, and now, when I'd met someone who was related to him—and to me—I'd acted like a nut job, calling him names and throwing peaches at him. And he wasn't a thief. Since Uncle Tinsley didn't mind Joe Wyatt taking the peaches, he wasn't actually stealing. At least, that was one way of looking at it.

"I think I need to go apologize to Joe Wyatt," I said. "And maybe meet the other Wyatts."

"Not a bad idea," Uncle Tinsley said. "They're good people. The father's disabled and doesn't do too much these days. The mother works the night shift. She's the one holding the family together." He scratched his chin. "I suppose I could drive you over there."

Something about the way Uncle Tinsley said that made me realize he didn't want to do what he'd just volunteered to do. After all, he was a Holladay, the former owner of the mill. He'd be paying a visit to the millworking family of the man who got his sister pregnant. It would be awkward for him to drop me off without coming in but probably more awkward to sit down with the Wyatts and shoot the breeze over a glass of lemonade.

"I'll go on my own," I said. "It will be a chance for me to see Byler up close on foot."

"Good plan," Uncle Tinsley said. "Better yet, Charlotte's old bicycle has to be around here someplace. You could ride it into town."

I went up to the bird wing to tell Liz about the Wyatts. She was sitting in a chair by a window, reading another book she'd found in Uncle Tinsley's library, this one by Edgar Allan Poe.

When I told her about the Wyatts, Liz jumped up and hugged me. "You're trembling," she said.

"I know, I know. I'm nervous," I said. "What if they're weirdos? What if they think I'm a weirdo?"

"It'll be fine. Do you want me to come?"

"Would you?"

"Of course, Beanstalker, you weirdo. We're in this together."

CHAPTER EIGHT

The next morning, Uncle Tinsley found the bike Mom rode as a kid. It was in the equipment shed, where he also found his old bike, but it needed a new tire, so Liz and I decided to ride double.

Mom's bike was a terrific Schwinn like they didn't make anymore, Uncle Tinsley said. It had a heavy red frame, fat tires, reflectors on the wheels, a speedometer, a horn, and a chrome rack behind the seat. Uncle Tinsley wiped it down, pumped air in the tires, oiled the chain, and drew us a map of the part of town where the Wyatts lived, explaining that it was known as the mill hill, or just the hill. With Liz pedaling and me sitting behind her on the chrome rack, we set off for the hill.

The day was hot and sticky, the sky hazy, and the rack dug into my behind, but along the way, we rode through cool stretches of woods where the branches of these big old trees reached out all the way across the road to create a sort of canopy, and you felt like you were going through a tunnel, with patches of sunlight occasionally flickering between the leaves.

• • •

The mill hill was in the north part of town, just past the mill, at the base of a wooded mountain. The houses were identical boxes, many of them with the original white paint now all faded, but some had been painted blue or yellow or green or pink or had aluminum or tar-paper siding. Chairs and couches lined porches, auto parts were crammed into some of the little yards, and one grimy house had a faded rebel flag hanging out a window. But you could see that keeping up appearances was important to a lot of the folks on the hill. Some used whitewashed tires as planters for pansies or had colorful pinwheels spinning in the breeze or little cement statues of squirrels and dwarves. We passed one woman out sweeping her dirt yard with a broom.

The Wyatts' house was one that clearly showed pride of ownership. The sky-blue paint was fading, but the front yard was mowed, the bushes around the foundation were evenly pruned, and little rocks lined the path from the front steps to the sidewalk.

Liz stepped back, letting me go first. I knocked on the door, and it was opened almost immediately by a big woman with a wide mouth and twinkling green eyes. Her dark hair, which had a streak of white, was gathered in a loose bun, and she was wearing an apron over a baggy dress. She smiled at me curiously.

"Mrs. Wyatt?" I asked.

"I reckon I am." She was drying her hands on a dish towel. They were big hands, like a man's. "You all selling something?"

"I'm Bean Holladay. Charlotte's daughter."

She let out a shriek of joy, dropped the dish towel, then wrapped her arms around me in a spine-crushing hug.

I introduced Liz, who held out her hand in greeting.

"This ain't a shaking family, it's a hugging family!" Mrs. Wyatt shouted as she enveloped Liz in another crushing hug. She pulled us into the house, hollering for Clarence to come and meet his nieces. "And don't you be Mrs. Wyatt–ing me," she told us. "I'm your Aunt Al."

The front door led into the kitchen. A small boy sitting at the table stared at us with wide, unblinking eyes. There was a big coal cooking stove with two freshly baked pies on top of it. Plates, bowls, and pots were stacked on the shelves according to size, and ladles and stirring spoons hung on a rack above the stove. You could tell Aunt Al ran a very tight ship. The walls were hung with needlepoint and small varnished boards with Bible verses or sayings like A SCRIPTURE A DAY KEEPS THE DEVIL AWAY and YOU CAN'T HAVE A RAINBOW WITHOUT A LITTLE RAIN.

I asked if Joe was there. "I met him yesterday, but I didn't know he was my cousin."

"Where'd you meet him?"

"In Uncle Tinsley's orchard."

"So you're the peach thrower?" Aunt Al threw back her head and let out a huge laugh. "I heard you got quite an arm on you." Joe was out and about, she said, and usually didn't come home until dinnertime, but he was surely going to be sorry he missed this. She had four children, she went on. Joe was thirteen, her middle boy. She introduced the kid at the table as her youngest, Earl. He was five, she said, and he was different, not much strength, and he'd never really learned to talk—so far, anyway. Her eldest, Truman, who was twenty, was serving his country overseas. Her daughter, Ruth, who was sixteen, had gone down to North Carolina to help out one of Aunt Al's sisters, who had three children to look after but had been taken down with meningitis.

A man came out of the back room, moving carefully like he was hurt, and Aunt Al introduced him as her husband, our Uncle Clarence.

"Charlotte's daughters? You don't say." He was thin and slightly bent, his gaunt cheeks had deep lines, and his gray hair was crew-cut. He studied Liz. "You I remember," he said. Then he looked at me. "You I never laid eyes on. That momma of yours got you out of town before I had a chance to see my brother's only child."

"Well, now you got your chance," Aunt Al said. "Be sweet."

"Glad to meet you, Uncle Clarence," I said. I wondered if he was going to hug me, like Aunt Al had. But he just stood there looking at me suspiciously.

"Where's your momma?" he asked.

"She stayed in California," I said. "We're just here for a visit."

"Decided not to come, did she? Now, why don't that surprise me?" Uncle Clarence started coughing.

"Don't be getting all cantankerous, Clarence," Aunt Al said. "Go sit down and catch your breath." Uncle Clarence left the room coughing.

"My husband can be a little crotchety," Aunt Al told us. "He's a good man, but his lot ain't been an easy one—what with his bad back and the white lung he got from working in the mill—and he's sour on a lot of people. He also worries hisself sick about Truman being over in Vietnam, but he ain't going to admit it. We've lost three Byler boys to the war, and I pray for my son and all those boys over there every night. Anyways, how about some pie?"

She cut us each a fat slice. "Best peaches in the county," she said with a grin.

"And you can't beat the price," I said.

Aunt Al burst into laughter again. "You're going to fit right in, Bean."

We sat down at the kitchen table next to Earl and dug into the pie, which was unbelievably yummy.

"How's your momma doing?"

"She's fine," Liz said.

"She ain't been back to Byler in years, has she?"

"Not since Bean was a baby," Liz said.

"Can't say I fault her for that."

"Did my dad look like Uncle Clarence?" I asked.

"Different as night and day, though you could still tell they was brothers. You never seen a picture of your poppa?"

I shook my head.

Aunt Al studied the dish towel that she seemed to carry everywhere, then folded it into a neat square. "I got something to show you." She left the room and came back with a thick scrapbook. Sitting next to me, she started paging through it, then pointed to a black-and-white photograph of a young man leaning in a doorway with his arms crossed and his hip cocked. "There he is," she said. "Charlie. Your daddy."

She slid the album over toward me. I almost heard the blood rushing in my head. I started to touch the photograph but realized that my hands were damp with nervous sweat, so I wiped them on Aunt Al's dish towel. Then I bent down until my face was inches away from the picture. I wanted to take in every detail about my dad.

He was wearing a tight-fitting white T-shirt with a pack of cigarettes folded into one of the sleeves. He had wiry muscles and dark hair, just like mine, though it was slicked back the way they did in those days. He had dark eyes, also just like mine. What struck me most was his crooked grin, like he saw the world in his own special way and got a kick out of it.

"He sure was handsome," I said.

"Oh, he was a looker, all right," Aunt Al said. "The ladies all loved Charlie. It wasn't just his looks. It was mainly the way he lit up the room."

"What do you mean?"

Aunt Al eyed me. "You don't know too much about your daddy, do you, sugar?"

I shook my head.

Charlie had been a loom fixer at the mill, Aunt Al said. He could repair anything. Had a head for it. He never got much in the way of a formal education, but he was real smart and all the time on the go. He always had to be doing something. And when Charlie arrived at a party, that was when it started.

"You got his spark, I do believe," Aunt Al told me. But Charlie Wyatt also had the wild streak that ran in their family, she went on, and that's what got him killed.

"I thought he died in a mill accident," Liz said. "That's what Mom told us."

Aunt Al looked like she was considering something. "No, hon," she finally said. "Your daddy was shot."

"What?"

"Gunned down in cold blood by the brother of the man he'd killed."

I stared at Aunt Al.

"You're old enough," she said. "You ought to know."

After Liz's dad ran off, Aunt Al explained, Charlotte left Richmond and came home to Mayfield, changing her name back to Holladay. She was feeling pretty mixed up about it all and dated around a bit. Then she and Charlie became sweet on each other. She ended up in a family way, and Charlie wanted to marry her, not just because it was the honorable thing to do but because he loved her. But Charlotte's father, Mercer Holladay, was of no mind to let his little girl marry one of the loom fixers from his very own mill. Charlotte also seemed to feel that, as much fun as he was, Charlie was beneath her station.

Charlie was still hoping to change Charlotte's mind when, one night at Gibson's pool hall, a fellow name Ernie Mullens said something about Charlotte being a loose woman—to put it politely. When Ernie refused to apologize, Charlie took after him. Then Ernie pulled out a knife. Charlie whacked Ernie upside the head with his pool cue, and Ernie fell against the pool table, cracking his skull. It killed him dead. The jury decided it was a case of self-defense. After the trial, Ernie's brother, Bucky, swore he was going to kill Charlie, and lots of people urged him to get out of town, but he refused. Two weeks later, Bucky Mullens shot Charlie Wyatt down on Holladay Avenue in broad daylight.

"Your daddy was murdered," Aunt Al said, "because he defended your momma's honor."

Her Clarence had sworn revenge, she went on, but Bucky was sent to the penitentiary, and when he got out, he left the state before anyone knew about it. Aunt Al said she was glad it had turned out that way, but Bucky disappearing was one more thing that had made Clarence mad at the world.

Aunt Al took the photograph of my dad out of the scrapbook and placed it in my hand. "This is for you."

"I feel like everything's changed," I said to Liz. We were walking back to Mayfield, pushing the Schwinn, because I wanted to talk. "Now I know who my dad was."

"And now you know who you are," Liz said. "You're Charlie Wyatt's girl."

"Yeah," I said. I had my dad's eyes and hair—and Aunt Al said I had his spark. "I'm Charlie Wyatt's girl."

As we walked along, we passed the house where the woman had been sweeping her dirt yard. The hardpacked dirt looked as smooth as terra-cotta tile. The woman was sitting on her porch. She waved, and I waved back.

"Now you're waving at people you don't know," Liz said, and grinned. "You've gone native."

We reached the bottom of the mill hill. "I think I like the way my dad died," I said.

"It was better than some dumb mill accident," Liz said.

"Like Aunt Al said, he was defending Mom's honor."

"He wasn't just another linthead—not that there's anything wrong with that."

"I feel like I've got a lot to ask Mom," I said. "So when in the heck is she ever going to call?"

"She'll call."

CHAPTER NINE

When we got home, Uncle Tinsley was sitting at the dining room table, working on his big genealogical chart of the Holladay family.

"How did it go, Bean?" he asked.

"Well, she found out how her dad died," Liz said.

"Did you know?" I asked.

"Of course," he said. He pointed to a name on the chart. "Charles Joseph Wyatt, 1932 to 1957."

"Why didn't you tell me?"

"It wasn't my place," he said. "But all of Byler sure knew about it. Didn't talk about anything else for months. Or years, it seemed."

Millworkers drinking beer in pool halls were always getting in knockdowns and knife fights, he said, and from time to time, they killed each other. That was no big deal. However, this particular incident involved Charlotte Holladay, the daughter of Mercer Holladay, the man practically everyone in town worked for. By the time Bucky Mullens came to stand trial, Charlotte was showing, and everyone knew she was carrying the child of the pool-hall-brawling linthead Bucky had killed. It was quite the scandal, and Mother and Father were mortified. So were he and Martha. They all felt that the Holladay name—the name on the darned mill, the name on the main street through town—was soiled. Mother stopped going to the garden club, Father stayed off the golf course. Every time Uncle Tinsley walked through town, he said, he knew people were chortling behind his back.

Mother and Father, he went on, couldn't help letting Charlotte know how they felt. She had come home when her marriage fell apart and expected to be supported. At the same time, she had declared that since she was an adult, she was going to do whatever she pleased. As a result, she brought shame on the entire family. Charlotte, for her part, felt the family had turned on her, and she hated Mother and Father, as well as him and Martha, for feeling the way they did.

"And so not long after you were born, Bean, she left Byler, vowing never to return," Uncle Tinsley said. "It was one of the few times in her life she showed good judgment."

That night I couldn't sleep. I was lying there chewing on everything I'd learned that day about Mom and my dad. I had always wanted to know more about my family, but I hadn't bargained for this.

In times like these, having your own room really stunk, because there was no one to talk to. I got up and carried my pillow into Liz's room, crawling under the covers next to her. She wrapped an arm around me.

"I actually know something about my dad now," I said. "It really gives you a lot to think about. Maybe, when Mom gets here, you should talk to her about getting in touch with your dad."

"No," Liz said sharply. "After the way he walked out on Mom and me, I will never have anything to do with him. Ever." She took a deep breath. "In a way, you're lucky. Your dad's dead. Mine left."

We lay there in silence for a while. I was waiting for Liz to say something smart and Liz-like that would help me make sense of everything we'd learned that day. Instead, she began coming up with jokey wordplay the way she did when something upset her and she needed to make light of it.

Liz started with the word "lintheads." First she spoonerized it as "hint leads." Then she said that lintheads were people who had no heads of their own, so people with spare heads lent heads to them. Sometimes they charged for the heads, in which case the people were known as rent heads, and once their money was gone, they were called spent heads. If the heads were damaged, they were called dent heads or bent heads.

"That's not funny," I said.

Liz was quiet for a moment. "You're right," she said.

CHAPTER TEN

The next morning, I was pulling weeds in the flower beds around the koi pond, still thinking about being Charlie Wyatt's daughter and how Mom's getting pregnant with me had created so many problems for everyone. The sound of a woodpecker hammering in the sycamores made me look up, and through the opening in the big dark bushes, I saw Joe Wyatt walking up the driveway, his burlap bag over his shoulder. I stood up. When he saw me, he headed my way, ambling along like he was out for a stroll and just happened to run into me.

"Hey," he said when he was a few feet away.

"Hey," I said.

"Ma said I should come over and say hello, seeing as how we're related and all."

I looked at him and realized he had the same dark eyes as my dad and me. "I guess we're cousins."

"Guess so."

"Sorry about calling you a thief."

He looked down, and I could see a grin spreading across his face. "Been called worse," he said. "Anyway, cuz, you particular to blackberries?"

Cuz. I liked that. "You bet I am."

"Well, then, let's go get us some."

I ran up to the barn to find my own sack.

It was the end of June, and the humidity had kept climbing. The ground was damp from rain the night before, and we crossed the big pasture, squishing in the mud where the land was poorly drained. Grasshoppers, butterflies, and little birds skittered up out of the grass in front of us. We came to a rusting barbed-wire fence line separating the pasture from the woods. Since blackberries loved the sun, Joe said, the best places to find them were along the sides of trails and where the forest met up with the fields. Walking the fence line, we soon came across huge clumps of thorny, brambly bushes thick with fat, dark berries. The first one I ate was so sour, I spit it out. Joe explained that you only picked the ones that came off when you barely touched them. The ones you had to pull weren't ripe enough to eat.

We made our way up the hill along the fence line, picking blackberries and eating as many as we kept. Joe told me that he spent much of the summer in the woods picking wineberries, mulberries, blackberries, and pawpaws—which some folks called hillbilly bananas—and raiding orchards for cherries, peaches, and apples, as well as now and then sneaking into someone's garden for a haul of tomatoes, cucumbers, potatoes, and beans.

"Only if they've got more than enough," he said. "I never take what would be missed. That would be stealing."

"It's more like scavenging," I said. "Like what birds and raccoons do."

"There you go, cuz. Though I got to admit, not everyone looks on it kindly."

From time to time, he said, farmers who spotted him in their orchards or cornfields took potshots at him. On one occasion, he was up in an apple tree in the backyard of this dentist's fancy house in Byler, and when the family came out to have lunch on the patio, he had to sit in the tree without moving a muscle for an hour until they left, still as a squirrel hoping the hunter wouldn't notice him. The worst that had ever happened was when someone's yard dog came after him and he lost part of a finger before making it over the fence. Joe grinned at the memory and held up his hand. "Wasn't a picking finger."

When our bags were full, we headed back down the hedgerow to Mayfield. The woods beyond the fence were quiet in the midday heat. At the barn we stopped to get a drink from the faucet above the watering trough, sticking our heads under the spigot, the water splashing on our faces.

"Maybe we can do some more scavenging, cuz," Joe said, wiping his chin.

"Sure, cuz," I said, wiping mine.

He walked down the drive, and I turned to the house. As I reached the front porch, Liz came out of the door.

"Mom called," she said. "She'll be here in a couple of days."

CHAPTER ELEVEN

That afternoon Liz and I sat out by the koi pond, talking about Mom's arrival and feasting on blackberries until our fingers were stained. It was about time Mom called. It had been five weeks and two days since she had the Mark Parker meltdown and took off. As much as I liked Byler and as thrilled as I was to know Uncle Tinsley and to have met my dad's family—even that grump Uncle Clarence—I really missed Mom. We were, as she always said, a tribe of three. All we needed was each other. I had tons of things I wanted to discuss with Mom, mostly about my dad, and Liz and I also wanted to know what the plan was. Would we be going back to Lost Lake? Or somewhere else?

"Maybe we could stay here for a while," I told Liz.

"Maybe," she said. "It's sort of Mom's house, too."

Ever since we'd arrived, we'd been straightening up Uncle Tinsley's stuff, but with a place like Mayfield, there was always more to do. Two days after Mom called, we were putting away jars and boxes when we heard the sound of the Dart coming up the driveway.

Liz and I rushed through the door, across the big porch, and down the steps just as Mom got out of the car, which was pulling a little white-and-orange trailer. She had on her red velvet jacket even though it was summer, and her hair was teased up the way she did it when she was going to an audition. We had a three-way hug in the middle of the driveway, laughing and whooping, with Mom going on about "my darlings," "my babies," and "my precious girls."

Uncle Tinsley came out of the house and leaned against one of the porch columns, watching us with his arms crossed. "Nice of you to finally drop in, Char," he said.

"Nice to see you, too, Tin," Mom said.

Mom and Uncle Tinsley stood there looking at each other, so I started jabbering on about all the fun things we'd been doing, staying in her old rooms in the bird wing, clearing the koi pond, riding the Farmall, eating peaches, and gathering blackberries.

Uncle Tinsley cut me off. "Where have you been, Char?" he asked. "How could you go off and leave these kids alone?"

"Don't pass judgment on me," Mom told him.

"Now, please, no fighting," Liz said.

"Yes, let's be civil," Mom said.

We all went into the house, and Mom looked around at the clutter. "Jesus, Tin. What would Mother say?"

"What would she say about someone abandoning her children? But as you said, let's be civil."

Uncle Tinsley went into the kitchen to make a pot of tea. Mom started walking around the living room, picking up her mother's crystal vases and porcelain figurines, her father's old leather-covered binoculars, the family photographs in their sterling frames. She'd tried so hard to put this place and her past out of her life, she said, and now she was back in the middle of it again. She laughed and shook her head.

Uncle Tinsley came in with the tea service on the silver tray.

"Being back here is all too dark and strange," Mom said. "I feel the old chill. Mother was always so cold and distant. She never truly loved me. All she cared about were appearances and being proper. And Father loved me for the wrong reasons. It was all very inappropriate."

"Charlotte, that's nonsense," Uncle Tinsley said. "This was always a warm house. You were Daddy's little girl—at least until your divorce—and you loved it. Nothing inappropriate ever happened under this roof."

"That's what we had to pretend. We had to pretend it was perfect. We were all experts at pretending."

"Don't be ridiculous," Uncle Tinsley said. "You've always exaggerated everything. You've always had to create your little dramas."

Mom turned to us. "See what I mean, girls? See what happens around here when you try to speak the truth? You get attacked."

"Let's just have tea," Uncle Tinsley said.

We all sat down. Liz poured and passed the cups around.

Mom stared into her tea. "Byler," she said. "Everyone in this town lives in the past. All they ever talk about is the weather and the Bulldogs. It's like they don't know or care about what's happening in the outside world. Are they even aware that their president is a war criminal?"

"The weather's important if you live off what you grow," Uncle Tinsley said. "And some people think President Nixon's doing a pretty good job trying to wind up a war he didn't start. First Republican I ever voted for." He stirred sugar into his tea and cleared his throat. "What is the plan for you and the girls?"

"I don't like plans," Mom said. "I like options. We have several options, and we're going to consider them all."

"What are the options?" Liz asked.

"You could stay here," Uncle Tinsley said. He took a sip of tea. "For a while."

"I don't consider that an option," Mom said.

Uncle Tinsley set down his teacup. "Char, you need to give these girls some stability."

"What do you know about looking after children?" Mom asked with a tight smile.

"That's not fair," Uncle Tinsley said. "I do know if Martha and I had been blessed enough to have children, we never would have gone off and left them."

Mom slammed her teacup down so hard I thought she'd break it, then she stood up and leaned over Uncle Tinsley. When anyone criticized Mom, she went on the attack, and that was what she did now. She was raising two daughters completely on her own, she said, and they were turning out darned well. He had no idea of the sacrifices she'd made. In any event, she was an independent woman. She had her own music career. She made her own decisions. She wasn't going to stand here and be judged by her brother, a broken-down old hermit still living in the house where he was born in a dead-end mill town. He'd never even had the wherewithal to get the hell out of Byler, and she had not come back to this godforsaken place to answer to him.

"Get your things, girls," she said. "We're going."

Liz and I glanced at each other, not sure what to say. I wanted to tell Mom how good Uncle Tinsley had been to us, but I was afraid she'd think I was taking his side, and that might make things worse.

"Didn't you hear me?" Mom asked.

We climbed the stairs to the bird wing.

"Jeez, they hate each other," I said.

"You'd think they'd at least be polite," Liz said.

"They're supposed to be the grown-ups," I said, and added, "I sort of don't want to go. We just met the Wyatts, and I really like them."

"Me, too. But it's not up to us."

. . .

Uncle Tinsley was sitting at a writing table, scribbling on a piece of paper, when we came downstairs carrying the two-tone deb-phase suitcases. He folded the paper and passed it to Liz.

"The telephone number," he said. "Byler two-four-six-eight. Call if you need me." He kissed us each on the cheek. "You two take care of yourselves."

"Thanks for letting me bury Fido near Aunt Martha," I said. "At first I thought you were a little grouchy, but now I think you're neat."

And then we walked out the door.

CHAPTER TWELVE

Mom drove as if we were fleeing the scene of a crime, passing cars on the road to Byler and running the stoplight on the south side of town. She was gripping the steering wheel as if her life depended on it and talking a mile a minute. Mayfield had really gone downhill, she said. Mother would have been appalled. It looked like Tinsley had become a complete recluse, though he had always been a bit of a crank. Boy, seeing that place sure brought back memories—bad memories. Same thing with this entire hopeless loser of a town. Nothing but bad memories.

"I like Mayfield," I said. "I like Byler, too."

"Try growing up here," Mom said. She reached into her purse and took out a pack of cigarettes.

"You're smoking?" Liz asked.

"It's coming back to this place. It's made me a little tense."

Mom lit the cigarette with the car's push-in lighter. We turned up Holladay Avenue. The Fourth of July was a few days away, and workers were hanging flags from every lamppost.

"God bless America," Mom said sarcastically. "With everything this country's done in Vietnam, I don't see how anyone could be feeling very patriotic."

We crossed the clanking iron bridge over the river. "I met the Wyatts," I said.

Mom didn't respond.

"Aunt Al told me about my dad getting shot." I bit my lip. "You said he died in an accident."

Mom took a drag on her cigarette and exhaled. Liz rolled down her window.

"I told you that for your own good, Bean," Mom said. "You were too young to understand."

Getting the hell out of Byler was another thing she had done for the good of her daughters, she said. There was no way she was going to let us grow up in a finger-wagging, narrow-minded town where everyone would whisper about me being the illegitimate child of a hotheaded loom fixer who killed someone and then went and got killed himself. "Not to mention that everyone in town saw yours truly as the slut who caused it all."

"But Mom," I said, "he was defending your honor."

"Maybe that's what he thought he was doing, but he made everything so much worse. By the time it was all over, Charlotte Holladay didn't have any honor left to defend." Mom took a long draw on her cigarette. "Charlotte the Harlot."

Anyway, she went on, she didn't want to think or talk about the past. She hated it. The past didn't matter, like where you came from or who you'd been didn't matter. What mattered was the future: where you were going and who you were going to become. "I've figured out the future for us," she said. "New York City!"

What had happened, she went on, was that she'd been down in San Diego with friends for a little group support, then went on to Baja to spend time alone on the beach looking for signs about what direction to take next. She hadn't seen any signs, but then she got back to Lost Lake and found Liz's message about us going off to visit the Mad Hatter and the Dormouse. That, she realized, was the sign. She needed to put California behind her and follow her daughters to the East Coast. She'd rented the U-Haul and thrown most of the stuff from our bungalow inside.

"Don't you see, Liz?" Mom asked, sounding almost giddy. "When I read your note about the other side of the Looking Glass, it hit me. That's New York City! If you're a performer, New York and L.A., they're the two sides of the Looking Glass."

Liz and I glanced at each other. We were all crowded in the front seat because Mom had crammed guitars and boxes of sheet music into the back.

"Are we being realistic?" Liz asked.

"Realism, schmealism," Mom said. Was Gauguin being realistic when he set out for the South Pacific? Was Marco Polo being realistic when he headed off for China? Was that skinny kid with the raspy voice being realistic when he dropped out of college and left Minneapolis for Greenwich Village after changing his name to Bob Dylan? "No one who dares to be great and reach for the stars worries about being realistic."

New York was where the real scene was, Mom said, much more than L.A., which was nothing but a bunch of slick producers making empty promises and desperate starlets willing to believe them. Mom started going on about Greenwich Village, Washington Square, and the Chelsea Hotel, blues bars and folk clubs, mimes in whiteface and violinists in graffiti-covered subway stations. As she talked, she became more and more animated, and it occurred to me that she wasn't going to mention the Mark Parker business or the fact that she'd walked out on us—and we weren't supposed to, either.

"What we're on now isn't just a car trip," Mom said. It was a holiday, she explained. A way of celebrating the forthcoming New York Adventures of the Tribe of Three. "I've got a surprise for you."

"What's the surprise?" Liz asked.

"I can't tell you, or it won't be a surprise," Mom said, and then she giggled. "But it's in Richmond."

We reached Richmond late in the afternoon. Mom drove up a tree-lined avenue, past a bunch of monuments of men on horseback, and stopped the Dart with the orange-and-white trailer behind it in front of a building that looked like some kind of Mediterranean palace. A man in a crimson coat with tails walked up and stood looking dubiously at the Dart and the U-Haul.

Mom turned to us. "This is the surprise. Mother and I used to stay here when we came into Richmond to shop."

She opened the car door and extended her hand to the doorman in a ladylike way. After a pause, he took her hand and, with a slight bow, helped her out of the car.

"Welcome to the Hotel Madison," he said.

"It's good to be back," Mom said.

We followed Mom out of the car. The doorman glanced down at my sneakers, which were caked with the orange mud of Byler. Mom led us up the carpeted stairs into a cavernous lobby. Rows of marble columns with big dark veins running through the stone lined both sides of the room. There was a soaring ceiling, two stories high, with a gigantic stained-glass skylight in the middle. Everywhere you looked, there were chandeliers, statues, overstuffed chairs, Persian rugs, paintings, and balconies. I'd never seen anything like it.

"Can we afford to stay here?" Liz asked.

"We can't afford not to stay here," Mom said. "After what we've been through, we not only deserve it, we need it."

Mom had been talking almost nonstop since we left Mayfield. Now she went on about the hotel's Corinthian columns and the sweeping staircase that, she said, had been used in a scene from *Gone with the Wind*. When she and her mother stayed here, she told us, they'd shop for her wardrobe for the school year, and afterward, they'd take tea and sandwiches in the tearoom, where ladies were required to wear white gloves. Her eyes were glowing.

I thought of pointing out to Mom what she'd said earlier, that she had nothing but bad memories of growing up, that she'd always hated the white-glove set. I thought better of it. She was enjoying herself too much. Besides, Mom was always contradicting herself.

At the check-in counter, Mom asked for two adjoining rooms. "Mom!" Liz whispered. "Two rooms?"

"We can't crowd up in a place like this," Mom said. "This is not some neon-lit fleabag motel. This is the Madison!"

A bellboy in a brimless hat brought our two-toned suitcases up to the rooms on a trolley. Mom made a show of presenting him with a ten-dollar tip. "Let's freshen up, then go shopping," she said. "If we're going to eat in the main dining room, we'll need proper clothes."

Liz unlocked the door to our room. It was extravagantly furnished, with a fireplace and burgundy velvet drapes pulled back with little tassels. We lay down on the four-poster bed. The mattress was so soft that you sank into it.

"Mom's never been like this before," I said.

"Not this bad," Liz said.

"She won't shut up."

"I noticed."

"Maybe it's just a mood and it'll pass." I plumped up one of the oversize pillows and leaned against it. "Mom and Uncle Tinsley have such different memories of growing up at Mayfield."

"Like they grew up in two different houses."

"What Mom said about her dad being inappropriate is creepy. Do you think it's true?"

"I think Mom believes it, but that doesn't mean it's true. Maybe she just needed someone to blame for the way everything turned out. Maybe something happened and she blew it out of proportion. Or maybe it's true. I don't think we'll ever know."

After a while, Mom knocked on our door. "Ladies," she called out, "time to hit the shops."

She was still wearing her red velvet jacket, but she had teased her hair even higher and had put on glossy lipstick and thick, dark eyeliner. She was also still talking a mile a minute. As we rode the elevator down, she explained that the hotel's main dining room was so fancy that men were required to wear a jacket and tie, and if they showed up in shirtsleeves, the maître d' provided them with the proper apparel from a collection of jackets and ties kept in the coat room.

Mom led us back through the main lobby, which was now bustling with smartly dressed guests checking in, uniformed bellboys stacking luggage, and dapper waiters in tuxes hurrying along with champagne buckets and silver trays of martinis. Liz and I were still wearing the cutoffs and T-shirts we had put on that morning at Mayfield, and I felt seriously out of place.

We followed Mom down a corridor lined with stores that had glittering plate-glass windows in brass frames displaying everything from jewelry and perfumes to fancy carved pipes and imported cigars. Mom directed us into a dress shop. "My mother took me to this very store when I was your age," she said.

There were racks of clothes, tables of shoes and handbags, and headless mannequins wearing expensive-looking pink and green summer dresses. Mom began holding up pairs of shoes and pulling dresses off the rack, saying things like "This was meant for you,

Bean," and "You'd look fabulous in these, Liz," and "This has my name written all over it."

The clerk came over, a slightly older woman with half-moon glasses hanging on a gold chain around her neck. She smiled, but like the doorman, she glanced down at my mud-caked sneakers. "Is there anything in particular I can help you with?" she asked.

"We need ensembles for dinner," Mom said. "We checked in on impulse without bringing much in the way of clothes. We're looking for something a little formal but also *très* chic."

The clerk nodded. "I know precisely what you have in mind," she said. She asked our sizes and started holding up various dresses while Mom oohed and aahed over them. Soon there was a pile of possibilities draped over a rack.

Liz fingered one and looked at the price tag. "Mom, this costs eighty dollars," she said. "It's sort of out of our price range."

Mom glared at Liz. "That's not for you to say," she said. "I'm the mother."

The clerk looked between Mom and Liz as if she couldn't decide whom to believe and where this was headed.

"Do you have any bargain racks?" I asked.

The clerk gave me a pained expression. "We're not that kind of establishment," she said. "There is a Dollar General on Broad Street."

"Now, girls, you're not to worry about money," Mom said. "We need outfits for dinner." She looked at the clerk. "They've been staying with their tightwad uncle and have picked up his penny-pinching habits."

"We can't afford this, Mom," Liz said. "You know that."

"We don't need to eat in the restaurant," I said. "We can order room service. Or takeout."

Mom looked at Liz and me. Her smile disappeared, and her face darkened. "How dare you?" she said. "How dare you question my authority?"

She was trying to do something nice for us, Mom went on, something that would lift our spirits, and this was the thanks she got? What a couple of ingrates. Thanks. Thanks a lot. She had driven all the way across the country to get us, and what did we do to show our gratitude? We publicly embarrassed her in a store where she'd been shopping since she was a girl. She'd had it. Had it with the two of us.

Knocking the dresses off the rack, Mom stormed out of the store.

"My goodness," the clerk said.

We followed Mom out to the busy corridor, but she had disappeared.

"She must have gone back to her room," Liz said.

We crossed the lobby, rode the elevator up to our floor, and walked down the hushed, carpeted hallway. A waiter passed us, pushing a cart loaded with plates and bowls covered by silver lids. The food smelled delicious and made me realize I was hungry. We hadn't eaten since breakfast, and I wondered what we were going to do for dinner. The idea of room service started to seem mighty appealing.

We stopped at Mom's door, and Liz knocked. "Mom?" she called out. There was no answer. Liz knocked again. "Mom, we know you're in there."

"We're sorry," I said. "We'll be good."

There was still no answer.

Liz kept knocking.

"Go away!" Mom shouted.

"We love you, Mom," Liz said.

"You don't love me. You hate me!"

"Please, Mom," Liz said. "We do love you. We're just trying to be realistic."

"Go away!" Mom screamed again.

The door shook with a bang and the sound of shattering glass. Mom had thrown something. Then she started sobbing hysterically.

We headed back to the lobby. There was a line of people standing at the reception desk, but Liz went right to the front, and I followed.

The clerk had polished black hair and was writing busily in a ledger. "The line starts back there," he said without looking up.

"We have a bit of an emergency," Liz told him.

The clerk looked up and raised his eyebrows.

"Our mom has locked herself in her room and won't come out," Liz said. "We need help."

We trooped up to Mom's room with the clerk and a security guard. She was still crying and refusing to open the door. The clerk went to a house phone and sent for a doctor. When the doctor arrived in his white jacket, the security guard took out a master key, opened the door, and led him into the room. Liz and I followed.

Mom was lying on the bed with a pillow over her head. The doctor, a small man with a mild Southern manner, stroked her shoulder. Mom took the pillow off her face and stared at the ceiling. Her makeup was smeared. Liz and I were standing by the wall, but Mom didn't look over at us. Liz put her arm around my shoulders.

Mom let out a loud sigh. "No one understands how hard it is to be me," she told the doctor.

The doctor murmured in agreement. He told Mom he was going to give her a shot that would make her feel a lot better, and after that she could probably use a couple of days of rest and observation at Commonwealth Medical. Mom closed her eyes and squeezed the doctor's hand.

The clerk ushered Liz and me out into the hall. "Now, what are we going to do with you two?" he asked.

"We have an uncle in Byler," Liz said.

"I think we'd better call him," the clerk said.

After talking to Uncle Tinsley, the clerk ordered us each a ginger ale that came with a maraschino cherry, as well as a plate of little sand-wiches—turkey, shrimp salad, cucumber—with the crusts cut off, and we ate them at a tiny table in the enormous column-filled lobby. An ambulance had arrived at the back entrance for Mom, the clerk told us, and the doctor had helped her into it. The bellboy brought our suitcases down, and after we finished our sandwiches, we sat there waiting. The clerk kept coming over to see if we were all right. As the hours passed, the bustling lobby grew quieter, and by the time Uncle Tinsley showed up, pushing through the revolving doors just before midnight, it was deserted except for our new friend the clerk straightening things up behind the counter and a janitor pol-ishing the marble floor with a big electric buffing machine.

Uncle Tinsley's footsteps echoed off the high ceiling as he walked through the lobby toward us. "I was hoping to see you again," he said, "but I never imagined it would be this soon."

CHAPTER THIRTEEN

Mom had me a little worried, but to be honest, I was relieved to be back in Byler. I hadn't been looking forward to moving to New York City, where, according to Uncle Tinsley, if you screamed for help, all people did was close their windows.

After a couple of days, Mom called. She was feeling a lot better. She'd had a little bit of a meltdown, she admitted, but that was due to the stress of going back to Byler after all those years. She talked to Uncle Tinsley, and they decided that what made the most sense was for Liz and me to stay in Byler for the time being. Mom said she would go on to New York by herself, and once she'd gotten settled in, she would send for us.

"How long do you think it will take Mom to get settled in?" I asked Liz.

We were getting ready for bed, brushing our teeth in the birdwing bathroom. To save money on toothpaste, Uncle Tinsley mixed together salt and baking soda. Once you got used to the taste, it did make your whole mouth feel well scrubbed.

"There's getting settled in," Liz said, "and then there's getting a grip on things."

"How long will that take?"

Liz rinsed and spit. "We might be here a while."

The next morning, Liz told me she hadn't slept all that well because she'd been thinking about our situation. It was entirely possible, she said, that for whatever reason, Mom wouldn't be ready to send for us by the time summer was over. That would mean we'd go to school here in Byler. We didn't want to be a burden to Uncle Tinsley, who was clearly set in his widower ways. Plus, although he lived in a grand house and his family used to run the town, the collars of his shirts were worn through and he had holes in his socks. It was obvious his tight budget didn't include providing for the two nieces who'd shown up on his doorstep unannounced and uninvited.

"We need to get jobs," Liz said.

I thought that was a great idea. We could both babysit. I might be able to make some money delivering *Grit* magazine, like I had in Lost Lake. We could mow lawns or pick up branches in people's yards. Maybe we could even get store jobs working cash registers or bagging groceries.

At breakfast, we told Uncle Tinsley about our plan. We thought he'd love the idea, but as soon as Liz started explaining, he began to wave his hands as if to dismiss the whole thing. "You girls are Holladays," he said. "You can't go around begging for work like a couple of hired hands." He dropped his voice. "Or coloreds," he added. "Mother would roll over in her grave."

Uncle Tinsley said he believed that girls from good families needed to develop discipline, a sense of responsibility for themselves and their community, and they got that by joining church committees or volunteering as candy stripers at the hospital. "Holladays don't work for other people," he said. "Other people work for Holladays."

"But we might still be here when school starts," Liz said.

"That's a distinct possibility," Uncle Tinsley said. "And I welcome it. We're all Holladays."

"We'll need school clothes," I added.

"Clothes?" he said. "You need clothes? We've got all the clothes you need. Follow me."

Uncle Tinsley led us up the stairs to the little maids' rooms on the third floor and started opening musty trunks and cedar-lined closets stuffed with mothball-smelling clothes: fur-collared overcoats, polka-dotted dresses, tweed jackets, ruffled silk blouses, knee-length pleated plaid skirts.

"These are all of the finest quality, hand-tailored, imported from England and France," he said.

"But Uncle Tinsley," I said, "they're kind of old-timey. People don't wear clothes like this anymore."

"That's the shame of it," he said. "Because they don't make clothes like this anymore. It's all blue jeans and polyester. Never worn a pair of blue jeans in my life. Farmer clothes."

"But that's what everyone wears today," I said. "They wear blue jeans."

"And that's why we need to get jobs," Liz said. "To buy some."

"We need spending money," I said.

"People think they need all sorts of things they don't really need," Uncle Tinsley said. "If there's something you really need, we can talk about it. But you don't need clothes. We have clothes."

"Are you saying we're not allowed to get jobs?" Liz asked.

"If you don't need clothes, you don't need jobs." Uncle Tinsley's face softened. "You do need to get out of the house. And I need to concentrate on my research. Take the bikes, go into town, visit the library, make friends, make yourselves useful. But don't forget, you're Holladays."

Liz and I walked up to the barn. We'd had a hot spell recently, but an early-morning shower had brought some relief, and the wilting butterfly bushes had sprung back to life.

"Uncle Tinsley's wrong," Liz said. "We do need to get jobs. And not just for clothes. We need our own money."

"But Uncle Tinsley will get mad."

"I think Uncle Tinsley doesn't really mind us getting jobs," Liz said. "He just doesn't want to know about it. He wants to pretend we're all still living back in the day."

Uncle Tinsley had patched the flat tire on the bike he'd ridden as a kid. It was a Schwinn, like Mom's, only it was a guy's bike and it was blue, with a headlight and a saddlebag. Liz and I got the bikes out of the garage and rode into town to look for work.

We had forgotten that it was the Fourth of July. A parade was getting under way, and people were lined up along Holladay Avenue, entire families sitting in folding chairs and on the curb, eating Popsicles, shading their eyes against the bright sun, and waving enthusiastically as the Byler High School band marched along in red-and-white uniforms. It was followed by the pom-pom-waving cheerleaders and baton-twirling majorettes, red-coated foxhunters on horseback, a fire truck, and a float with waving women in worn sequined gowns. Finally, a group of older men in a variety of military uniforms turned up the avenue, all of them looking very serious and proud, those in the lead using both hands to hold big American flags out in front of them. Right in the middle of the group was Uncle Clarence, dressed in a green uniform, moving stiffly and looking a little short of breath but keeping pace. As the flags passed, most of the people in the crowd stood up and saluted.

"Here come the patriots," Liz whispered in that sarcastic tone she'd picked up from Mom.

I kept quiet. Mom, who'd gone to antiwar rallies where protesters burned flags, had been telling us for years about everything wrong with America—the war, the pollution, the discrimination, the violence—but here were all these people, including Uncle Clarence, showing real pride in the flag and the country. Who was right? They both had their points. Were they both right? Was there such a thing as completely right and completely wrong? Liz seemed to think so. I usually had pretty strong opinions, but now I wasn't so sure. This was complicated.

When the parade passed, the people in the crowd started folding up their chairs and spilling onto Holladay Avenue. We walked along pushing our bikes. Ahead, we saw the Wyatts coming up the street. Joe was carrying Earl, who held a little American flag. Uncle Clarence had medals above the breast pocket of his green uniform, and he wore one of those skinny army caps with patches and pins covering both sides.

"I do love Independence Day," Aunt Al said after giving us both hugs. "Reminds you how lucky we are to be Americans. When my Truman comes home, he'll be marching alongside Clarence in that parade."

"But he's thinking of reenlisting," Joe said.

"Why?" Liz asked. "We're losing the war."

"We're losing the war here at home with all these goddamned spoiled draft-dodging protesters," Uncle Clarence said. "We're not losing the war over there. Our boys are just trying to figure out how to win. They're doing a hell of a fine job. Truman himself says so." He turned on his heel and stalked off.

"I didn't mean to upset him," Liz said. "Doesn't everyone know we're losing?"

We all started walking up Holladay Avenue toward the hill. "People have different views," Aunt Al said. "It's a touchy subject around here. There's a tradition of service in these parts. You do what your country asks you to do, and you do it with pride."

"I'm enlisting when I graduate," Joe said. "Not waiting to be drafted."

"My Clarence was in Korea," Aunt Al went on. "So was your daddy, Bean. Got the Silver Star."

"What's that?"

"A medal," Aunt Al said. "Charlie was a hero. He ran out into enemy fire to save a wounded buddy."

"You're enlisting?" Liz asked Joe.

"That's what guys around here do," Joe said. "I want to fix helicopters and learn to fly them, like Truman."

Liz stared at him in disbelief, and I was afraid she was going to say something sarcastic, so I changed the subject. "We're going to go looking for jobs," I told Aunt Al.

"That's a tall order," she said. There was not a lot of work around Byler these days, she explained. The folks on the hill sure didn't have money to spare. She and Clarence couldn't even afford a car, and neither could a lot of the neighbors. Over on Davis Street and East Street, where the doctors and the lawyers and the judges and the bankers lived, most people had coloreds who did the cooking and washing and gardening. However, there were retired folks around town who may have the odd job or yard work.

"Sometimes I get little jobs, but I make more money selling fruit and scrap metal," Joe said.

"Still," Aunt Al added, "you might land something, God willing and the creek don't rise."

• • •

Liz and I spent the next couple of days knocking on doors all over Byler. Most of the folks on the hill apologetically explained that in times like these, they were lucky if they could pay their bills each month. They couldn't afford to fork over hard-earned cash to kids for jobs that they could do themselves. Our luck wasn't much better at the fancier houses on East Street and Davis Street. A lot of times, black maids in uniforms answered the doors, and some of them seemed surprised when they learned we were looking for the kind of work they were doing. One older lady did hire us to rake her yard, but after two hours' work she gave us only a quarter each, acting like she was being extravagantly generous.

At the end of the second day, Liz decided to check out the Byler Library and I rode over to the Wyatts' to tell Aunt Al that the job search wasn't going so well.

"Don't be discouraged," she said. "And wait right here. I got a surprise for you." She disappeared down the hall and came back with a ring box. I opened it, and hanging from a little red, white, and blue ribbon was a star-shaped medal.

"Charlie Wyatt's Silver Star," she said.

I picked up the medal. The star was gold and had a small wreath in the middle surrounding a tiny second star that was silver. "A war hero," I said. "Did he have a lot of war stories?"

"Charlie was quite the talker, but one thing he never did like to talk about was how he got this Silver Star. Or, for that matter, anything about that danged war. Charlie never wore that star, and he never told people about it. He saved one buddy, but there were plenty others he couldn't save, and it weighed on him."

Little Earl, who was sitting next to Aunt Al, stretched out his hand, and I passed the medal to him. He held it up, then put the star in his mouth. Aunt Al took it back, polished it with her dish towel, and passed it to me. "Uncle Clarence was keeping this in memory of his kid brother. But it's yours now."

"I don't want to take it if it's important to Uncle Clarence," I said.

"No," Aunt Al said. "We talked, and Clarence thought about it and decided that Charlie would want his little girl to have it."

Charlie and Clarence had always been close, Aunt Al went on. Their parents were sharecroppers who had been killed in a tractor accident. It happened one night when they were trying to bring in the tobacco crop during a big storm and the tractor turned over on a hillside. At the time, Charlie was six and Clarence was eleven. None of their relatives could afford to feed both boys, and since Charlie was too young to earn his keep, no one wanted him. Clarence told the family taking him in that he would do the work of two hands if they took Charlie as well. The family agreed on a trial basis, and Clarence worked himself to the bone, dropping out of school to take on the responsibilities of a full-grown man. The brothers stayed together, but those years hardened Clarence, and when he went to work at the mill, most of the women thought he was downright mean.

"I saw the hurt orphan inside the bitter man," Aunt Al said. "Clarence just wasn't used to being cared for."

"I should thank him for the star," I said.

"He's out tending to his garden."

I walked through the Wyatts' small, dark living room, which was behind the kitchen, and out the back door. Uncle Clarence, wearing a battered straw hat, was kneeling in a few dirt rows of green beans, staked tomatoes, and cucumber vines, working a trowel around the base of the plants.

"Uncle Clarence," I said. "Thank you for giving me my dad's Silver Star."

Uncle Clarence didn't look up.

"Aunt Al said you two were close," I added.

He nodded. Then he put the trowel down and turned toward me. "Damned shame about your momma going crazy," he said, "but that woman should have the word 'trouble' tattooed on her forehead. Meeting your momma was the worst thing that ever happened to your daddy."

CHAPTER FOURTEEN

Liz and I continued our job hunt the next day. Most of the houses in Byler were old, both the grand ones and the dinky ones, but late in the afternoon, we turned down a street that had newer ranches and split-levels with breezeways and asphalt driveways and little saplings surrounded by pine-needle mulch. One of the houses had a chain-link fence around the front yard with a bunch of hubcaps hanging on it. A shiny black car was parked in the driveway and a man had his head under the hood, fiddling with the engine, while a girl sat in the driver's seat.

The man shouted at the girl to turn the engine over, but she gave it too much gas and when the engine roared, he jerked his head up, banging it on the hood. He started cussing loudly, yelling that the girl was trying to kill him, and then he turned around and saw us.

"Sorry, ladies. Didn't know you were there," he said. "I'm trying to fix this damned engine, and my girl here's not being much help."

He was a big man. Not fat, just big, like a bull. He pulled up his T-shirt and used it to wipe his face, exposing his broad, hairy belly, then wiped his hands on his jeans.

"Maybe we can help," Liz said.

"We're looking for work," I said.

"That so? What kind of work?"

The man walked over to where we were standing. His walk was lumbering but also strangely light-footed, as though he could move very quickly if he needed to. His arms were thick as hams, his fingers were thick, too, and his neck was actually thicker than his head. He had short blond hair, small but very bright blue eyes, and a broad nose with flaring nostrils.

"Any kind of work," Liz said. "Yard work, babysitting, house-cleaning."

The man was looking us up and down. "I haven't seen you two around before."

"We've only been here a few weeks," I said.

"Your family move here?" he asked.

"We're just kind of visiting," Liz said.

"Kind of visiting," he said. "What's that mean?"

"We're staying with our uncle for a while," I said.

"Why are you doing that?"

"Well, we're just spending the summer with him," Liz said.

"We were born here," I said. "But we haven't been back since we were little."

Liz gave me the look that said I was talking too much, but I didn't see how we were going to get jobs if we didn't answer the man's questions.

"Oh, really?" he said. "And who's your uncle?"

"Tinsley Holladay," I said.

"Oh, really?" he said again, leaning in like he was suddenly interested. He was so big that when he got close and looked down on us, it felt like he was swallowing up the sky. "So you're Tinsley Holladay's nieces?" He smiled, as if the idea of that was amusing. "Well, Tinsley's nieces, do you have names?"

"I'm Liz, and this is my sister, Bean."

"Bean? What kind of name is that?"

"A nickname," I said. "It rhymes with my real name, Jean. Liz is always rhyming and giving things her own names."

"Okay, Liz and Bean-rhymes-with-Jean, I'm Jerry Maddox. And that's my girl, Cindy." He motioned at her with his finger. "Cindy, come over here and meet Tinsley Holladay's nieces."

The girl got out of the car. She was a few years younger than me, thin with blond hair like her dad's that came down to her shoulders, and she walked with a slight limp. Mr. Maddox put his arm around her. Liz and I said hi, and I smiled at Cindy. She said hi, but she didn't smile back, just stared at us with the same blue eyes as her father's.

"Well, I might have some work for Tinsley Holladay's nieces," Mr. Maddox said. "I just might. Either of you ever been behind the wheel of a car?"

"Mom has let me drive up and down the driveway," Liz said.

"Mom? That would be Tinsley Holladay's sister."

"Yes," Liz said. "That's right."

"Charlotte Holladay, if I'm not mistaken."

"Do you know her?" I asked.

"Never met her, but I've heard of her." He smiled again, and it seemed that what Uncle Tinsley said was true—everyone in town knew Mom's story.

Mr. Maddox had Liz get in the driver's seat where Cindy had been. Liz had the privilege, he told us, of sitting behind the wheel of a Pontiac Le Mans, one of the classiest cars Detroit had ever turned out, but only the real buffs appreciated it, the suckers falling for the GTO just because it cost more. He had Liz turn the engine on and off, then operate the turn signal and tap the brakes while he had me walk around the Le Mans, checking all the lights. Then he told Liz to gun the engine. He checked the timing, adjusted the carburetor, tested the belts, and had me hold the funnel while he added oil. Cindy stood by silently, watching it all.

Finally satisfied, Mr. Maddox stood up and slammed down the hood. "All tuned up and ready to go," he said. "You girls are good at taking orders." He pulled a wad of money out of his pants pocket and riffled through it. "Looking for something small, but all I have is tens and twenties," he said. "Oh, here we go." He pulled out two fives and passed one to each of us. "I think we can work together," he said. "Come back Saturday after lunch."

"I told you we'd get jobs," Liz said on the way home. She was practically crowing. "Didn't I say that, Bean?"

"Sure did. You're always right."

Halfway back to the house, we passed the field with the two emus. Usually, they were out of sight or on the far side of the field, but now they were walking along the fence line right by the road.

"Look," I said. "They want to meet us."

"Mom would call it a sign," Liz said.

We stopped to watch the emus. They moved slowly and deliberately, their long necks swaying from side to side as they cocked their heads. They had curling turquoise stripes on the sides of their heads, tiny stunted wings, and big, scaly feet with these sharp-taloned toes. A gurgly drumming noise that didn't sound like any birdcall I'd ever heard came from deep in their throats.

"They're so weird," I said.

"Beautifully weird."

"They're too big to be birds. They have wings, but they can't fly. They look like they shouldn't exist."

"That's what makes them so special."

CHAPTER FIFTEEN

When we showed up at the Maddoxes' on Saturday, Cindy answered the door. I started to say hello, but she turned away and called out, "They're here."

We followed Cindy into the house. The living room was filled with boxes and appliances, including a portable black-and-white TV on top of a console color TV. Both TVs were on and tuned to different stations, but the sound on the black-and-white TV was turned down. A pregnant woman with mousy blond hair sat on a black Naugahyde couch, nursing a large baby. She looked up at us and shouted, "Jerry."

Mr. Maddox came out of the back, introduced the woman as his wife, Doris, and gestured to us to follow him down the hall. One of the funny things about the Maddox house was that there wasn't a single thing up on the walls: no pictures, no posters, no bulletin boards, no family photographs, no happy sayings or Bible verses, just these bare hospital-white walls.

Mr. Maddox led us into a bedroom that had been converted into an office, with more boxes and putty-colored metal filing cabinets and a metal desk. He sat down behind the desk and pointed at two folding chairs in front of it. "Take a seat, ladies," he said. He picked up a stack of folders, tapped them on the desktop, and slipped them into a drawer. "A lot of people work for me," he went on, "and I always ask them about their backgrounds." He was a foreman at the mill, he explained, but he also had outside business dealings that involved complicated and sensitive financial and legal matters. He needed to be able to trust the people who worked for him and had access to his home and this office, where he handled the outside dealings. In order to fully trust the people who worked for him, he needed to know who they were. Due diligence, he called it, standard operating procedure for savvy businessmen. "I can't have some surprise come out and bite me in the ass after I've hired someone. It's a two-way street, of course. Any questions about me or my qualifications as an employer?" He paused. "No? Well, then, tell me about yourselves."

Liz and I looked at each other. She started hesitantly explaining the part-time jobs we'd held, but Mr. Maddox also wanted to know about our backgrounds, our schooling, our chores, Mom's rules, Mom herself. Mr. Maddox listened intently, and the moment he sensed Liz was being evasive about something, he zeroed in with pointed questions. When Liz told him that some of the information was personal and irrelevant, he said that lots of jobs required security clearance and background checks, and this was one of them. He would treat everything we told him with the utmost confidence. "You can trust Jerry Maddox," he said.

It seemed impossible not to answer his questions. The funny thing was, nothing seemed to surprise or disturb him. In fact, he was sympathetic and understanding. He said Mom sounded like a talented and fascinating individual, and he confided that his own mom was a complicated woman herself—very smart, but boy, did she run hot and cold, and when he came home at day's end, he never knew whether he was in for a hugging or a whipping.

That really got us talking, and soon Mr. Maddox had wormed the whole story out of us—Mom taking off, the bandersnatches, the cross-country bus trip. He wanted to know exactly why Mom had left and exactly why she'd had a meltdown, so I ended up telling him about Mark Parker, the boyfriend who kind of, sort of didn't really exist. I also told him how we'd dodged the odious Perv in New Orleans, thinking that the way Liz and I had handled it would impress him.

That was the very word he used. "I'm impressed," he said. He was leaning back with his hands clasped behind his head. "I like people who know how to deal with difficult situations. You're hired."

So that was how Liz and I began working for the Maddoxes.

CHAPTER SIXTEEN

I worked mostly for Doris Maddox. She had light freckles, and eyebrows and eyelashes that were completely white, and she kept her mousy blond hair in a short ponytail. She was a few years younger than Mom and was the sort of woman Mom would have said could be quite pretty if she'd just fix herself up a little, but she wore a faded cotton housedress and walked on the backs of her bedroom slippers like it was too much trouble to get them all the way on her feet.

In addition to her daughter, Cindy, Doris had two boys—a toddler, Jerry Jr., and Randy, the baby. She was pregnant with her fourth child and spent most of her time sitting on the couch, watching TV—game shows in the morning, soap operas in the afternoon—while smoking Salems, drinking RC Colas, and nursing Randy. When Mr. Maddox was in the room, Doris said very little, but once he'd left, she became more talkative, mostly complaining about the morons on the game shows or the sluts in the stories, as she called the soap operas. She also complained about Mr. Maddox, how he was always telling her what to do and staying out all hours with God knows who.

Doris had me take care of Randy when she wasn't nursing him, and also look after Jerry Jr., who was three. My duties included changing their Pampers and heating Randy's little jars of Gerber baby food and Jerry Jr.'s SpaghettiOs—that and baloney-and-cheese sandwiches were all he would eat—as well as running to the store for Doris's RCs and Salems. I also washed and folded the clothes, cleaned the bathroom, and mopped the floors. Doris told me I was a good, hard worker because I was willing to get down on my hands and knees to scrub. "Most whites just won't do that, you know."

Mr. Maddox was infatuated with the latest gadgets and high-tech gizmos and the house was full of trash compactors, air sanitizers, vacuum cleaners, popcorn poppers, transistor radios, and hi-fi systems. Most of the boxes throughout the house contained appliances, though a lot had never been opened. The family had two dishwashers because Mr. Maddox had decided that was more efficient. You could be using one set of dishes while the other was being washed, he said, then load the empty washer and take the clean dishes from the other washer right to the table without having to waste time putting them away in the cupboard.

Mr. Maddox was always thinking like that. He'd figure out more efficient and improved ways of doing things, then order everybody to do it his new way. That was why he'd been hired at the mill, he told us, to increase efficiency. He'd had to kick some butt to do it, but he'd kicked the butt, and it had gotten done.

Mr. Maddox was fascinated by the law. He subscribed to several newspapers and clipped out articles about lawsuits, bankruptcies, swindles, and foreclosures. His side dealings included buying up and renting out old millhouses. He had several houses on one street and was trying to get the town to change its name to Maddox Avenue. He also had a business loaning money to millworkers who needed to get to the next paycheck, and from time to time, he said, he was forced to take legal action against people who owed him money or were trying to stiff him or thought they could play him for a fool.

A lot of Mr. Maddox's business dealings required meetings. While I stayed at the house helping out Doris, Liz accompanied Mr. Maddox in the black Le Mans to collect rents and take meetings at bars, coffee shops, and offices, where he introduced her as his personal assistant, Liz Holladay of the Holladay family. Liz carried his briefcase, passed him documents when he asked for them, and took notes. Back at the house, she would file paperwork, call to set up his appointments, and answer Mr. Maddox's phone. He told her to tell everyone who called that he was in a meeting, so he could dodge the people he didn't want to talk to and impress those he did.

We never worked regular hours. Instead, Mr. Maddox would tell us when he'd need us next. And we never received regular pay. Mr. Maddox paid us what he thought we deserved depending on how hard we'd worked that day. Liz thought we should be paid by the hour, but Mr. Maddox said in his experience, that encouraged laziness, and people were more motivated to work hard if they were paid by the job.

Mr. Maddox also bought us clothes. We showed up for work one morning, and he presented each of us with a pale blue dress, saying they were a bonus. A week later, he actually took Liz to the store and had her try on several outfits before choosing the one he liked best.

We didn't have to wear the pale blue dresses every day, only when Mr. Maddox told us to. I didn't particularly like the dress, which felt like a uniform. I would rather have gotten my bonus in cash, but Mr. Maddox said since I was working in his house and Liz was representing him in meetings with his business associates, we needed to dress in a way that he felt was appropriate. And, he added, the cost of the clothes was more than any cash bonus he would have given us, so we were coming out ahead. "I'm doing you a big favor here," he said.

One thing about Mr. Maddox, he always made it darned hard to argue with him.

CHAPTER SEVENTEEN

We hadn't been working for the Maddoxes long when it dawned on me that Doris and the kids hardly ever left the house except to go into the front yard. Some days I'd sit on the front steps watching Cindy, Jerry Jr., and Randy and studying the extensive hubcap collection that hung on the chain-link fence. There was something hypnotic about those rows and rows of hubcaps—shiny and bold, like shields, with spokes or arrowheads or sunburst patterns—and when they caught the sun, they were almost blinding.

The funny thing was, even when the kids were out in the yard, they didn't really play. They just sat on the grass or in the plastic toy cars bleached by the Virginia sun, staring straight ahead, and I couldn't for the life of me get them to pretend to drive or even make car noises.

But they didn't even go into the yard that often. One reason was because Mr. Maddox and Doris had a fixation about germs and bacteria. That was why they were always having me scrub down their walls, floors, and countertops and why they had more cleaning products than I knew existed: ammonia, Clorox, Lysol, different cleaners for carpets, leather, glass, wood, sinks, toilets, upholstery, chrome, brass, even a special aerosol spray to remove stains from neckties.

Cindy Maddox was the most obsessed with the idea of contamination. She wouldn't eat her food if other food had touched it. The grease from the burger wasn't allowed to run onto the potatoes, the canned corn couldn't bump up against the meat loaf, and she wouldn't eat eggs at all because the white and the yolk had shared the shell. Cindy didn't like her toys to be touched, either. Most of her dolls were still in their boxes, lined up on a shelf in her room, staring out from behind the cellophane.

Cindy was the only Maddox kid who was school-age. Her parents homeschooled her, however, because Doris was afraid she'd catch germs. Cindy hadn't done well on the last exam she'd been given, so even though it was summer, she had schoolwork. But Cindy wasn't really interested in learning, and Doris wasn't really interested in teaching. The two of them usually sat on the Naugahyde couch, watching TV together. Sometimes Doris had Liz or me read to Cindy. Cindy loved being read to. She also loved the way Liz would change the ending to a story if Cindy found it upsetting, having the little match girl survive instead of freezing to death, or saving the one-legged tin soldier and the paper ballerina rather than letting them wind up in the fire.

Doris wanted me to tutor Cindy, who knew how to read on her own but didn't seem to enjoy it. One day I had her read aloud from *The Yearling*. She made it through a chapter just fine, but when I asked her what she thought of it, she went completely blank. I asked her a few more questions and realized she didn't understand a darned thing about what she'd just read. She had no problem with the individual words but couldn't string them together to mean anything. She treated the words like she did her food, keeping each one separate.

I was trying to explain to Cindy how words depended on other words for their meaning—how the bark of a dog is different from the bark of a tree—when I heard Mr. Maddox start shouting at Doris in the bedroom. He was going on about how she didn't need any new clothes. Who was she trying to impress? Or was she trying to seduce someone? I looked at Cindy, who acted as if she didn't hear anything at all.

Mr. Maddox came into the living room carrying a cardboard box and he handed it to me. "Put this in the Le Mans," he said.

Inside the box were Doris's three faded housedresses and her one pair of street shoes. Doris appeared in the hallway in her nightgown. "Those are my clothes," she said. "I don't have anything to wear."

"They're not your clothes," Mr. Maddox told her. "They're Jerry Maddox's clothes. Who bought them? Jerry Maddox. Who worked his butt off to pay for them? Jerry Maddox. So who do they belong to?"

"Jerry Maddox," Doris said.

"That's correct. I just let you wear them when I want. It's like this house." He swung his arm around. "Who owns it? Jerry Maddox. But I let you live here." He turned back to me. "Now go put that box in the car."

I felt like I was being drawn into the middle of the fight. Since I worked mainly for Doris, I glanced at her to see what she wanted me to do, half expecting her to tell me to give her the box. She was just standing there looking defeated, so I carried the box out to the breezeway and put it in the backseat of the Le Mans.

As I closed the car door, Mr. Maddox stepped outside. "You think I was being hard on Doris, don't you?" he said. "Not for nothing. She's one of those people who needs to be disciplined." Doris was fast when he first met her, Mr. Maddox went on. She wore too much makeup, her skirts were way too short, and she let men take advantage of her. "I had to step in to protect her from herself. I still do. If I let her go out whenever she wants, she'll fall back into her old ways. Without her clothes, she can't go out. If she can't go out, she can't get in trouble. I'm not being mean. I'm doing it for her own good. You see?"

He was looking at me with that direct fixed stare. I just nodded.

CHAPTER EIGHTEEN

Mr. Maddox had said he didn't need me working for Doris the next couple of days, but he wanted Liz to come back, so the following morning, I rode my Schwinn over to the Wyatts' to see if Joe was up to a little fruit scavenging.

Joe was finishing breakfast. Aunt Al made me a plate, too—gravy over biscuits and eggs fried in bacon fat until they were crispy as french fries. She poured Joe a cup of coffee, which he drank black, and asked if I wanted some.

"Ugh," I said. "Kids don't drink coffee."

" 'Round here they do," Joe said.

Aunt Al gave me a cup of milk, then added a little coffee and two heaping teaspoons of sugar. "Try this," she said.

I took a sip. The milk and sugar cut the bitterness of the coffee, making it like a soda-fountain drink with a tiny kick.

"Did you all ever find yourselves any work?" Aunt Al asked.

"Sure did," I said. "Your boss at the mill, Mr. Maddox, he's our boss, too, now. He hired me and Liz to work around his house."

"Is that a fact?" Aunt Al set down her coffee. "I'm not too sure how I feel about that. Jerry Maddox can ride people hard. Sure does at the mill, where they all hate him. My Ruthie used to work for that family, but she just finally couldn't take it anymore. And she gets along with everyone."

"Mr. Maddox was the only one who offered me and Liz a job," I said. "He hasn't been too hard on us, but he does boss his wife around something awful."

"That man would boss the calf out of the cow. Your Uncle Tinsley don't mind you working for him?"

"We haven't exactly told Uncle Tinsley," I said, and took a glug of my milk-with-coffee. "He didn't want us to get jobs. We're Holladays, he said, and Holladays don't work for other people. But we need the money."

"I hear you there," she said. "But you ought to know about the history between Mr. Maddox and your uncle."

Mr. Maddox, Aunt Al explained, was one of the men the new mill owners from Chicago had brought in to run the place. Uncle Tinsley had worked out an arrangement with the buyers to stay on as a consultant, seeing as how he knew the operations of the mill firsthand and had a history with the clients and the workers. But in no time, he and Mr. Maddox butted heads. Mr. Maddox's job was running the shop floor, and the new owners had told him to do everything he could to cut costs and raise production. He followed people around with a stopwatch, pushing them to work faster and eliminate any unnecessary movements, to fold each pair of socks in two and a half seconds, not three, hollering at them for taking bathroom breaks and insisting they eat lunch at their workstations. He announced that, every month, he was going to fire the five slowest workers until he'd cut the number of employees by half.

It was at Mr. Maddox's recommendation that the owners did away with the baseball team and the free hams at Christmas. He then got them to sell off the houses that the mill rented to the workers, buying up a lot of them himself on the cheap and raising the rent.

The mill had never been an easy place, Aunt Al said, but for the most part, all the workers got along. They felt they were in the same boat. But after Mr. Maddox showed up and started firing people, former friends turned on one another, even selling out or ratting on their coworkers so they could keep their jobs and feed their families.

Mr. Holladay insisted that a lot of Mr. Maddox's changes were doing more harm than good, Aunt Al said. He felt that Mr. Maddox was making the workers more miserable, which was making them less motivated. That meant they'd take less pride in the product, and from time to time, they would even sabotage the machinery just to get a few minutes' breather from the backbreaking pace. He and Mr. Maddox kept locking horns, arguing about the best way to run the mill. At one point they got into a shouting match on the shop floor. Mr. Holladay took his complaints to the new owners, but they sided with Mr. Maddox and forced Mr. Holladay out of the mill.

"The mill with his name on it," Aunt Al said. "The mill his family had founded, owned, and operated for the better part of a century. After that, a lot of people around Byler started avoiding your uncle."

"But he didn't do anything wrong," I said.

"True enough. But Mr. Maddox won the fight, and he was holding all the cards."

"I guess that's why Uncle Tinsley sort of keeps to himself."

"He lost his parents and his wife and his mill all in the space of a few short years," Aunt Al said. "The poor man's just had too much taken from him."

I finished off the last bite of my eggs and biscuits. "Maybe we should tell Uncle Tinsley that we're working for Mr. Maddox," I said.

I took my plate over to the sink and rinsed it. "I feel bad. He's been good to us, and we're sneaking around behind his back."

"I'm none too big on giving advice," Aunt Al said. "Most times when folks ask for advice, they already know what they should do. They just want to hear it from someone else."

"Enough of this jawboning," Joe said. "Let's go get us some apples, cuz."

In the bird wing that night, I told Liz what Aunt Al had said about the bad blood between Mr. Maddox and Uncle Tinsley. "It doesn't feel right working for someone Uncle Tinsley hates."

"We need the money."

"Still, he's letting us stay here and sharing his stew, and we're lying to him."

"We're not lying, we're just not telling him everything," Liz said. Look, she went on, if Uncle Tinsley would be realistic, admit that we needed money for school clothes and school supplies, that would be one thing. But as long as he was going to pretend we could wear debutante clothes from the forties and didn't need to worry about buying schoolbooks and cafeteria lunches, then we had to do what we had to do. "You don't need to tell people everything. Keeping something to yourself is not the same as lying."

Liz had a point, but I still felt funny about it.

The next afternoon, when Liz came back from work, she said she'd asked Mr. Maddox about his clash with Uncle Tinsley. Mr. Maddox had told her that he and Uncle Tinsley had indeed had some disagreements over how the mill should be run. Uncle Tinsley lost the argument, Mr. Maddox said. He hadn't mentioned it before because he didn't want to sound like he was badmouthing our uncle. But he wasn't too surprised to find out that Uncle Tinsley, or someone else around town, was badmouthing Jerry Maddox, and he'd be happy to give us the real story if we wanted to hear it.

"I think we should take him up on his offer," Liz said.

CHAPTER NINETEEN

I was glad Mr. Maddox was willing to give his side of the story. After all, he was the boss, and we were the ones who needed the money. He didn't owe us any explanation, and it made me feel like he cared what we thought of him.

Sometimes Mr. Maddox worked the day shift at the mill, but sometimes he worked nights and weekends, which gave him weekdays to conduct other business. This particular week, he was working afternoons but had his mornings free, so the next day after breakfast, Liz and I pedaled our bikes into town and parked them in Mr. Maddox's carport, next to his polished black Le Mans. As usual, Doris had the TV on and she and the kids were on the Naugahyde couch, watching cartoons.

Mr. Maddox was in his office, sitting at his desk, feeding sheets of paper into a machine that shredded them into spaghetti-thin strips and spewed them into the wastebasket.

"Never just wad papers up and throw them out," Mr. Maddox said. "Your enemies will go through your trash to find anything they can use against you. Even harmless stuff. They can twist and distort it. You have to protect yourself."

Mr. Maddox shredded the last sheet of paper. His desk was clean, and that was the way he liked it. One of Liz's jobs was to make sure all his papers were filed away in the correct folders in the filing cabinets, which he kept locked.

"So you want to hear what happened between me and your uncle?" he asked. "That doesn't surprise me. Only thing that surprises me is that it took this long."

Mr. Maddox got up and closed the door. "I'd be happy to tell you," he said, "but you tell me something first." He took the two folding chairs out of the closet and had us sit down. Then he rolled his chair over until he was a few inches away from us. "Does your Uncle Tinsley know you're working for me?"

Liz and I exchanged glances. "Not exactly," she said.

"I was willing to bet that would be the case."

"We wanted to tell him," I said, "but . . ."

"But he probably wouldn't be too happy," Mr. Maddox said.

"We love Uncle Tinsley—" Liz began.

"But sometimes Uncle Tinsley doesn't see things the way they really are," Mr. Maddox said. "Sometimes Uncle Tinsley doesn't see what needs to be done."

"Exactly," Liz said.

"So I think it's a good idea that you don't tell him," Mr. Maddox said. He smiled that smile he got when he found a situation privately amusing. "Let's keep it between ourselves."

"But other people already know," Liz said. "You keep introducing me as Tinsley Holladay's niece."

"Also, I told my Aunt Al—Al Wyatt," I said. "Joe Wyatt, too."

"The Wyatts," Mr. Maddox said. "Wife works the late shift. Husband's a shirker who claims he's got white lung. That girl of theirs used to do some babysitting for us, but things started going missing, so we had to tell her to hit the road." He leaned back and slapped the arms of his chair. "Anyway, just because a few people know you're working for me doesn't mean your uncle will find out. He doesn't get around much these days. And if he does find out, we'll handle the matter when it comes up. But I think this gives you an idea of the headaches I had dealing with him."

Mr. Maddox explained that the Chicago company brought him in because the mill was losing money. The new owners said there were two choices: cut costs by thirty percent and try to eke out a profit, or shut down the mill for good, disassemble the entire operation, and sell it—looms and all—to a factory in Asia.

"People at the mill hated me for firing their friends," Mr. Maddox said. "The fact of the matter is, they should have been down on their hands and knees, kissing any part of my body I wanted kissed, thanking me for saving some of their jobs. The slope heads in Asia are willing to work for twenty cents an hour, and they're eating our asses alive. Meanwhile, I have your uncle with his panties in a twist, pissing and moaning about keeping the baseball team going and how the quality of the bath towels isn't what it used to be. As if people give a shit about quality these days. They're looking for something to dry their butts with, and all they care about is price."

Mr. Maddox leaned forward, his thick arms on his knees, looking back and forth between me and Liz with his intense blue eyes. "So," he said, "Uncle Tinsley had to go." He smiled again. "The news that he was getting the boot spun him around like a top," he said. He pointed his forefinger in the air and made a circling motion. "Woo, woo, woo. Round and round. Like a faggoty little ballerina."

Mr. Maddox stood up, raised his arms above his head, and did a mincing pirouette. Then he sat back down. "Don't get me wrong, I think your uncle's a great guy, but you have to admit his judgment sometimes sucks." He looked at the two of us. "Well, don't you?"

I shifted in my seat. Liz studied her fingernails. There wasn't a whole lot to say.

CHAPTER TWENTY

Mom called once a week and talked first to Liz, then to me. Life in New York was exciting, she said, but also more challenging than she'd expected. It was expensive, for one thing. The only affordable apartment she could find had a bathtub in the kitchen and was in a rough neighborhood with a crummy school. Lots of kids in New York went to private schools, but they were way beyond our budget. Liz and I rightly belonged in one of those special public schools for gifted students, she explained, but it was too late to apply this year, so what we needed to do was start the school year in Byler—Uncle Tinsley had said he'd be happy to have us stay on at Mayfield—then, once she'd found a cheap apartment in a neighborhood with a good school, she'd bring us up to New York, and the Tribe of Three would be together again.

That was fine by me. Frankly, Mom had begun to get on my nerves. By now, it was early August, and whenever I felt like talking to a grown-up, I'd go see Aunt Al. We'd sit with Earl at the kitchen table while she nursed a glass of the iced tea she made by the potful and talked about things like the time when she was a girl on the family farm and the corn didn't sprout because of a drought, so her pa made the kids dig up the kernels to plant the next year. She also told me stories about my dad, like the time he built an entire car out of junkyard parts, the time he held Ruth upside down over a bridge so she wouldn't have a fear of heights, and the time he gave Aunt Al a ride on his motorcycle and she accidentally stuck her foot in the spokes, ripping her shoe to pieces.

Uncle Clarence was a certifiable curmudgeon, and I suppose Aunt Al was right that it was on account of his hard life. But it seemed to me that Aunt Al also had it really tough—working the late shift at what Mom would call a dead-end job, coming home to make her family breakfast, grabbing a few hours' sleep, and getting up to make them dinner. Her grouchy husband was disabled, one son was off at war, her youngest wasn't quite right, but she never complained. Instead, she was always talking about how blessed she was and how many wonderful things Jesus had brought into her life, what with people like me showing up out of the blue. But her greatest blessings were her kids, and most of Aunt Al's conversations came around to them—Truman, the proud serviceman; Joe, who could do anything he set his mind to; Ruthie, who had spent the summer nursing Aunt Al's sister and was going to get herself a good office job; and her little special Earl. She loved them all, and they loved her back. "I swear, they think I hung the moon and scattered the stars," she told me more than once.

One day shortly after Mom told me we should start school in Byler, I biked over to the Wyatts'. When I walked into the kitchen, Aunt Al was sitting at the table reading a letter. It was from Ruth, she said. Aunt Al's sister had recovered from meningitis, Ruth hoped to be home in a few days, and she was looking forward to meeting Liz and me. Then Aunt Al opened a shoe box on the kitchen counter and pulled out a bundle of thin blue aerograms wrapped with a rubber band. "Truman's letters," she said. "He writes me every week, without fail."

In Truman's most recent letter, he'd told her that he'd become sweet on a nice Vietnamese girl. He was thinking of asking her to marry him and bringing her back to Virginia, and he wanted Aunt Al to write back with her thoughts on it all. "If you'd asked me a couple of years ago, I might have said I don't rightly know if Byler is ready for that, but a lot's been changing around here these days, so I told him to pray on it, and if that's what the Lord tells him to do, I'll welcome that girl with open arms."

Aunt Al carefully replaced the bundle of aerograms in the shoe box, along with Ruth's letter.

"I've got news, too," I said. "It looks like Liz and I are going to Byler High this fall."

"Honey!" Aunt Al gave me one of her big hugs. "I'm so glad you're staying with us instead of going off to the big city."

"Mom said life in New York was more challenging than she'd expected."

"That's one word for it." Aunt Al laughed. "Speaking of challenges, you're in for quite a time. This is the year that, like it or not, we're integrating."

Back in the fifties, she went on, the Supreme Court had ruled that black kids were allowed to attend white schools. In almost all Southern towns, however, black kids kept going to the black school, and white kids kept going to the white school.

As Aunt Al was talking, Uncle Clarence came in from the garden. Pulling off his straw hat and wiping his forehead, he filled a water glass at the sink and took a gulp. "Everyone was free to attend whatever school they wanted, and people chose to go to school with their own kind," he said. "That's natural. White ducks flock with white ducks, and mallards flock with mallards. It's called freedom of choice. What's more American than that?"

"The Supreme Court disagreed," Aunt Al said. Last year the court ordered the forced integration of all Southern schools. So the Byler superintendent was closing down Nelson High, which had been the black school for fifty years, and turning it into the vocational school. Beginning this year, the kids from Nelson would be going to Byler High.

"It's the doing of those damned Harvards," Uncle Clarence said. "They started this war and told our boys to fight it, then they changed their minds about the war and went around spitting on our boys for serving their country. And now the Harvards want to come down here and tell us how to run our schools." He coughed and tossed the rest of his water in the sink. "Now I'm all riled up, so I best get the hell back to my tomatoes." He picked up his straw hat and muttered on his way out, "Ducks got more sense than that Supreme my-ass Court."

CHAPTER TWENTY-ONE

Later that week, on a morning when Mr. Maddox didn't have any work for either of us, Liz and I rode over to the mill hill. While we were parking our bikes in the Wyatts' front yard, a tall young woman around Liz's age came running out the door. She had a wide smile just like Aunt Al's and long dark hair held back by barrettes, and she wore those plastic cat's-eye glasses that you saw on old ladies.

"You must be Liz and Bean," she cried out, wiping her hands on her apron and giving us both a bone-crushing Wyatt hug. "I'm Ruth, and I been just dying to meet you all for the longest time."

Ruth led us into the house, explaining that the harvest season was under way and she and her mom were in the middle of canning. The kitchen table was piled with red, green, orange, and yellow tomatoes. Earl was lining up rows of mason jars on the counter while Aunt Al stirred a big steaming pot.

"Uncle Clarence grew all these tomatoes?" I asked.

"Everything Daddy grows, we eat fresh," Ruth said.

"With all these mouths to feed, it don't go far," Aunt Al said. "Joe brings me my canning tomatoes." She started spooning stewed tomatoes into the jars. "I know some people may wag their finger at what my boy does," she said, "but the food he brings home helps keep this family fed, and those darned farmers are always growing more than they can sell anyway."

"Ma told me you all will be going to Byler High this fall," Ruth said. "A lot of the white folks, including Daddy, are making a heck of a fuss about integration."

"I don't get it," I said. "What's the big deal? There were always Mexican kids in the schools in California, and they were just like everyone else, except they had darker skin and ate spicier food."

"It's a little more complicated in these parts," Aunt Al said.

"A few people in Byler are saying this integration thing could actually be good," Ruth went on. The Byler High football team would get all those big, strong, fast black boys from Nelson, she explained, and they might take us to state. At the same time, she said, white players would have to be cut from the team to make room for the blacks. The Byler High cheerleaders, who all had boyfriends on the team, were saying that they'd quit the squad if their boyfriends were cut because they didn't want to be cheering for a bunch of coloreds who stole their boyfriends' positions.

The cheerleaders all came from well-to-do families, Ruth said. They were the daughters of the doctors, the lawyers, the car dealer, the man who owned the country club. Mill hill boys sometimes made it onto the football team, but no girl from the hill had ever become a cheerleader. It simply didn't happen. A cheerleader had to be a certain type, and that type just wasn't found on the hill. All the girls on the hill knew this, so they never even tried out.

"Until now," Ruth said. "Because if some of the cheerleaders who are the right type quit, saying they aren't cheering for any niggers— pardon my French, that's the word the girls use, I know you're not supposed to call them that—other girls will have a chance to make the squad." She started screwing lids on the jars Aunt Al had filled. "And that there's the silver lining in the whole integration thing. So

I'm planning to try out for the cheerleading squad. I don't have any problem cheering for the colored boys."

A bunch of the other hill girls were going to try out as well, and they were all meeting in a little while to practice. "Why don't you all come practice with us?" Ruth asked.

"You bet," I said.

"Sure," Liz said in that voice she used when her heart wasn't really in something.

"Well, okay, then," Ruth said. "But we'll need to fix your hair."

"You all go on," Aunt Al said. "I'll finish up here."

Ruth led us to the back of the house, where part of the porch had been turned into a tiny bedroom with a slanted ceiling. The three of us could scarcely fit in. On her dresser was a photograph of a guy wearing black-rimmed glasses and a khaki uniform. Ruth picked it up. "This is Truman," she said.

Liz and I studied the photograph. Truman had a serious expression, dark eyes, and wide lips.

"He's got eyes like yours and Bean's," Liz said.

"Most of us Wyatts got those same dark eyes," Ruth said. "There's an old rumor we got some Jew blood in the family, but Mom says it's just black Irish."

"He looks smart," I said. "Not like a soldier."

"That came out wrong, in typical Bean fashion," Liz said. "She meant it as a compliment."

Ruth laughed. "Truman is smart. Maybe that's also the Jew blood. The other soldiers call him Poindexter the Professor because of his glasses and the books he's all the time reading."

Ruth put the photograph back. She said she wanted to show us her hope chest, for when she got married. She pulled a small trunk out from under the bed and opened it. Inside were dish towels, bath towels, place mats, a blanket, and an oven mitt. She was planning for the future, she said, but she wasn't counting entirely on marriage. She was a top student in the secretarial track at Byler High and could type ninety-five words a minute. She had no intention of working at the mill, she said, not to disparage her ma, of course. It was her ma who encouraged her to get herself a good office job.

"I've been doing some office work for Mr. Maddox," Liz said.

"I heard," Ruth said. "I worked for that family for a while. Watch yourself around him."

"What for?" I asked.

"Just watch yourself."

I looked at Liz to see if she was going to say anything about Mr. Maddox telling us he had to fire Ruth. Liz gave me an almost unnoticeable shake of the head, like she thought the whole subject was too awkward to bring up, and then she said, "So what is this we're supposed to do with our hair?"

"You can't have it flopping all over the place if you're going to be a cheerleader," Ruth said, and opened a jewelry box full of barrettes and ponytail holders. She carefully sorted through and found a pair of baubles and barrettes that matched the blue shirt I was wearing, then a set that matched Liz's yellow shorts. She brushed my hair back, pulling it into a ponytail so tight that I felt like it was stretching my eyebrows back. Then she turned to Liz, whose reddish-blond hair was thick and wavy and fell halfway down her back.

"I never wear a ponytail," Liz said.

"You do if you're a cheerleader," Ruth said.

She pulled back Liz's hair into another tight ponytail and used barrettes to pin the stray ringlets in place. Without all of her flowing hair, Liz's face looked smaller and a little forlorn. She studied herself in the mirror inside the lid of the jewelry box. "I'm not sure this is me."

"You look real cute," Ruth said. "All nice and tidied up."

• • •

A little while later, a group of about eight girls showed up at the Wyatts'. Ruth had us form a line on the street in front of the house. She took off her cat's-eye glasses and set them on the front steps, saying she cheered without them even though she could barely see, because there was no way on God's green earth she'd make the squad wearing glasses that everyone knew came from the state's free clinic. Without those ugly glasses, Ruth's dark eyes were large and beautiful, but she sure did blink a lot.

Ruth stood facing us. She knew the words for all the chants, and she knew the moves and the names for the moves. She showed us the eagle, the Russian jump, the candlestick, the pike, and the bow-and-arrow, calling out the names in a loud, energetic voice. I had always been a little uncoordinated, but I gave it my best shot, and to tell the truth, it was actually fun. Liz, however, started out half-heartedly, flapping a limp hand when she should have been pumping with her entire arm, and the little enthusiasm she had steadily dwindled until she gave up altogether and went to sit on the Wyatts' steps.

Ruth finished up by showing us the cartwheel split, which was the finale for some of the big cheers. It was difficult, she explained, but required if you wanted to make the squad. All of us except Liz lined up to try it, but none of the other girls was as coordinated and flexible as Ruth, and they couldn't get their legs either up or apart. When it came my turn, Ruth stood next to me and grabbed me by the waist as I came through the cartwheel, then lowered me to the ground for the split.

"You've got it, Bean!" she said. She turned to Liz. "Now, don't be discouraged," she called out. "Practice makes perfect. Come back tomorrow, and we'll work on it some more."

"Right," Liz said. She started pulling out the barrettes and pony-tail holder.

"You can keep those for next time," Ruth said.

"We can get our own," Liz said. "If we need them."

I wasn't used to wearing a ponytail, but I liked it. It made me feel ready for action. However, the way Liz included me in her answer made me think I had to give my barrettes and holder back, too, so I pulled them out. "Uncle Tinsley's got a ball of rubber bands on his desk," I said. "I can use those."

The other girls wandered up the street, and Ruth went inside to help Aunt Al finish up the canning. After a drink of water from the Wyatts' garden hose, Liz and I got on our bikes.

"So you're going to become a cheerleader now?" she asked.

"Maybe. What's wrong with that?"

"All that rah-rah stuff. It's excruciating."

CHAPTER TWENTY-TWO

When we showed up for work one day shortly after that cheer-leading practice, Mr. Maddox ushered us into his office and closed the door. He handed each of us a thin little booklet with a blue leath-erlike cover and fancy gold lettering that said BYLER NATIONAL BANK.

"I opened up a savings account for each of you," he said. "These are your very own passbooks."

I turned to the first page of mine. JEAN HOLLADAY was typed on the first line, along with JEROME T. MADDOX. There were columns marked "Deposits," "Withdrawals," "Interest," and "Balance." The deposit column had $20.00 typed in blue ink, and so did the bal-ance column.

Now, Mr. Maddox explained, he could deposit our pay directly into our accounts from one of his own accounts. It would be simpler and more efficient, not to mention safer, because there was no chance that the deposited money could be lost or stolen. It would allow us not only to save money but to earn interest, accumulating wealth rather than squandering our earnings on soda pops and records.

Liz was examining her book. "It all looks very official," she said.

"It's a rite of passage," Mr. Maddox said. "Like getting your driv-er's license. Since neither of you girls has a dad—and Tinsley Holladay, whatever his virtues, ain't much help in that department—I'm stepping up to show you the way things work. Welcome to the real world."

"If it's my passbook, why is your name on it?" I asked.

"They're joint accounts," Mr. Maddox said. He needed to be able to make direct deposits. He didn't expect us to know all this because we'd never had savings accounts, but that was banking. "This is my way of helping you move along to becoming an adult, understanding the way the system works."

"But I like getting money," I said. It was fun fingering the worn bills that had passed through hundreds or even thousands of other people's hands, looking at the eye over the pyramid, wondering what the heck that was all about, and studying the signatures and serial numbers and complicated little scrolly stuff. "If your money's locked away in some bank, you can't look at it and feel it and count it," I said. "I like cash."

"Cash is what smart investors call 'stupid money,' " Mr. Maddox said. "It's just sitting in your pocket, tempting you to piss it away. It's not working for you. You got to make your money work for you."

"Maybe so. But I still like getting cash."

"You'll be earning interest, Bean," Liz said.

"There, someone's using her brain," he said. "And not just interest but interest on the interest. Compound interest, is what that's called."

"I don't care. I just want the money."

"Your choice. But it's the loser's choice. Typical Holladay."

CHAPTER TWENTY-THREE

I didn't make the cheerleading squad.

Tryouts were held a couple of weeks before school began, and I could tell from the moment I got to the gym just how seriously the other girls took cheerleading. They were wearing the red-and-white Byler colors, they had their hair held back with little baubles in the shape of bulldogs, the school mascot, and some had bulldogs painted on their cheeks. They limbered up with stretches, handstands, and backflips, the black girls in one group and the whites in another. The white girls eyed me suspiciously as a newcomer. The JV coach barely looked my way when it came my turn, as if she already knew which girls she would pick.

Afterward, I sat in the bleachers to watch the varsity tryouts. Three of the girls who'd been on the squad had followed through with their threat to quit, which meant there would be three open slots for girls from the mill hill and Nelson High.

Ruth took her turn late in the morning, and I thought she nailed it. She had taken off her cat's-eye glasses, but that didn't affect her performance at all. Her voice was loud, her routine was flawless, and she was so limber that when she did her final cartwheel split, everyone heard the slap of her thighs against the gym's wooden floor. There was no way she wasn't making the squad, I thought. Then the black girls took their turns. Six of them had been varsity cheerleaders at Nelson, and they really knew their stuff. They acted sassy, swinging their hips and shaking their heads, almost like they were dancing, and I wondered if that would help them or hurt them, judged against the white girls.

The results were posted a couple of days later, and Ruth made the team. So did two of the black girls. When I went over to the Wyatts' to congratulate Ruth, she gave me a big Wyatt hug. Folks on the hill, Aunt Al told me, were over the moon that one of their own had finally up and made the cheering squad. The cheerleading coach's selections had also created a lot of grumbling. Some whites in Byler had been willing to accept a single black cheerleader but thought that two was too many. At the same time, the Nelson students felt they should have had at least three cheerleading slots, since they were half the school now and had supplied key new players for the football team. A black girl and a white girl had gotten into a catfight over it in front of the Rexall.

"Don't quite know what this bodes for the school year," Aunt Al said.

Aunt Al was mixing up a bowl of pimento cheese for sandwiches when Uncle Clarence came through the front door, clutching a bottle in a paper bag. He had a huge grin on his face, and he was doing a bent-legged jig. He kissed Aunt Al and his kids and hugged me, talking all the while in the tones of a preacher man, asking how everybody was doing on this glorious day, going on about his beautiful daughter and how the mill hill finally got itself a cheerleader. "That there's reason for a celebration. Let's celebrate. Let's have us some music. Somebody get me my guitar!"

Joe came back with an ancient guitar, the body worn black in places from years and years of playing. Uncle Clarence took a long slug from the bottle, then picked up the guitar and started to play it like nobody I'd ever heard. He didn't seem to be thinking about what he was doing. He was plucking and strumming and twanging away, almost like he was in a trance, the music flowing up out of him.

I was stunned. This crazy dancing guitar player wasn't the Uncle Clarence I knew.

"There's mean drunks and there's sad drunks," Aunt Al said. "When my Clarence drinks, the spirit moves him. He's a dancing drunk."

The rest of the Wyatts started clapping and shouting and jigging, and I joined in. We all circled around Uncle Clarence, who was playing so fast that his hands were a blur. Then he threw his head back and began to howl.

CHAPTER TWENTY-FOUR

Doris's pregnancy was getting along, and one day in late August, Mr. Maddox told me she had a doctor's appointment. He wanted Liz to stay at the house to answer the phone, but I needed to come with them to take care of Randy, the baby, while the doctor saw Doris.

Mr. Maddox had given Doris her clothes back a few days after he had me put them in his car, and she was wearing one of her flowered housedresses. He told her to get in back of the Le Mans with the baby, and he had me sit up front next to him. He gunned the car and it shot out of the driveway, the tires squealing. We were just going to a routine checkup, and we weren't even late, but Mr. Maddox drove like a demon, swerving through turns so hard it threw you against the door, tailgating the car in front, passing in no-passing zones, and keeping up a running commentary about all the incompetent fools and idiots in his way.

About halfway to the hospital, Mr. Maddox pulled into the parking lot of a convenience store. "I'm getting chips and sodas for everyone," he announced. "What do you want?"

"You decide, honey," Doris said.

"I want an orange soda," I said. "Nehi, Orange Crush, or Fanta, it doesn't matter. And Cheetos. Not the puffy baked ones but the crunchy fried ones."

"Sit tight," Mr. Maddox said, and climbed out of the car.

A couple of minutes later, he returned carrying a brown paper bag. He got into the car, reached into the bag, and handed me an RC Cola and a little cardboard cylinder.

"What's this?" I asked.

"Chips and soda." He passed Doris the same.

"This isn't what I asked for," I said. "I asked for orange soda and Cheetos."

"That's RC, which is the best cola on the market, and those are Pringles. They're just out, and they're better than Cheetos."

"But that's not what I wanted."

"I asked what you wanted, but I didn't tell you that I was going to get you what you wanted," he said. "You have to pay attention to exactly what I'm saying. That's important if you're working for me."

I examined the container of Pringles, which had a little tab on the tin lid. I pulled back the tab, and it let out a whoosh. Inside was a perfect stack of saddle-shaped chips. I ate one. "This tastes funny," I said.

"What are you talking about?" Mr. Maddox asked. "Pringles taste better than Cheetos. But it's not just the taste. They're far superior in every way." He started lecturing me about the technological advances that Pringles represented. They were uniform in shape, he said, and they didn't break and crumble, because they were stacked neatly inside the cylinder instead of rattling around in a bag that was filled mostly with air. You didn't have to deal with the sharp edges or burned spots that you sometimes found on regular potato chips. With Pringles, you knew precisely what you were getting. Consistency of product. Pringles were the wave of the future. "What's more, you don't get that orange crap on your fingers."

"I like that orange crap," I said. "It goes with the orange soda that I also asked for but didn't get." And, I continued, Cheetos were in fact better than Pringles—in my opinion, anyway. They came in a variety of sizes, so you could choose big or little, depending on your mood at the moment. And they came in all sorts of different shapes, so you could have fun trying to figure out what each one looked like.

Mr. Maddox was gripping the steering wheel, and I could see a vein on his temple pulsing, like his head was going to explode.

"That's about the stupidest thing I've ever heard," he said. "You don't know what you're talking about." He pointed a thick finger at my face. "I'm telling you, Pringles are better than Cheetos."

"He's right, you know," Doris piped in. "Jerry knows what he's talking about. You'd be best off listening to him rather than trying to argue. And just be grateful he bought you anything at all."

Mr. Maddox nodded. "You made a bad choice about the Cheetos, so I had to overrule it. That's what I have to do when the people around me make bad choices." He paused. "So shut up and eat your damned Pringles."

Later that afternoon, when Liz and I were riding our bicycles side by side back to Mayfield, I told her about the Cheetos-versus-Pringles debate.

"I don't see why he got so bent out of shape," I said. "If he thinks Pringles are better than Cheetos, that's his opinion, but if I like Cheetos, that's my opinion. If I have a fact wrong, that's one thing. But an opinion isn't a fact. And he can't tell me my opinion is wrong."

"Bean, you're getting all worked up over a bunch of snacks," Liz said. "It's not important."

"He can't tell me what to think."

"He sure can, especially if you're working for him—but that

doesn't mean you have to think it. At the same time, you don't have to tell him you disagree. You don't have to argue."

"In other words, I should just shut up and eat the damned Pringles?"

"Choose your battles," she said. "It's like with Mom. Sometimes it's better to go along with what they say."

That was what she did with Mr. Maddox, Liz said. He had strong opinions on just about everything, and what worked best was simply to listen. Mr. Maddox had told Liz he knew he could be a hothead, and one of the reasons he liked her was that she didn't get upset when he got a little out of control. She knew how to handle herself. He also trusted and respected her, and that was why he gave her real responsibilities. He had let her see confidential legal papers about the lawsuits he was involved in.

"Like what?" I asked.

"I can't discuss them," she said. "Mr. Maddox swore me to secrecy."

"Even with me?" I asked. Liz and I always shared everything.

"Even with you."

CHAPTER TWENTY-FIVE

By the end of summer, Liz and I had saved up enough money for new clothes. Mr. Maddox had been paying me in cash, as I wanted, and I had been keeping it in a cigar box in the little white cradle, along with the photograph of my dad and his Silver Star. Liz withdrew some money from her savings account, and one afternoon shortly before school began, we went down to Kresge on Holladay Avenue. I thought we should get several cheap sets of clothes, but Liz insisted that, in addition to jeans and T-shirts, we needed to invest in at least one really striking outfit. She kept saying it was important to make a good first impression at a new school. Liz picked out a bright orange-and-purple skirt and a shiny purple shirt for herself. For me, she found a pair of lime-green pants and a matching lime-green vest. "You need to make a statement," she said.

On the first day of school, we each put on our one really striking outfit, and even though there was a bus stop within walking distance of Mayfield, Uncle Tinsley drove us to Byler High in the Woody. He also believed in making a good first impression.

The school was a big brick building, three stories high, with limestone pillars and trim. Hundreds of students were milling around under the huge poplar trees in front of the school, all the black kids in one group and all the white kids in another. As soon as we pulled up, I realized that we had made a terrible mistake clothes-wise. All of the white kids were wearing faded jeans, sneakers, and T-shirts, while all of the black kids had on flashy, bright clothes, like the ones Liz and I were wearing.

"We're dressed like the black kids!" I blurted out.

Uncle Tinsley chuckled. "Well, I do believe you are," he said. "These days, the coloreds dress better than the whites."

"Everyone will point and stare," I said. "We need to go home and change."

"It's too late," Liz said. "Anyway, like Mom is always saying, who wants to blend in when you can stand out?"

We certainly stood out. The other kids, both black and white, were eyeing me, giggling, and doing slack-jawed double takes as I walked from class to class. "Hey, Day-Glo Girl!" some white boy shouted.

That night I hung the lime-green pants in the closet, next to Mom's debutante gowns. Tomorrow I'd put on jeans and a T-shirt. Liz said she was going to do the same, but I knew that even if I never wore those pants again, they'd made an unforgettable first impression. From here on out, I was sure, I would be known as Day-Glo Girl.

CHAPTER TWENTY-SIX

Byler High was one old building. Unlike the flat, modern schools I'd been to in California, it had stairways and high ceilings and was musty as well as noisy, with lockers slamming and bells ringing between periods and students yelling in the crowded halls. It quickly became clear that kids who'd known each other all their lives had no interest in meeting a new girl. Even if I gave them my friendliest smile, they quickly looked away. Maybe it was because of integration, but there was also a lot of pushing and shoving in the halls and stairways. You could tell that Byler High was filled with riled-up kids itching for a fight.

When I was in sixth grade, I'd thought junior high would be hard, with changing classes, thick books, and mysterious subjects like algebra. Liz was the smart one, not me. But despite the intimidating names, such as literature and comprehension, social studies, and home economics, the courses themselves were no big deal. Literature and comprehension was just reading. Social studies was just news with a little history thrown in. And the first thing we learned in home economics—required for all seventh-grade girls—was how to set a table. Knife on the right side of the plate, facing in; spoon next to that; forks on the left, lined up in the order they were to be used.

Our teacher, Mrs. Thompson, was a big, slow-moving woman with a powdered face and earrings that always matched her necklace. She said she was teaching us "survival skills" that every woman needed to know. But you were never going to die because you put the spoon on the left side of the plate. The seventh-grade guys got to take shop and learn all these interesting, useful things, like how to fix a flat tire, how to wire a lamp, how to build a bookcase. When I told Mrs. Thompson that fixing a flat tire—not setting a table—was my idea of a survival skill, she said that was a man's job.

We weren't even learning practical stuff, like how to keep a budget or how to sew on a missing button. It was all about being proper, knowing where the water glass stood in relation to the juice glass, and the need for correct foundation garments. Mom wouldn't be caught dead in a girdle, and some of her friends didn't wear bras, but Mrs. Thompson was always going on about how you should never be able to see a woman's body jiggle under her clothes, which was why all women should wear girdles—an essential foundation garment—and it was a shame in this day and age that so many of them had stopped.

It was so boring I couldn't even listen. I would have flunked the first test, except Mrs. Thompson said she'd give us bonus points for every kitchen utensil we could name. Most of the girls listed five or six, but I really went to town, coming up with everything I could think of, from pizza slicers to cheese graters to nutcrackers, swizzle sticks to apple peelers to rolling pins. I ended up with thirty-seven.

"This doesn't seem right," Mrs. Thompson said after she graded the test. "You're one of my poorest students, but you got the best score in the class simply because of your bonus answers."

"You made the rules," I said.

* * *

Soon after that first test, I learned that you could get out of home ec one day a week if you joined the pep squad. So, without really knowing what the pep squad was, I decided to volunteer. Our job, it turned out, was to help the cheerleaders rev up the crowds during pregame pep rallies on Fridays, the day of the football games, and then at the games that evening. We also made the spirit stick— a painted broomstick gussied up with Bulldog doohickeys—which was awarded to the class that showed the most spirit during rallies, and we painted the posters that went up in the hallways before each game.

Byler's first game that year was against the Big Creek Owls. When we met in the gym, Terri Pruitt, the senior who was the leader of the squad, said we needed to come up with owl-themed posters. When I told Liz about it, she rattled off a string of really neat owl puns and rhymes we could use—"Pluck the Owls," "Disembowel the Owls," "Befoul the Owls," "Owls Are Foul Fowls," and best of all, "Bulldogs Growl, Owls Howl."

"Why don't you join the pep squad?" I told Liz. "You'd be great."

"I don't think so," she said. "The whole thing's too tribal."

At the next meeting of the pep squad, I read out Liz's list of slogans. Terri loved "Bulldogs Growl, Owls Howl." She said we could make a big banner by spray-painting the words on an old sheet and hanging it on the gym wall for Friday's pep rally. She turned to Vanessa Johnson, the one black girl on the pep squad, who was also in my English class. "Vanessa, you can help Bean," Terri said.

"So I'm the help?" Vanessa asked. She was taller than most of the girls, with long, athletic arms and legs. She crossed those arms slowly and stared at Terri.

"We're all helping each other, okay?"

Terri found the sheet and spray paint and had us take them outside. As we walked down the hall, I started telling Vanessa that we should outline the words in pencil first, to make sure we got them centered and they didn't scrunch up at the end.

"Who put you in charge?" she asked.

"That's not fair," I said. "It was just an idea."

Vanessa put her hands on her hips. "Fair? You want to talk about what's fair and what's not fair? What's not fair is having your own school closed down and being forced to go to the cracker school."

"What do you mean? I thought the black kids wanted to go to the white schools. I thought that was the whole point."

"Why would we want to go to the white school when we had our own school?" At Nelson they had their own football team, Vanessa said, their own cheerleading squad and pep squad, their own school colors, their own homecoming king and queen. Nelson families took pride in the school, and on weekends, they would come in to mop and polish the place. Some of the families even painted their cars in the school's purple and silver colors. But now the Nelson kids had to give up those colors. And the former Nelson students knew none of them would ever be elected class president at Byler, or named homecoming king or queen, or be declared "Most Likely to Succeed." Byler would never be their school.

"If that's how you feel, why did you join the pep squad?"

"I didn't make JV cheerleader, even though I was better than the white girls who did," she said. "That doesn't mean I'm going to just sit in the bleachers." Her sister, Leticia, she explained, was one of the two Nelson cheerleaders chosen for the Byler squad. Vanessa said she would be at every game, cheering on Leticia and rooting for the

Nelson boys on the Byler team. Then she looked me squarely in the eye. "And I ain't giving up. I'm going to make cheerleader myself next year."

I held up the sheet. "Then I guess we should get cracking on this banner."

"The cracker wants to get cracking," she said, and for the first time, she smiled.

CHAPTER TWENTY-SEVEN

The following Saturday, I was down in the basement of the Maddoxes' house, folding laundry, when Mr. Maddox appeared at the top of the stairs. He clambered down the steps and came over, moving in that strangely light-footed way he had for such a large man.

"Keeping busy," he said. "I like that. You work for me, you keep busy."

"Thanks," I said. "I folded the big stuff, and now I'm matching the socks."

Mr. Maddox stretched his arm out and propped himself against the basement wall. He was towering over me, and I felt a little boxed in. He had come so near that I could feel his breath on my face. I could also smell him. He didn't stink, but I wasn't used to being so close to a grown man, and his smell made me think of sweat and work, muscle and meat. I didn't dislike it, but it was a little unsettling.

"Another thing I like about you," he said, "is that you're not scared of me. I'm a big guy, and I know some people get nervous when I'm standing next to them like this."

"Nope," I said. "Not me."

"No," he said. "You're not afraid." He'd had his right arm cocked on his hip, and now he reached over and put his hand on my shoulder. It was a hot September day, and I was wearing a sleeveless shirt. His enormous hand was so rough and calloused that I thought I could feel the individual ridges of his fingerprints.

"You take your responsibilities seriously," he went on, "and you don't make a big deal out of little things. Unlike Doris. She's always making a huge deal over dumb little things. You've got a good sense of humor; you're fun to be around. You've got spunk, and you're mature for your age. How old are you again?"

"Twelve."

"Twelve? That's all? That's hard to believe. You look and act much older than that." Mr. Maddox suddenly slipped his thick thumb into my armpit and stroked it. "And you've already got your peach fuzz coming in."

I jerked back. "Cut it out!"

Mr. Maddox held my shoulder with his thumb still in my armpit for just a moment longer, then dropped his hand and laughed. "Now, don't go getting all stupid on me," he said. "I didn't do anything wrong. I was just commenting on your coming-of-age. I got a wife and daughter, I grew up with sisters, and I know all about women and their cycles and when they start developing. This is just nature. I'm an adult, and you're on the way to becoming one. If we're going to have a working relationship, the way grown-ups do, we need to be able to talk about things like this. For example, maybe someday you won't be able to come to work for me because you started your cycle and got cramps, and you'll need to tell me that. Happens all the time at the mill."

I looked down at the pile of unfolded socks. I couldn't think of anything to say. I didn't want to get all stupid and blow it out of proportion. Even though Mr. Maddox sticking his thumb in my armpit felt completely wrong, I couldn't disagree with a single thing he said.

Mr. Maddox reached over and pushed my chin up. "You're not

mad at me, are you?" he asked. "I thought we were just talking about growing up. Look, if you're mad, you should say something. If you think I did you wrong, you can do me wrong. You can call me a name. Any name you want." He paused. "Or you can hit me. Go ahead, hit me." He spread out his arms. "Right here in the stomach. Hard as you can." He waited a moment. Then he pointed at his jaw. "Or right here in the face if you want."

"No, thanks."

"Don't want to hit me? Why not?" He paused again. "I know you're not scared of me, so I guess you're not mad at me. Good." He took out his roll of bills and pulled off a twenty. "Here's for your day's work," he said, and headed back up the stairs.

Twenty dollars was way more than Mr. Maddox usually paid me for a day's work. The whole thing had been creepy, and by taking the money, I felt I was letting him buy me off. But twenty dollars was a lot of money. Mr. Maddox knew I needed it, and he knew I'd take it. I put the money in my pocket, finished matching the socks, and left without saying goodbye to anyone.

"I don't like Mr. Maddox," I told Liz that night.

"You don't have to like him," she said. "You just have to know how to handle him."

I had been planning to tell Liz what had happened, but it was sort of embarrassing. Also, when I played it through in my head, Mr. Maddox hadn't actually done anything wrong, and if he had, he'd more or less apologized. I kept telling myself that I didn't want to make a bigger deal out of it than it was. From now on, I just had to figure out how to handle him. Like Liz did.

CHAPTER TWENTY-EIGHT

Usually Mom called once a week, but every now and then she called a few days late or skipped a week. When that happened, she'd apologize, saying she meant to call, but you know how crazy the music world can get.

The time wasn't quite right yet for Liz and me to come up to New York, Mom told us, but we weren't going to be stuck at Mayfield forever. Besides, it was good for us to be exposed to life in Byler. It would help us understand her, what she had to put up with and why she made the decision to leave. It would make us grateful that she'd taken pains to raise us among open-minded nonconformists instead of people who treated you like a pariah if you didn't do everything exactly the way they did.

When I told Mom I joined the pep squad, she sighed. "Why would you want to do that?" she asked. She'd been a cheerleader herself, she said, and she shuddered to remember it. Football was barbaric. And cheerleading was a way of brainwashing women into thinking that the men were the stars and the most women could expect out of life was to stand on the sidelines and cheer them on.

"Don't be someone else's little cheerleader," Mom said. "Be the star of your own show. Even if there's no audience."

I knew Mom had a point. Still, I liked being on the pep squad. It was fun, and I'd made some friends. What was wrong with that? Also, I'd figured out that school spirit was important in Byler, and if you didn't show any, you wouldn't get very far.

Liz, however, took Mom's advice to heart. She'd been leaning in that direction anyway and was glad to have Mom's perspective to support her own views. I'd been trying my best to make things work out at Byler, but you couldn't say the same about Liz. She was constantly making comments about quaint local customs, dropping Latin phrases, correcting other kids' grammar, and grimacing at the sound of country music. After the first day of school, Liz and I had worn blue jeans, but after a couple of weeks, she'd gone back to outfits that made her stand out, including the orange-and-purple skirt, a beret, and recently, even some of Mom's old clothes—the very ones Uncle Tinsley had wanted us to wear—like a tweed hunting jacket and riding breeches. It had been years since I'd been in the same school with Liz, and while I was in the habit of thinking of her as brilliant and beautiful and all-around perfect, it was clear the other kids at Byler thought she acted peculiar and put on airs.

In California, we'd never paid much attention to school sports. The only people who really cared were the kids on the teams. But in Byler, the entire town was obsessed with the Bulldogs. Signs cheering on the team appeared in the storefronts along Holladay Avenue. People painted Bulldog slogans on the windows of their cars and houses and planted red and white flowers in their gardens. Grownups standing on street corners discussed the team's prospects and debated the strengths and weaknesses of individual players. Teachers interrupted class to talk about the upcoming game. And everyone treated the members of the team like gods.

On the day of a game, you were supposed to wear red and white to school. It wasn't a rule, but everyone did it, Terri Pruitt told me. I put on a red-and-white T-shirt the day the Bulldogs were scheduled to play the Owls in the season opener. Liz made a point of wearing her orange-and-purple skirt, saying that she was a nonconformist, like Mom. She had to put on that blue dress when Maddox wanted and go along with whatever he said, but that was because she was on his payroll. No one at Byler High was going to tell her what to wear or who to cheer for.

Everyone at Byler was required to attend the pep rally, held the day of game. I got out of home ec to decorate the gym. All the kids and teachers were wearing red and white, including the former Nelson students. Each class sat together, and they all competed to cheer the loudest, with the noisiest class winning the spirit stick and the privilege of waving it around at the game that night. When it was the seventh-graders' turn, Vanessa and I stood in front of the class, waving our arms and pumping our fists in the air. One kid stood up and shouted, "You go, Day-Glo Girl!" I just grinned and pumped my fists even harder, and I'll admit I was downright proud when we won that spirit stick.

The game started in the early evening. The floodlights around the football field had been turned on even though there was still plenty of light left. A hot wind blew across the field, and a half-moon hung in the silver sky.

The entire Wyatt family showed up early to get seats down front so they could cheer Ruth on. Joe, who was carrying Earl, waved at me. Liz didn't come—she said she agreed with Mom, football was barbaric—but Uncle Tinsley showed up, wearing a gray felt hat and an old red-and-white varsity jacket with a big *B* on it. He walked over to where I was standing on the sidelines with the pep squad. "Class of '48," he said. "We swept the division." He winked. "Go get 'em, Bulldogs."

The bleachers filled up quickly, and just like in the school cafeteria, the blacks and the whites sat separately. After the band came out, the Bulldogs were introduced one by one, each running onto the field when his name was called. The white fans cheered for the white Byler players, but they stayed pretty quiet for the black players who'd been at Nelson. At the same time, the blacks in the bleachers cheered for the black players but not the white ones.

When the Owls took the field, their fans cheered for the entire team, but the Owls had only one black player. One of the things people had been talking about before the game was that the Owls had always been a weak team, but Big Creek was a tiny town up in the mountains, and hardly any blacks lived there, so the team hadn't had the integration issues Byler was going through.

At the start of the game, the crowd was enthusiastic, cheering every time the Bulldogs completed a pass or made a tackle and booing every time the Owls advanced. The cheerleaders were in position along the sidelines, kicking and jumping around and shaking their pom-poms, while the pep squad ran back and forth in front of the bleachers, pumping the crowd, yelling, "Bulldogs growl, Owls howl!"

Everyone was having a blast, and it didn't seem to me that you had to be a barbarian to enjoy the game. By the second quarter, however, the Bulldogs had fallen behind by two touchdowns, and the mood of the crowd turned sour. I didn't know much about football—the rules seemed incredibly confusing—but I did know we were losing. During a time-out, I asked Ruth what was going on. The Bulldogs weren't playing like a team, she explained. Dale Scarberry, the white quarterback, was passing only to the white receivers, and the new black players weren't blocking for their white teammates. If that kept up, the Bulldogs would be massacred.

When Dale Scarberry threw a pass that was picked off by one of the Owls, I was surprised to hear the Byler fans—both the students and the adults—start booing their own team. They kept it up every time another Bulldog made a mistake, not just booing but cussing and shouting things like "You're stinking up the field!" "Idiot!" "Bench him!" "You suck!" and "Shit for brains!"

The Owls scored again, and that was when things got really ugly. We pep squadders were still jumping and pumping, trying to get the crowd back on our side, when someone threw a paper bag of garbage on the field. I dashed out to pick it up, and when I got back to the sideline, I saw a white man in the bleachers stand up and hurl a hamburger at Vanessa Johnson's sister, Leticia, as she was raising her pom-poms over her head with a big grin. The hamburger hit her in the chest, leaving a greasy mark on her pretty red-and-white uniform.

Leticia ignored it—she even went on smiling—and all the cheerleaders continued their routine. Then a white man I recognized from the hill stood up and threw a big cup filled with ice and cola. When it hit Leticia on the shoulder, the lid flew off, drenching her uniform. Leticia kept going, kicking up and cheering as vigorously as before, though she had stopped smiling.

Aunt Al turned to face the two white men. "Hey, now, that ain't right!" she shouted.

At that point, a black man standing on the bleacher steps hurled a soda cup at Ruth. It hit her on the shoulder, the drink splattering down her uniform.

That was too much for Joe. He sprang up and charged toward the black man, but other blacks knocked him down before he got there. A bunch of white fans started jumping across the bleacher seats to defend Joe, and then all hell broke loose, people everywhere throwing drinks and food, shouting, trading punches, and tackling one another, women cursing and pulling hair, babies crying and kids screaming, the seventh-grader with the spirit stick smacking some guy on the head with it. The ruckus went on until the police rushed into the bleachers with their nightsticks out and broke it up.

We lost the game 36 to 6.

CHAPTER TWENTY-NINE

In school on Monday, all anyone could talk about was the game. Some white students were outraged about the brawl in the bleachers, calling it shameful and disgraceful, but they blamed it on integration, saying this was what was going to happen when you mixed black and white; nothing good could come of it. Some black kids were just as disgusted, although they were saying the ruckus wasn't their fault, fights had never erupted at Nelson games, and they'd just been defending themselves. Most students were less upset about the brawl than about the shellacking the Bulldogs had taken at the hands of the Big Creek Owls, whom they usually creamed. Integration was supposed to improve the team, kids were saying, but now we couldn't even beat those pencil necks from Big Creek.

The principal, at the end of his morning announcements over the P.A. system, mentioned the need for "mutual respect and school unity." But it wasn't until English class, after lunch, that any of my teachers directly raised the subject.

My English teacher, Miss Jarvis, a thin-lipped young woman who got very excited about the readings she assigned, told us that she thought we ought to discuss what had happened at the game.

"The whites started it," said Vanessa Johnson. "Throwing that Coke at my sister."

"Stuff always gets thrown at games," said Tinky Brewster, a kid from the hill. "It's just like you all to make it a racial thing."

"We're not simply going to trade accusations here," Miss Jarvis said. "But I'd like people's views on what we can do to make integration a success at Byler High."

White kids started saying the problem was that blacks were always carrying on about prejudice and slavery, even though blacks were freed a hundred years ago. And blacks could have black pride, but if you started talking about white pride, all of a sudden it was racist. How come we can't use the N-word, but they can call us honkies? Anyway, a bunch of the white kids from the hill said, none of their families had owned slaves. In fact, they went on, most of their great-great-grandparents had been indentured servants, but you never heard people complaining about the Irish being enslaved. I was looking around guiltily to see if anyone was going to mention the old Holladay cotton plantation. No one did, and I sure wasn't about to bring it up.

Slavery might have ended a hundred years ago, the black kids replied, but until recently, they couldn't eat in the Bulldog Diner, and even today, they got glared at when they did. They started getting hired at Holladay Textiles only a few years ago, and they were still given the worst jobs. The real problem, the black students said, was that whites were scared that blacks were taking over sports and music. They wanted blacks to shut up, stop demanding their rights, and go back to cleaning toilets, washing clothes, and cooking food for white people.

"Well, we're not going to resolve this issue in a day," Miss Jarvis said. Instead, she wanted us to read a book about racial conflict in a small Southern town. It was called *To Kill a Mockingbird*.

• • •

I liked *To Kill a Mockingbird,* but I didn't think it was the most amazing book ever written, the way Miss Jarvis did. The best part, I thought, wasn't the stuff about race but the way Scout and the two boys snooped around the big haunted house where the scary recluse lived. That really reminded me of being a kid.

For all of Miss Jarvis's singing its praises as great literature, a lot of the kids in the class had real problems with the book. The white ones said they knew blacks shouldn't be lynched, and they didn't need a book preaching to them about it. Some resented the way the book divided the town into good respectable whites and bad white-trash types. The black kids, for their part, wondered why the hero had to be a noble white guy trying to save a helpless black guy and why the head of the lynch mob was described by the noble white guy as basically a decent man who happened to have a blind spot when it came to hanging innocent blacks. They also didn't like the way that all the good blacks knew their place and made their children stand up when the noble white guy walked by. It was all that Stepin-Fetchit-yass-suh-no-suh stuff.

"No one's challenging the system," Vanessa said.

"This discussion isn't going the way I'd anticipated," Miss Jarvis said. What she wanted us to do, she went on, was to put our thoughts down on paper.

When Uncle Tinsley heard about the assignment, his eyes lit up. "*To Kill a Mockingbird* is a fine book in its own way," he said. "But if you really want to understand Southern race relations, you need to read the great historian C. Vann Woodward."

Uncle Tinsley was sitting at his desk in the library. He pulled out a book from the floor-to-ceiling bookcase behind him and passed it to me. The title was *The Strange Career of Jim Crow*.

I started reading, but the writing was so complicated that I got bogged down on the very first page. Uncle Tinsley grabbed the book back and flipped through it, eagerly explaining the ideas and quoting sentences while I took notes.

Because blacks and whites in the South had lived together under slavery, Uncle Tinsley said, they got along better after the Civil War than blacks and whites up north, where the races hadn't mixed nearly as much. Legal segregation started first in the North and it was hypocritical of Northerners to blame it all on the South. In fact, the Jim Crow laws began in the South only at the turn of the century. Around that time, outsiders started using what C. Vann Woodward called "negrophobia" to turn poor whites against poor blacks, when the two groups should have been natural allies.

Uncle Tinsley helped me write up the paper—basically dictating large chunks of it—and had me read it to him. A little way in, he cut me off. I needed to throw myself into the presentation, he said. He'd been in the drama club at Washington and Lee, and he showed me how to gesture for emphasis and use what he called pregnant pauses.

The next day, when it was my turn to read my essay to the class, I didn't know if the other kids would be interested in or even understand what Uncle Tinsley had helped me write—I barely understood it myself—and that made me so nervous, the paper was shaking in my hands. It didn't help that Uncle Tinsley had me throw in fancy words and phrases like "white man's burden" and "negrophobia."

I tried to use the gestures he had shown me, but I forgot the pregnant pauses. Instead, I started rushing through the essay, and my gestures got a little wild. When I finished the paper, I looked up. Some kids were whispering or doodling, and a few were smirking, but most seemed bewildered.

Tinky Brewster raised his hand. "What's 'negrophobia'?" he asked.

"You don't have to know what it means to know it's a highfalutin word for people who don't like black folks," Vanessa piped up from the back of the class. "Bean, you one crazy-ass white girl."

The entire class cracked up.

"Now, Vanessa," Miss Jarvis said, starting to get teacherly, but then, looking at the class, she changed her mind. "Well, at least you've finally found one thing you can all agree on."

CHAPTER THIRTY

Liz and I were scrounging around in the attic one afternoon, opening trunks and chests to see what was inside, when we came across an old guitar. Mice had chewed at the neck, but Liz toyed with the tuning pegs and declared that the sound wasn't half bad. When we brought it downstairs, Uncle Tinsley told us it was Mom's first guitar, from when she was about Liz's age and decided she wanted to become a folksinger. Liz took the guitar into the music shop in town, where the clerk put on new strings and tuned it. Liz started spending afternoons in the bird wing, strumming away on it.

Mom had tried to teach us both to play the guitar. I was hopeless. Tone-deaf, Mom said. Liz showed real potential, but she couldn't take any sort of criticism, and Mom was always telling her what she was doing wrong and moving her fingers to the correct position. Great musicians bent the rules, Mom said, but before you could bend the rules, you had to learn them, so she was always badgering Liz to practice and Liz finally said, "I've had it."

Now, since Mom wasn't around looking over her shoulder, Liz could have fun picking out notes and chords, following songs on the radio, and figuring out what worked and what didn't without someone getting exasperated every time she hit a wrong note.

After a while, Liz decided she needed a guitar in better working condition. The music store in Byler had a used Silvertone in the window for a good price—at $110, the clerk said it was a steal—and Liz decided to buy it with the money in her passbook savings account. Since the peach-fuzz business, I had wanted to avoid Mr. Maddox, so I hadn't been working much, but Liz was still doing his filing and helping in his office, and she had socked away nearly two hundred dollars in her account.

One Monday afternoon in November, shortly after I'd read my "Negrophobia Essay"—as everyone in class had taken to calling it—Liz biked into town with plans to go to the bank, withdraw the money, and bring back the guitar that day. The guitar had a strap, and she was going to bike home with it slung upside down across her back. She was pretty excited.

By the time the light started fading, it was chilly enough to see your breath. I had put on a navy pea coat of Mom's that I found in the attic—unlike most of the stuff, it didn't look old-timey—and was out in front of the house raking leaves into big piles you could jump on when Liz came pedaling up the driveway. She didn't have the guitar.

"What happened?" I asked. "Did someone else already buy it?"

"My money wasn't in the bank," Liz said. "Mr. Maddox took it out."

She parked the bike under the carriage overhang, and we sat down on the front steps. After going to the bank, she'd gone over to the Maddoxes' to find out what the heck had happened to her money. Mr. Maddox told her that he'd moved the money out of her account, since the interest rate was so low, and instead invested it in T-bills, which had a much higher rate of interest but couldn't be liquidated until maturity—one year out. It was a shrewd move, he said, and if he hadn't been so busy, he would have explained it to her before. When Liz told him she wanted the money to buy a guitar, Mr. Maddox said she was a fool to waste her money on a passing fancy. Most kids who decided they wanted to play a musical instrument lost interest after a couple of months, he said, and they or their parents were out the cost of the damn thing while it just took up space in a closet.

"I can't believe it," Liz said. "That's my money. Mr. Maddox can't tell me what to do with it."

The very moment Liz uttered those words, Uncle Tinsley came out of the house carrying a ladle. Dinner was ready.

"Mr. Maddox?" he asked. "Jerry Maddox? What about Jerry Maddox?"

Liz and I looked at each other. It was one thing to avoid telling Uncle Tinsley what we'd been up to. It was another thing to outright lie now that he'd asked point-blank.

"Mr. Maddox won't give me my money," Liz said again.

"What do you mean?" Uncle Tinsley asked.

"We've been working for him," Liz said.

"It was the only job we could get," I added.

Uncle Tinsley looked at the two of us for a long moment without saying anything. Then he sat down next to us, put the ladle on the step, and pressed his fingers against his temples. I couldn't tell if he was upset or angry, disgusted or worried. Maybe he was feeling all those things at once.

"We needed money for clothes," Liz said.

"And we wanted to help out with the expenses," I said.

Uncle Tinsley took a deep breath. "Holladays working for Maddoxes," he said. "I never thought it would come to that." He looked over at us. "And you kept it from me."

"We just didn't want to upset you," I said.

"Well, now I know, and now I'm about as upset as I could possibly be," he said. "So you might as well tell me the whole story."

Liz and I explained it all, how we hadn't wanted to be a burden, so we'd gone looking for jobs and Mr. Maddox was the only one who'd give us work, how he'd set up the passbook savings accounts but now when Liz went to get her money to buy the guitar, Mr. Maddox had invested it in these T-bills and so she couldn't have it.

Uncle Tinsley took another deep breath and let the air out with a sigh. Now he seemed more tired than anything else. "If you'd come to me in the first place, I could have told you something like this would have happened sooner or later with Maddox. It always does. He's a vile snake." He stood up. "I don't want you to ever have anything to do with him again."

"What about my money?" Liz asked.

"Forget the money," he said.

"But it's two hundred dollars."

"Write it off to experience."

CHAPTER THIRTY-ONE

I'd been sharing Liz's room ever since the day I'd found out about my dad. That night, when Liz turned out the lights in the bird wing, the moon was so full and bright, it cast shadows across the floor. We lay side by side in bed, staring up at the ceiling.

"I'm going to get my money," Liz suddenly said.

"How?" I asked. "Uncle Tinsley told us not to have anything to do with Mr. Maddox."

"I don't care," she said. "That money's mine. I worked for it."

"But Uncle Tinsley said—"

"I don't care what Uncle Tinsley said," Liz went on. "What does he know? He lives shut up in this old house, eating his venison stew. He doesn't know what it's like to need a job. He never has." She sat up and looked out the window. "That money's mine. I need it. I earned it. I'm going to get it."

After school on Tuesday, Liz got on the blue Schwinn and rode into town to see Mr. Maddox. I expected her back in an hour or two. By dinnertime, she still hadn't returned. I went into the kitchen, where

Uncle Tinsley was opening a can of tomatoes to stretch out the stew. He dumped it into the big copper pot and gave the stew a taste. "Needs a little zing," he said. "Where's Liz?"

"She had some stuff to do. She should be back soon."

"I see," Uncle Tinsley said. He poured some vinegar into the pot and then ladled out the stew.

I carried the bowls to the table. After he'd said his usual blessing and eaten a few bites, Uncle Tinsley put down his spoon. "What stuff?" he asked.

"What stuff?"

"You said Liz had some stuff to do. What stuff?" He was eyeing me intently.

I looked at my spoon, trying to figure out what to say. "You know, stuff."

"No, I don't know."

"Errands and things."

"Bean, you're a terrible liar. Absolutely terrible. Your eyes are darting around all over the place. Now look at me square and tell me where Liz is."

I raised my eyes and felt my lower lip quivering.

"I guess you don't need to tell me. There are only two things I've asked both of you not to do since you got here. One was not to get jobs, and you went out and got them. The other was to forget the money, and the very next day, Liz goes to get it."

"Please don't be mad at us, Uncle Tinsley. Liz just wanted to get her money. It was hers. And please don't kick us out."

"I'm not going to kick you out, Bean," Uncle Tinsley said. "I guess we'll just have to wait and hear what she has to say."

Through the rest of dinner, Uncle Tinsley kept glancing at his watch. "It's late," he said at one point. "She really shouldn't be out this late." A couple of minutes later, he said, "I'm going to ground that girl until her hair turns white." He added, "What she really needs is a good old-fashioned whipping."

We were rinsing out the bowls at the kitchen sink when we heard a knock at the door. I ran to see who it was, turning on the porch light. When I opened the door, a strange man stood there with his arm around Liz. She was crying. Her eyes were puffy and red, she had bruises on her cheek and chin, and her shirt was torn. She was looking down, holding a soft drink cup with both hands and sucking on the straw, but the drink was all gone and the ice cubes were rattling around.

"Liz?" I said. She didn't look up, and when I tried to hug her, she turned away.

Uncle Tinsley had come up behind me. "What happened here?" he asked.

"Mr. Holladay, I didn't know she was your niece," the man said. He was skinny, with black hair and a mustache, and he wore a blue mechanic's jacket with the name Wayne stitched on the pocket. "What happened wasn't right, Mr. Holladay. Wayne Clemmons, by the way." He extended his hand and Uncle Tinsley shook it.

"What did happen?"

Wayne explained that he worked at a garage but also ran a one-man car service part-time, Byler not needing a lot of taxis. Jerry Maddox occasionally hired him because, although Mr. Maddox had that fancy Le Mans, he got a charge out of being driven to business meetings, like he was a big shot with a chauffeur. "Mr. Maddox said it enhances the aura."

"Get to the point, Wayne."

Wayne had been at the garage late that afternoon when Mr. Maddox drove up with this young woman. He said the carburetor on the Le Mans was acting up, but he had some meetings he needed to attend, and he wanted Wayne to drive him and the girl around. As they were getting in the car, Wayne said, Mr. Maddox pulled him aside and said the girl was a hooker and he might be getting a little backseat action between meetings.

"Sweet Jesus," Uncle Tinsley said.

They started driving around town, Wayne continued, stopping at various places with him and the girl waiting in the car while Mr. Maddox went inside. As evening came on, the girl started complaining to Mr. Maddox about not getting her money, saying things like "It's my money, I earned it." Mr. Maddox kept telling her she'd get the money, but first she needed to do what he wanted. Wayne figured it was just a hooker and a john haggling over the fee. The argument grew more heated, with the girl getting louder and angrier. Then, in the rearview mirror, Wayne saw Mr. Maddox backhand her, and she started crying. Mr. Maddox caught Wayne's glance. "Keep your eyes on the road," he said. "I don't pay you to watch, I pay you to drive."

By then it was dark. As Wayne drove through town, he heard the two of them struggling, the girl begging Mr. Maddox to stop and him backhanding her a couple more times. Then they came to a red light. The girl suddenly jumped out of the car. Mr. Maddox jumped out after her, but the girl ran around the car and jumped back in next to Wayne, locking the door. "Go!" she screamed.

Wayne took off, leaving Mr. Maddox at the street corner. The girl was sobbing. Her shirt was half torn off, and she was holding it together with both hands. Wayne said he mentioned, by way of showing some sympathy, that whoring could be a rough line of work, but the girl said Tinsley Holladay was her uncle and she wanted Wayne to take her to Mayfield. That, Wayne said, was when he realized she wasn't a hooker after all.

"She was awful upset, Mr. Holladay," Wayne said. "But I was in 'Nam, and I know how to deal with people losing it. So I stopped at the Park 'N Eat and got her a Coke. I think that helped calm her." Wayne kept looking back and forth between me and Uncle Tinsley, like he wanted our reaction. His adrenaline seemed to be pumping.

"Thank you for doing this," Uncle Tinsley said. "I know it wasn't easy, but you did the right thing."

"Mr. Maddox has got to be pretty pissed with me, but I don't care. I'm pretty pissed with him. What he did was wrong. It was wrong—and I'll testify to that."

I didn't know what to say. I tried to hug Liz again, and this time she didn't turn away, but her body was completely rigid. Her shoulders felt so thin and frail that it seemed I'd crush her bones if I hugged too tightly. Then she let her cup drop, the ice scattering across the floor, and collapsed in my arms. I felt that if I didn't hold her up, she'd fall to the floor as well.

"Thank you for all you've done, Wayne," Uncle Tinsley said. "You're a good man." He was usually tight with money, but he took a twenty-dollar bill from his wallet and offered it to Wayne.

"I couldn't accept, sir," Wayne said. "I didn't do it for the money."

"I insist. After what happened, Maddox certainly isn't going to pay you."

"Well, then, thank you very much."

"Thank you, Wayne," Uncle Tinsley said. "We can handle it from here."

He opened the door. Wayne walked out, giving Liz and me that nod that said, I got you covered.

I squeezed Liz again. "Liz, are you okay?"

She shook her head.

"What are we going to do?" I asked Uncle Tinsley.

"Let's get Liz cleaned up and into bed," he said.

"Shouldn't we call the police first?"

"I don't know if that's such a good idea," Uncle Tinsley said.

"We've got to do something," I said.

"I told you two to stay away from Maddox, but you wouldn't listen, and this is where it's gotten us."

"Still, we've got to do something," I said. I gave Liz a gentle shake. "Don't you think?" I asked her.

"I don't know," Liz said. "I just don't know."

"Don't you want to press charges?" I asked. I kept thinking about Wayne saying he'd testify. It sounded like he thought going to the cops was a foregone conclusion.

"I don't know," she said again.

"What's done is done," Uncle Tinsley said. "You can't undo it by pressing charges. It'll only create more trouble—and more scandal."

"What do you want to do, Liz?"

"I just want to take a bath."

CHAPTER THIRTY-TWO

I ran Liz a bath. I worried I might be destroying evidence or something, but Liz really wanted that bath. She also wanted the water as hot as it could be, and she asked me to stay.

"What happened, Liz? Did he actually—"

"He tried to. But I don't want to talk about it."

"Are you okay?"

"No."

"Shouldn't we go to the hospital?"

"That's the last thing I want to do."

"But you might be hurt."

"I don't want anyone examining me."

"Are you worried about getting pregnant?"

"No. He didn't . . . I said I don't want to talk about it."

When Liz climbed into the tub, she kept on her underwear. She didn't explain why, but I understood.

"You were smart, Liz," I said. "You got away from Maddox just like we got away from that perv in New Orleans."

"I'm not smart," she said. "If I was smart, I never would have gotten in the car."

"Don't think about it like that. You did get away."

After the bath, Liz got into bed and pulled the covers up over her head, saying she wanted to be alone. I went back downstairs. Uncle Tinsley was in the living room, poking at the fire he'd built. I tried calling Mom to ask what we should do about pressing charges, but there was no answer.

"We should go to the police," I said.

"That's not a good idea," Uncle Tinsley said.

"Or at least talk to a lawyer."

"These things are best kept in the family."

"It's worse than Wayne said. Liz told me Maddox tried to rape her."

"Oh Christ," he said. "That poor girl." He ran his hand through his hair. "Still, nothing you can do will undo the damage. It'll only make things worse."

"But Maddox can't get away with this."

"You don't know Maddox," he said. We may have been working for Maddox, he continued, but we didn't understand what kind of man he really was. Maddox loved nothing better than a fight. A lot of people think a fight is over when they knock their opponent down, but people like Maddox think that's the time to start kicking hard.

Maddox did a lot of his fighting in the courthouse, Uncle Tinsley went on. The county clerk had a docket a mile long, listing all the cases he'd been involved in. He sued neighbors over boundary disputes. He sued doctors for malpractice. He sued dry cleaners, claiming they shrank his clothes. He sued mechanics, claiming they didn't fix his car. He sued town officials if there was a pothole on his street. While most people saw the court as a place to seek justice, Maddox saw it as a place to take down anyone who happened to stand in his way or get on his wrong side.

This was something Maddox had learned years ago, Uncle Tinsley said, when he was living in a boardinghouse in Rhode Island and stole some jewelry from his landlady. The police searched his room and found the jewelry, and Maddox was convicted. Then along came a civil rights lawyer who argued that the police didn't have the right to search Maddox's room without his permission. The case went all the way to the Rhode Island Supreme Court. Maddox won, although everyone knew he was guilty as sin. And that was when Maddox became a voracious student of the law, because he realized that guilt and innocence were incidental, that people who understood the law could also figure out how to bend the law.

"He brags about winning that case," Uncle Tinsley said. "He fights dirty. That's why you don't want to tangle with Maddox."

"What do we do? Pretend nothing happened?"

Uncle Tinsley gave the burning logs a hard jab with the poker, and sparks flew up into the chimney.

I went back up to the bird wing. Uncle Tinsley wanting to pretend nothing happened made me wonder if maybe what Mom had said about her family was true—they were all experts at pretending.

Liz still had the covers over her head. I took my dad's photo and his Silver Star from the cigar box that I kept in the white cradle and brought them into the bathroom to study them in the light.

I ran my finger over the tiny silver star that was inside the bigger gold star, and I wondered what advice my dad would give me if he were around. I looked at his crooked grin and the cocky way his arms were crossed as he leaned against the doorframe, and I knew the one thing Charlie Wyatt would never do. He would never pretend nothing happened.

CHAPTER THIRTY-THREE

The next morning, I woke up before Liz and went downstairs to make her a cup of tea. Uncle Tinsley was puttering around in the kitchen. He started talking about what a hard frost we'd had during the night, and how this time of year the birds, especially the blue jays, were always flying into windows and banging their heads on the glass. "Always startles me," he said. "Startles them more, I expect. Sometimes they just bounce off, sometimes they hit so hard, it knocks them senseless."

It was clear that Uncle Tinsley wasn't going to make any reference to what had happened with Maddox, in the hope that we would put it all behind us and get on with life. Lying in bed, I had decided during the night that Liz and I should at least see a lawyer. I didn't know much about the police and the courts and the law, but I did know that everyone got a lawyer, even the poor black guy in *To Kill a Mockingbird*. I figured Uncle Tinsley knew every lawyer in town, but since he wanted us to forget the whole thing, there was no point in asking him for a recommendation or telling him about the plan. I had a classmate, Billy Corbin, whose father was a lawyer. I could look him up in the phone book.

When I brought the cup of tea up to Liz, she was awake, lying in bed. Her face was even more swollen and bruised than the night before. "There's no way I'm going to school," she said.

"You don't have to," I said. I passed her the cup of tea and explained my plan for the two of us to go see Billy Corbin's dad.

"Whatever you think," Liz said. She sounded like she was in a daze.

Before leaving the house, I tried calling Mom again. I was certain she would want us to press charges, since she was always going on about women standing up for their rights. With Mom, however, you never knew how she'd react. I let the phone ring a long time, but there was still no answer. That made me wonder where the heck Mom was, because she wasn't exactly an early riser.

Instead of taking the bus to school, Liz and I walked into town. The sun was out, and it was melting the frost, though the grass was still white and stiff in places the sun hadn't reached. We passed the emus, who were on the far side of the field pecking at the grass, but we didn't stop to watch them.

When we got to Holladay Avenue, I found a phone booth and asked the operator to put in a collect call to Mom. There was no answer. I thought of going over to the hill and talking to Aunt Al, but she didn't like to give advice. Also, if she advised us to press charges and Mr. Maddox found out about it, he could make life real hard for her. Anyway, it seemed that the most important thing to do was talk to a lawyer.

I looked up Mr. Corbin's address in the phone book dangling from a chain. His office was over a shoe store, up a rickety flight of stairs, and his door had a frosted glass pane etched with WILLIAM T. CORBIN, ESQ., ATTORNEY AT LAW. When we knocked, there was no answer, and the door was locked.

"We'll just wait," I said. We sat down at the top of the stairs. After a while a man came climbing up, carrying two big briefcases. He looked tired, with circles under his eyes, and his suit was rumpled.

"Mr. Corbin?" I asked.

"The one and only. Who wants to know?"

"I'm Bean Holladay. This is my sister, Liz. We need to talk to you. About a legal matter."

He smiled. "Let me guess. Your mother grounded you, and you want me to appeal the ruling."

"It's serious," I said.

He took out a key and unlocked the door. "I suspect it is." He looked at Liz. "What happened to you?"

"That's what we're here to talk about," I said.

Mr. Corbin's office was a mess, with law books propped open and legal papers stacked everywhere. I took that as a good sign. Any lawyer who couldn't afford a secretary to keep his office neat must be honest.

Mr. Corbin had us sit in cracked leather chairs facing his desk while he shuffled some of the papers covering the surface. "Now, tell me what happened," he said.

I cleared my throat. "It's kind of complicated," I said.

"It usually is," he said.

"And awful," Liz added. It was the first thing she'd said since we'd got to town.

"You probably can't tell me anything I haven't heard before," he said. "And if a lawyer can't keep his mouth shut about things his clients tell him, he shouldn't be a lawyer."

"What do you charge?" I asked.

He smiled and shook his head. "Let's not worry about that at this point. Let's just hear what the problem is."

"It involves Jerry Maddox," I said.

Mr. Corbin raised his eyebrows. "Then I imagine it is complicated."

After that, the whole story came spilling out. Mr. Corbin listened quietly, his clasped hands propping up his chin.

"Wayne told us he'll testify," I said.

"What a mess," Mr. Corbin said, almost to himself. He pinched the bridge of his nose. "So, you didn't go to the hospital or to the police?"

"I wanted to talk to a lawyer first."

"Why isn't your uncle here with you?"

"He wants us to forget the whole thing ever happened."

"And you don't want to forget it? You want to file charges?"

"What I want is for my uncle to blow Mr. Maddox's brains out with his shotgun," I said.

"I'm going to pretend I didn't hear that."

"That isn't going to happen, so we came to find out what we're supposed to do, legal-wise."

"It's not really a question of what you're supposed to do. It's more a question of what you want to do." Mr. Corbin picked up a paper clip and pried it apart. We had two options, he went on. One, we could press charges, which would create a big stink and a nasty trial with a lot of god-awful publicity but might result in Mr. Maddox being punished for what he allegedly did. On the other hand, there was no guarantee of that. Two, we could decide it was an incident that involved bad judgment on the part of both parties—since Liz did voluntarily get into the back of the car with Mr. Maddox—and didn't need to be rehashed in a public courtroom with the entire town following every sordid detail.

"What's the right thing to do?" I asked.

"I can't decide that for you," he said. "You two have to decide that. And unfortunately, you don't have a choice between a good option and a bad option. Each option is bad in its own way."

"We can't just do nothing," I said.

"Why not?" Mr. Corbin asked.

"Because what Maddox did was wrong," I said, "and because then he'll be walking around laughing about how he got away with it." At that point, something occurred to me. "And he might do it again."

"Possibly."

"We can't let that happen."

"Do you think he'd try it again?" Liz asked.

I had been doing most of the talking and was surprised to hear her speak up.

Mr. Corbin shrugged. "Like I said, it's possible."

"I just don't want it to happen again," Liz said. "I'm scared of him doing it again. I'm scared of even running into him."

"You could always leave town," Mr. Corbin said. "Can't you go stay with your mother?"

"We tried that last summer," I said. "It didn't work out so well. Anyway, Maddox attacked my sister, and we're supposed to go into hiding? That's not right."

"No, it's not. It's an option, nonetheless."

"I don't know what to do," Liz said. "My thoughts keep jumbling up. Bean, what do you think?"

"The thing is," I said, "if we don't at least file charges, it will be like nothing ever happened."

"Legally speaking, that's true," Mr. Corbin said. "If you do file charges, you can always drop them later, but bear in mind that these things sometimes develop a momentum of their own."

"Well," I said, "if we don't want to pretend it never happened and we don't want to leave town and go into hiding, we have no choice. We have to file charges."

Mr. Corbin put down his paper clip. "Bean Holladay, how old are you?"

"Twelve. I'll be thirteen in April."

"You're a little young to be making a decision like this on your own. Should you decide to proceed, you need your uncle with you from here on in."

"He's going to be mad," I said.

"I'll call him." Mr. Corbin picked up the phone and dialed. "Tinsley," he said. "Bill Corbin here." He explained that Liz and I were in his office and that we'd decided to file charges against Jerry Maddox for the alleged assault the night before. He stopped and listened, then shook his head. "No, sir. It's not my advice. They came to me, and I outlined their options, and they made the decision." He listened again. Then he handed the phone to me. "He wants to talk to you."

"What the hell are you doing?" Uncle Tinsley asked.

"We're going to file charges," I said.

"I thought you were going to drop the whole matter."

"He'll think he can try it again. And what if he does? What are we supposed to do then? Just let him? Hide from him? We can't. So we're filing charges."

There was a long pause.

"I'll meet you at the sheriff's office."

Mr. Corbin called the sheriff's department and told them we were coming over. When I asked him how much we owed him, Mr. Corbin said he considered it pro bono. That meant free, Liz explained.

"So you'll be our lawyer?" I asked. "Pro bono?"

"If you press charges, the state's prosecutor becomes your lawyer," Mr. Corbin said. "You won't need me."

"Oh," I said.

The sheriff's department was in a low brick building with a flat roof. The deputy at the desk didn't seem particularly happy to see us. He called in another deputy. The other guy wasn't smiling, either. He had me wait in the lobby while he brought Liz into the back to take her statement.

A few minutes later, Uncle Tinsley came through the door wearing one of his tweed jackets and his gray felt hat. He sat down next to me in the row of orange plastic chairs. We didn't say anything. After a bit, he reached over and ruffled my hair.

Liz wasn't in the back for long.

"How'd it go?" I asked when she came out.

"They took some pictures, asked questions, and I answered them, okay?" she said. "Let's go home."

CHAPTER THIRTY-FOUR

By the time we got back to Mayfield, the school day was half over. Uncle Tinsley said, given everything that had happened, we might as well just stay home and unwind. A few hours later, we heard a car roar up the driveway. I went to the window and saw Maddox's black Le Mans screech to a stop. Doris Maddox got out, more pregnant than ever, and slammed the door behind her. Liz was up in the bird wing, but Uncle Tinsley and I went out to meet Doris, who was stalking over to the porch.

For a moment, I genuinely believed Doris had come to apologize and try to smooth things over. She was constantly complaining about what a no-count scoundrel her husband was—always tomcatting around, had a terrible temper, picked fights right and left, lied through his teeth. I thought Doris was going to say something like "Look, what my husband did was wrong, but he does provide for me and my kids, and if you go ahead with this, it will hurt my family."

But as soon as I saw Doris's face, I realized she had not come to make amends. Her mouth was tight and her eyes were all fired up.

"What the goddamn hell do you think you're doing?" she shouted. "How dare you? How dare you, after all we've done for you?"

The deputies, she said, had come to her house and arrested her husband, taking him down to the jail, where they fingerprinted him and put him in a cell. His lawyer was arranging bail even as she spoke, and Jerry would be out by the end of the day.

We didn't know what we were up against, Doris said. We had picked a fight with the wrong rhino. Her husband knew the law inside and out. He'd won countless lawsuits. He had fought a case all the way to the Supreme Court of the state of Rhode Island and had won. We would regret the day we started this. "No jury's going to believe you lying sluts."

At first I was stunned, but when Doris started threatening us and accusing us of lying, I got pretty steamed myself. "Don't you get all high and mighty," I said. "We have an eyewitness. He'll testify to what happened. Your husband hurt Liz, and now you're pretending he's a saint and talking about all you did for us?"

"Your sister's a whore!" Doris shouted. "My husband hired her as his personal secretary, he paid her, he trained her, he trusted her, he bought her nice clothes, and he treated her like a queen. We know the two of you were stealing from us. Your sister was drinking yesterday, and she put the moves on Jerry in the backseat of that car. When he turned her down, she made up this bullshit story. She was out to get him all along because he had your worthless uncle fired. You think you've got your evidence? Well, we've got our evidence. We have a vodka bottle with y'all's fingerprints all over it as proof."

I had no idea what she was talking about, since I'd never had a drink of vodka in my life and I was pretty sure Liz hadn't, either, but I pushed it out of my mind. "You can try to twist the facts as much as you want," I said. "But you know your husband did this. I don't care what a big shot he is, the truth will come out."

"When the truth about you two comes out," Doris said, "you won't be able to show your skanky faces in this town. Mark my words. My husband will destroy you!"

Doris climbed back into the Le Mans, slammed the door, jerked the car into reverse, then gunned it down the driveway, tires spraying gravel. I watched with my hands on my hips, fighting the urge to give her the finger because I knew Uncle Tinsley would find it appalling. "She thought she could scare us, but it didn't work, did it?"

"This is going to be a shit storm," Uncle Tinsley said.

It was the first time I had heard him use a curse word.

CHAPTER THIRTY-FIVE

That evening Liz announced there was absolutely no way she would consider going to school the next day. Neither Uncle Tinsley nor I tried to talk her into it.

The next morning, as soon as I got to the bus stop, I could tell that everyone knew. Word spread quickly in a small town like Byler. All it took was one deputy mentioning to his brother-in-law that Tinsley Holladay's niece had filed charges against Jerry Maddox, and within hours it was the talk of the barbershop and the beauty parlor. The other kids were clearly discussing it, and when they saw me, they started shushing each other, saying things like "Here she comes," "Dummy up," and "Where's the other one?"

When I got to school, there was time before first period to go to the library, which always had a copy of the *Byler Daily News*. I expected Maddox's arrest to be a big front-page story because the paper usually played up anything local, no matter how small—a horse getting stuck in a pond, someone's toolshed catching on fire, or a farmer growing a five-pound tomato. The story wasn't on the front page, or even the second or third page. I finally found it at the back, under a section called "Police Blotter." The headline was "Mill Boss Charged." The article said:

Jerry Maddox, 43, a foreman at Holladay Textiles, has been charged with the alleged assault of a local girl, 15, whose name is being withheld because of her age. He has been released on bail. No trial date has been set.

I was shocked. I thought the story was a big deal, certainly bigger news than a five-pound tomato, and it involved a Byler heavyweight. Sure, people were gossiping about it, but they didn't know the real story. I'd been counting on the whole town reading in official detail exactly what had happened. I thought that was one way to punish Maddox and make sure he never did it again.

The article didn't even say "attempted rape," as if the editors were afraid of spelling it out. "Assault." What did that mean? It could mean anything or nothing. From what people were going to read in the *Byler Daily News,* Maddox might as well have shoved some girl who sassed him in a parking-lot argument over a fender bender.

The rest of the day was just awful. In the halls, kids stared at me, looking away as soon as I caught their eye. Girls whispered and giggled and pointed. Guys smirked and in mocking, cheeping voices said things like "Help! Help! I'm being molested!"

On my way to English class, I ran into Vanessa. She saw me and shook her head. "Going to the law," she said. "Such a white thing to do."

"What would you do?" I asked.

"I wouldn't be getting into no car with Mr. Maddox in the first place," she said. "You climb in the backseat with the boss man, you got to expect something's going to happen. That's just the way it is."

Liz decided she wasn't going back to school the next day, either. In fact, she said, she was not leaving the house until the bruises on her face had gone away. It was Friday, the day after the article, and things in the halls at school went from bad to worse. Kids kept snickering behind my back, throwing wadded-up paper at my head, and tripping me.

The football game that night was against the Orange Hornets. I hadn't been much help to the pep squad that week, and Liz had hardly been in the mood to concoct any crowd-rousing rhymes or puns. At the beginning of the week, I had come up with "Orange You Scared?" but Terri Pruitt, the pep squad adviser, thought it might leave some kids scratching their heads. Still, the posters got made— the slogan was "Swat the Hornets"—and on Friday the whole school gathered in the gym for the weekly pep rally.

When it came time for me and Vanessa to rile up the seventh-graders so our class could win the spirit stick, we walked out onto the gym floor and started pumping our fists in the air. We got no reaction from the crowd. Most of the kids sitting in the bleachers were just staring, as if they couldn't believe I had the nerve to be out there. I kept trying to rev them up, and a few kids cheered halfheartedly, but then there was a boo, then a few more boos. Then the trash started coming—spit wads, a bag of Corn Nuts, pennies, a roll of Certs. I glanced at Vanessa. She was pushing right through it, wearing the same steely expression I'd seen on her sister's face after she got hit with the soda cup during the football game. I tried to follow Vanessa's example, ignoring the trash and the booing, but it only got louder and the cheering died out altogether, and I could see it was pointless to continue. I walked off the floor, leaving Vanessa to shake the spirit stick on her own.

Terri Pruitt was standing by the door. "Are you all right, Bean?" she asked.

I nodded. "But I think I'm quitting the pep squad."

She squeezed my shoulder. "It's probably for the best," she said.

• • •

That afternoon, before I boarded the bus in the parking lot for the ride home, a few boys from the hill started crowding around me, shoving me with their shoulders, and saying things like "I'm Jerry Maddox. Are you scared of me?" A teacher saw what was happening but looked away. Joe Wyatt also saw what was happening, and he came over.

"Hey, cuz, how you doing?" he said. Then he turned to the boys. "You all know she's my cousin, don't you?"

The boys backed off, but they had kept me from catching my bus, so Joe offered to walk me home. "Some people are jerks," he said.

We walked along in silence for a while. It was a crisp November afternoon, and out of town, on the road to Mayfield, you could smell the woodsmoke drifting from the farmhouse chimneys. "If you want to talk about it all, you can," he said. "If you don't want to talk about it all, we can talk about chestnuts."

By then the last thing I wanted to do was rehash the whole mess. "Let's talk about chestnuts," I said.

It was the time of the year for gathering chestnuts, Joe said. Most chestnut trees had died out during the great blight, but he knew where a few survivors were holding on up in the hills. After he gathered the chestnuts, his mom roasted them over a fire he made in an old oil drum. "Maybe tomorrow," he said, "we should go get us some chestnuts."

CHAPTER THIRTY-SIX

Liz hadn't set foot out of the house since going to the cops four days earlier. She'd hardly even left the bird wing and I'd been bringing up bowls of stew on the silver tray. She kept obsessing about whether filing the charges had been the right thing to do and whether the whole mess was all her fault because she'd been stupid enough to think she could get her money back if she got in the car with Mr. Maddox. She wondered whether we'd have been better off if the bandersnatches had taken us away back in Lost Lake.

"Don't think like that," I said.

"I can't help it," she said. "I can't control my thoughts." The argument going on inside her head was so heated, she said, that she felt like different voices were making the cases for and against her. One voice kept talking about Alice in Wonderland's "Eat Me" cake, saying a slice of it would make her grow so tall that people would be scared of her. Another voice recommended Alice's "Drink Me" bottle—a sip would make her so small, no one would notice her. She knew the voices weren't real, but that was what they sounded like, actual voices.

Liz and her voices had me worried. I'd kept trying to call Mom without any luck, but I figured she'd say what Liz needed was to get out of the house, breathe some fresh air, and clear her head. So on Saturday morning, I insisted that she come with me to the Wyatts' to gather chestnuts.

"I don't feel like it," Liz said. "And my face is still a mess."

"I don't care," I said. "You've got to get out."

"I don't want to."

"Too bad. You're getting out. You can't stay in here forever."

Liz was sitting in bed in her pajamas. I started pulling her clothes out of the chest of drawers, throwing them at her, and snapping my fingers to speed her up.

Uncle Tinsley was glad to see Liz up and dressed. To celebrate he opened a can of Vienna sausages to go with our poached eggs. After breakfast, we rode the Schwinns over to the hill. Aunt Al was, as always, in the kitchen. She had a pot of grits going and was grating cheese into it. As soon as she saw us, she gave us great big hugs, then offered us some grits. Liz said we'd already eaten and she was full.

"I've still got some room left," I said.

Aunt Al laughed and passed me a bowl.

"I hope you all know, I believe every word of your story," she said to Liz. The whole town was divided over the charges, she continued. "A lot of folks don't believe you—but there's a lot who do." Thing was, she went on, most of them that believed Liz wouldn't come out and say so. They were good people, Aunt Al said, but they were scared. They had jobs they couldn't afford to lose, and they didn't want to take sides against Jerry Maddox. But they were all too happy to see someone else stand up to him. "You're one gutsy girl."

"Or crazy," Liz said.

"It's not crazy," I said. "What would be crazy would be to pretend nothing happened."

Aunt Al patted my arm. "You got more than a lick of your dad in you, child."

Joe came into the kitchen carrying two flour sacks. "Go get another sack for Liz," Aunt Al said. "Come to think of it, get me one, too. I don't hardly get out of this house except to go do my shift at that dang mill."

Joe hoisted Earl onto his shoulders and led us up a trail through the woods behind the Wyatts' house. At first the ground was covered with dense brambles, but when we got farther into the woods, the brambles thinned out. The leaves had mostly fallen, the sun shining down through the naked branches, and you could see the dead tree trunks and downed limbs and thick vines twisting up into the treetops.

For a woman who spent most of her time in the kitchen, Aunt Al acted right at home in the woods, booking up the trail like a kid out exploring. When she was a girl, she told us, gathering chestnuts was her favorite chore. Her family's farm had been on the edge of a forest full of chestnut trees, some of them so big that three grown men locking hands couldn't wrap their arms all the way around the trunks. One big chestnut was right next to the house, and at first frost, she went on, the nuts came falling down so thick they sounded like a hard rain on the tin roof. She and her ten brothers and sisters would get up before dawn to gather chestnuts, which they sold in town to buy goods like shoes and calico.

In the thirties, when she was about eight, the blight that made its way from China started killing off the chestnuts in her neck of the woods. Within a few years, all the beautiful giant trees had become lurking dead hulks. "People said it looked like the end of the world, and in a way, it was," she said. The wild turkeys and deer that ate the chestnuts disappeared, and the farm families who hunted the game and counted on the chestnuts for a cash crop were forced off the land. They moved into towns like Byler, where they took jobs in the mills.

"There's a few chestnuts left," Aunt Al said. "Joe knows where some of them are, but he won't show them to most folks."

"They need to be left alone," Joe said.

After a while, the trail started sloping sharply uphill. When we came to an old tractor tire lying on the ground, we turned off the trail and pushed through the branches. After a few minutes, Joe pointed through the woods to a tree with dark bark. It had two straight trunks that soared upward and some yellowing toothy leaves still clung to the branches.

"The first time Joe showed me this tree," Aunt Al said, "I won't lie to you, I fell on my knees and cried like a baby."

When we reached the base of the tree, Joe set Earl on a fallen log, picked up a thorny chestnut hull, and held it out to me. It weighed almost nothing. He pointed out a rust-colored spot in the tree's bark, about the size of a saucer. "She's got the blight, but it ain't killed her yet," he said. He also pointed out four smaller chestnut trees and some young saplings sprouting out of an old stump. "I do believe they're figuring out a way to fight off that blight."

"Job, chapter fourteen, verse seven," Aunt Al said. " 'For there is hope for a tree, if it is cut down, that it will sprout again, and that its tender shoots will not cease.' "

I looked over at Liz. She was staring up at the twin trunks of the big chestnut rising to the sky. "What are you thinking about?" I asked her.

"How sad it must have been for the tree to stand there all those years while the blight was killing off her brothers and sisters," she said. "Do you think she wondered why she was the only one to survive?"

"Trees don't wonder about things," Joe said. "They just grow."

"Now, we don't know that for a fact," Aunt Al said. "What I do know is that wondering why you survived don't help you survive."

The woods were quiet except for an occasional squirrel stirring up the damp leaves when it darted along the forest floor. We all knelt down and started gathering chestnuts.

CHAPTER THIRTY-SEVEN

By Monday, Liz's face was looking a lot better, and although she didn't want to do it, Uncle Tinsley and I decided it was time for her to go back to school. Sitting in the bird wing, brooding and listening to her voices, wasn't doing her any good.

Liz took forever getting dressed that morning, moving like she was underwater, pulling socks on and then taking them off, shuffling through her shirts and saying she couldn't find the one she wanted. I was afraid we'd miss the bus and kept urging her to hurry up, telling her she was dawdling, but she insisted she was moving as fast as she could. We did miss the bus, and since Uncle Tinsley hated wasting gas on unnecessary car trips, we decided to walk to school. Classes had started by the time we arrived, and we both got tardies—our first.

I hadn't told Liz about the way I'd been teased since she filed the charges. It would give her one more reason not to return to school. When we walked down the hall, people made a point of avoiding her, leaning away and stepping back. Girls who had ignored her now went out of their way to whisper loud enough for her to hear, some of them giving little shrieks and saying things like "Here she comes!" and "Crazy Lizzie!" and "We've got to get away!" At lunch hour, a whole line of them fell in behind her, imitating her walk while the rest of the girls in the hallway cracked up, cupping their hands over their mouths.

That night Liz joked that she felt like Moses parting the Red Sea, but it was horrible. She started to hate coming to school, and every morning I had to drag her out of bed and get her dressed. At school, it just got worse, with the other girls openly taunting her, mimicking her voice, and tripping her when she walked by.

At the end of the week, I ran into Lisa Saunders standing with a group of girls on one of the stairway landings. Lisa was one of the cheerleaders who had quit the squad when the football team was integrated. She had a bony nose and wore her blond hair in a high ponytail. Her father owned the Chevy dealership, and she was one of the few kids at Byler who had her own car. If she wasn't with her boyfriend, who always had his arm around her, she was surrounded by other girls, all of them whispering together.

Lisa held a stack of mimeographed papers and was passing them out to the kids on the stairs. "Here, Bean, I'm taking applications for friends. Fill this out if you want."

There were several pages stapled together. The title said "Application for Friendship," and it looked like a test, with a bunch of questions and multiple-choice or fill-in-the-blank answers. Most were what you'd expect: "Name your favorite TV show." "Give the model and color of your dream car." But some were spiky, like "What teacher would you most like to see fired?" and "What member of your class would you least want to date?" I heard Lisa's friends giggling, but I didn't understand why until I got to the last page. The final question was:

If a boy goes on a date with Liz Holladay, what should he bring for protection?

A) A rubber
B) A bar of soap
C) A gun
D) Jerry Maddox

My face started burning and my hands clenched up like they needed to grab something and tear it to shreds and without thinking about what I was doing, I leaped at Lisa Saunders, shouting, "You think you're special, but I'm going to hurt you bad!"

After that, it was all a mess of hair I pulled on, skin I scratched at, arms I pounded against, and clothes I tore up. Lisa Saunders's fingers were in my face, clawing and scratching back, but it didn't hurt. All I felt was anger. We were rolling on the floor, grunting and screaming and kicking and gouging and flailing. Very quickly, other kids circled around to watch, cheering and hollering encouragement, not to me or even to Lisa but generally, to urge it all on. Fight! Fight! Hit her! Hit her good!

Then I felt a different pair of hands on me, a man's hands. The science teacher Mr. Belcher had pushed through the crowd, and he broke us apart. I was panting like a dog, shaking with rage, but I was glad to see that I had done some serious damage to Lisa Saunders. Her bony nose was bleeding, her mascara was running down her face, and I'd pulled out her ponytail holder along with a fistful of blond hair.

Lisa Saunders's friends began accusing me of starting the whole thing. When Mr. Belcher dragged both of us by the arm down to the principal's office, they followed behind, going on about how Bean Holladay jumped on Lisa out of the blue for no reason at all.

The principal was out, so Mr. Belcher shoved us into the office of Miss Clay, the vice principal. "Hall fight," he said.

Miss Clay looked up at us over her reading glasses. "Thank you,

Mr. Belcher," she said. "Take a seat, girls." She passed us a box of Kleenex. I started to explain about the friendship application, since that was what the fight was about, but Miss Clay cut me off. "That's neither here nor there." She launched into a lecture, saying how disappointed she was in us for engaging in such inappropriate behavior and going on about what was and wasn't proper conduct at Byler High. "Girls hitting each other," she said. "It's so unladylike."

"Unladylike?" I asked. "Do you think I care what's ladylike and what's not?"

I was still completely worked up. I had gotten even hotter when I realized that Miss Clay wasn't going to let me tell her about the repulsive friendship application. I went on to say that if the teachers had been doing their jobs and looking after their students instead of turning a blind eye when one of them got picked on, these girls wouldn't be going after my sister, and I wouldn't have to be defending her.

Miss Clay jerked off her reading glasses. "Don't use that tone of voice with me, young lady. You need to respect your elders."

"I respect people who do their jobs," I said. "Respecting people just because they're older is a bunch of malarkey. Jerry Maddox is older. Am I supposed to respect him?"

"Don't try to change the subject," she said. "Jerry Maddox has nothing to do with this."

"He sure as heck does," I said. "You know it, too, and if you pretend you don't, you've got your head up your butt just like all the rest of them."

"Jean Holladay, you have one ugly mouth on you. You're suspended."

"What?"

"You can spend the next three days at home, thinking about your behavior."

"What about her?" I pointed over at Lisa Saunders, who hadn't said a word and instead had been sitting there with her ankles crossed, daubing at her runny mascara with the Kleenex and doing her best to look innocent. "She was fighting, too. And she wrote that thing about Liz that I've been trying to explain to you."

"I'm not interested in whatever the two of you were squabbling about," Miss Clay said. "School officials never get to the bottom of these quarrels, and in my mind, we shouldn't try. You're not being suspended for fighting. You're being suspended for using unseemly language with the vice principal."

CHAPTER THIRTY-EIGHT

Uncle Tinsley was pretty upset when I told him I'd been suspended. "This is mortifying," he said. "Another first for the Holladay family." Once I explained that I'd been standing up for Liz, he said, "Well, I guess you did what you felt you had to do, but it won't exactly boost our standing in the community."

The funny thing was, it sort of did. When I got back to school at the end of November, the other kids treated me differently. Now I wasn't Day-Glo Girl, I was the Girl Who Beat Up Lisa Saunders. I guessed that it was, if nothing else, a step up. The teasing mostly stopped, and a few kids actually went out of their way to be friendly. It was as if they thought going to the cops and filing charges against Maddox was being a tattletale—like running to the teacher when someone picked on you—but throwing punches, now, that got their respect.

Kids continued to give Liz a hard time, but then the judge set a date in March for the trial, and it became clear to everyone in town that the case wasn't going to go away. That was when we realized we had a lot more to worry about than bony-nosed Lisa Saunders and her girlfriends.

Piles of garbage started appearing on the lawn and driveway at

Mayfield. We'd get up in the morning, and it would be strewn all over the place—used Pampers, empty bottles of RC and cans of SpaghettiOs, plastic bags, shredded paper, and those cylindrical Pringles containers. All that stuff practically had Maddox's name on it.

One day, on our way to the bus stop, Maddox's black Le Mans appeared out of nowhere. Maddox was behind the wheel, hunched forward like a racecar driver. He gunned the car toward Liz and me, swerving so close that we had to jump into the ditch to keep from getting hit. We felt the whoosh of air as the car passed. I picked up a rock and hurled it after him, but the Le Mans sped off and the rock missed.

After that, it seemed like Maddox cruised around looking for us almost every day, trying to run us off the road when he saw us walking home or riding our bikes into town. It got to the point where, whenever I went outside, I listened for the roar of the Le Mans. I started carrying around a pocketful of rocks, and I did give the car at least one good dent, but most of the time Maddox got away too quickly for me to score a hit.

We didn't tell Uncle Tinsley. We never seriously considered going to the police, either, since we wouldn't be able to prove anything, and so far, filing complaints against Maddox had only caused trouble. But Maddox's campaign was having an effect on Liz. She was terrified and didn't want to leave the house. She also started talking more and more about the voices and how they were warning her that Maddox was hiding behind every bush and tree.

I kept telling Liz—and myself—that the voices were temporary and would go away once Maddox got convicted and sent to prison. It was now December, with the trial three months away, and I was worried sick that Liz might fall apart by then. That made me wonder if we should drop the case. But if we pulled out now, Maddox would know he had terrorized us into giving up. We'd have to leave town, since I couldn't imagine riding my bike around Byler knowing I might run into the man and he'd give me that smile bullies give the people they push around. And leaving town wouldn't solve anything. Maddox would haunt Liz, and that might make the voices get worse.

I decided there was only one thing to do. I couldn't wait for the trial. I had to kill Jerry Maddox.

CHAPTER THIRTY-NINE

I didn't have a car to mow Maddox down, so I had to strategize. There was a ridge behind the Maddox house with a lot of boulders and big rocks. I'd noticed one in particular when I was working for the Maddoxes, and I'd thought at the time that if it ever rolled down, it might do some serious damage. It might even kill someone. So I decided to roll it down myself.

I would hide on the ridge until Maddox came out to the back porch, which he did every day to check the thermometer and put the stuff from his paper shredder into the trash cans, and then I'd send that rock barreling down the hill and crush him like a bug.

After school the next day, I rode the red Schwinn into Byler, left it at the library bike stand, and cut through the yard of one of Maddox's neighbors to the ridge behind his house. I scrambled up through the scrub pines to the rock, which was about as big as an armchair and had one side covered with lichen. I pushed on the rock to see how loose it was, and that was when I discovered I couldn't budge the thing. It must have weighed a ton.

I needed a partner.

• • •

Liz wasn't cut out for this type of assignment, and asking Uncle Tinsley was out of the question. The only person I could turn to was Joe Wyatt. I'd already told him all about Maddox's harassment campaign, of course, and so at school the next day, I explained my plan and asked if he'd be willing to help out.

"When do we do it, cuz?" he asked.

I told him how big and heavy the rock was. Joe didn't make such good grades in school, but he was really smart when it came to doing things, and he told me what we needed to do was lever the rock into motion. His dad, he said, had a tamping bar that would do the job.

The next day, Joe met me at the library, carrying the heavy iron bar. We circled up into the woods behind Maddox's house, and I showed Joe the rock. He worked the tamping bar under it, but it wouldn't budge, so he got a smaller rock that he used as a fulcrum, and with both of us pulling down on the long end of the bar, we worked the big rock forward.

"This'll do it," Joe said.

"Maddox is a goner," I said.

We sat down on the pine needles and waited.

After about an hour, we heard the whistle of the train and the wheels rumbling and screeching across the tracks that ran through the middle of Byler. After the noise died away, the back door opened. We jumped up and grabbed the handle of the tamping bar. But instead of Maddox coming out the door, it was Doris. She had just given birth and was carrying her pink-faced newborn in one arm and a bag of trash in the other.

I felt my whole body sag. All the energy that I had worked up to kill Maddox just drained out of me. As much as I hated Doris for siding with her husband, I wasn't about to kill her—and certainly not the new baby. That was when I realized I really didn't want to kill anyone, not even Maddox. Bad as he was, that just wasn't in me.

"Maybe this isn't such a good idea after all," I said.

"I was thinking the same thing," Joe said.

As we watched, Doris took the lid off the can, dropped the bag in, and replaced the lid without putting down the baby. Then she went back into the house, never once looking our way. Joe pulled the tamping bar out from underneath the rock. "That was a right nice fulcrum, though," he said. "Could have done it if we'd wanted to."

We headed across the hill, away from the house.

"Does this mean we're wimps?" I asked.

"Nah," Joe said. He kicked at a pinecone in his path. "You know, we could get Maddox where it really hurts."

"What do you mean?"

"The Le Mans."

CHAPTER FORTY

Joe and I talked about smashing the windshield, but we worried that the noise might bring Maddox running out of the house. Then he suggested keying the car, but we also nixed that idea because it would only do cosmetic damage, and Maddox could still cruise around, trying to mow us down. In the end, we decided that the best course of action would be to immobilize the Le Mans by slashing the tires. Maddox could buy new ones of course, but we'd have made a real statement—and we could always slash the new tires, too.

We waited until the weekend, when Maddox would probably be home. We needed the cover of darkness, so Joe told me to meet him at the library at dusk. He always carried his jackknife on him, he said, so I didn't need to worry about anything in the weapons department. He said he'd go over the day before and case Maddox's street and work out a plan of attack. We needed to wear dark clothes, he added. "Camouflage," he explained. Joe was putting a lot of thought into what he called "the operation."

When I rode up at the appointed time on Saturday, Joe was waiting at the library bike stand. He got on the Schwinn, and with me sitting on the rack behind, we pedaled over to Maddox's neighborhood as the sun was going down. It was a colorless December sunset, the sky all silvers and whites and grays.

When we got to Maddox's street, we could see the Le Mans parked in the breezeway down the block. Joe had me hide with the Schwinn behind a holly bush at the street corner. My job was to be the lookout and if anyone approached, either in a car or on foot, I was supposed to hoot like an owl. By then the sun had gone down, the streetlights had come on, and they cast pools of purplish light. While I waited at the holly bush, Joe casually walked down the street and looked around. When he saw that the coast was clear, he ducked behind a big rhododendron a few houses up from the Maddoxes'.

As I watched from over the holly, Joe scurried from bush to bush, stopping at each one to suss out the situation. When he reached the bush closest to Maddox's house, he dropped down on his stomach and shimmied over to the Le Mans.

Joe was out of my sight when a porch light flicked on at the house across the street from Maddox's. The front door opened and an older lady let out a little dog. I started hooting like crazy. At the sound of it, the little dog began to bark. Suddenly, Joe came running as fast as he could toward me. I had the bike ready to roll, kickstand up, when he reached me.

"Got two tires," he said breathlessly as he jumped on. I clambered aboard and pushed off with both feet while Joe stood up on the pedals, working them as fast as he could.

We circled around town instead of going through it, and fifteen minutes later, we got to the bottom of the mill hill. Joe was about to get off and walk the rest of the way home, and I was going to head back to Mayfield, when the squad car pulled up alongside us. The cop pointed to the side of the road. Joe stopped the bike, and the cop parked behind us and got out, leaving the engine running and the headlights on. As he walked toward us, he put on his broad-brimmed hat and adjusted the chin strap.

"What seems to be the hurry here?" he asked.

"Got to get home for dinner," Joe said.

"We had a report of some slashed tires over on Willow Lane," the cop said. "Know anything about it?"

"No, sir," Joe said.

"You're saying you didn't do it?"

"Yes, sir."

"You're denying it."

"Yes, sir."

"We're just bike riding," I said.

"I'm not talking to you," the cop said. He turned back to Joe. "Son, empty your pockets onto the hood of the car."

Joe sighed. He climbed off the bike and started taking stuff out of his pockets: keys, change, string, a few screws, a chestnut, and the jackknife.

The cop picked up the knife and opened it. "This is a concealed weapon," he said.

"It's my whittling knife," Joe said.

"It's a concealed lethal weapon," the cop said. "Follow me." He opened the back door of the squad car. "Get in."

People driving by slowed down and craned their necks to stare as Joe climbed into the backseat. I stood there straddling the Schwinn as the cop car pulled away. I wanted to wave to Joe, but he didn't look back.

CHAPTER FORTY-ONE

I pedaled through the darkness toward Mayfield. While Joe and I were planning and then carrying out the operation, slashing Maddox's tires seemed not only justifiable but something I obviously had to do to defend myself and Liz and to strike back against someone trying to kill us. But it occurred to me that if I tried to explain the tire-slashing operation to anyone, it was going to sound incredibly stupid, the kind of boneheaded crime that landed kids in juvie. Looking back, I almost couldn't believe it myself. On top of it all, I had gotten Joe into trouble. I kept thinking of him staring straight ahead as the squad car drove off.

I couldn't tell Uncle Tinsley or Liz about any of it, so I went to bed saying nothing. First thing next morning, I rode the Schwinn over to the Wyatts' house to find out what had happened to Joe. I never knocked anymore—Aunt Al insisted I come on in, seeing as I was family—and when I stepped inside, Joe was sitting at the kitchen table with Earl while Aunt Al fried eggs in bacon fat. I wanted to hug Joe, but he was acting all nonchalant and offhand. The cops, he said, had confiscated his knife and given him a lecture about staying on the right side of the law, but they didn't have any evidence that he'd done anything wrong, so they let him go.

"I swear, you'd think those deputies would have better ways to spend their time than bringing in mill hill boys for carrying around whittling knives," Aunt Al said. "Bean, you want an egg?"

"Sure do," I said. I sat down next to Joe. I felt giddy that we'd gotten away with the operation, though we couldn't say anything in front of Aunt Al. Joe poured me a cup of milk-with-coffee, and we just sat there grinning like a couple of crocodiles. Then Aunt Al passed me a crispy, glistening fat-fried egg.

We had finished breakfast and I was washing the plates at the sink, Aunt Al talking about how we might be in for our first snow of the season, when there was a hard knock on the door.

Joe went to answer it. Maddox was standing on the front step. It was a cold winter morning, but he wore no coat, just a hooded black sweatshirt with the hood pushed back. His hands were on his hips, and he shoved his finger in Joe's face. "I know it was you," he said.

"You know what was me?"

"Don't act all innocent with me, you little son of a bitch."

"Please, none of that language in my house," Aunt Al said. "What's this all about?"

Maddox pushed past Joe, entered the house, and looked over at me. "Why am I not surprised to see you here?" he asked.

"She's family," Aunt Al said. "She has every right to be here. Now, please, what's this all about?"

"I'll tell you what this is about. It's about criminal mischief and the wanton destruction of personal property. Your boy slashed my tires."

"Did not," Joe said.

"I know it was you," Maddox said. "At first I couldn't figure out who did it, but this morning a buddy on the force mentioned that the Wyatt boy had been picked up for carrying a knife, and that he'd been in the company of one of the Holladay sisters at the time, and that's when the light went on. It was you."

"He says he didn't do it," Aunt Al said. "If you had any proof, you'd charge him."

"Just because I don't have proof doesn't mean he didn't do it," Maddox said, "and doesn't mean he won't get what's coming to him."

Maddox's voice brought Uncle Clarence into the kitchen. "What's going on here?"

"Your boy needs a beating," Maddox said. "Firstly, for slashing my tires. Secondly, for lying about it."

"Is that true, son?" Uncle Clarence asked.

"He says he didn't do it," Aunt Al said.

"He didn't do it," I said. "He was with me last night. We were just riding around."

"You were probably in on it," Maddox said. He pointed at Aunt Al. "You work for the mill," he said. He turned to Uncle Clarence. "And you take the mill's disability checks. People who work for the mill and take the mill's money do what I say. And I say that boy needs a beating."

Maddox and Uncle Clarence looked at each other for a long moment. Then Uncle Clarence walked out of the room. He came back carrying a leather belt.

"Oh, Clarence," Aunt Al said. But she didn't try to stop him.

"Outside," Maddox said.

He led Joe and Uncle Clarence through the house and into the backyard. Joe was staring straight ahead saying nothing, like he'd done in the squad car. Aunt Al and I followed them outside. In the vegetable garden, the dead vines of Uncle Clarence's tomatoes were still tied to their stakes. Aunt Al clutched my arm when Uncle Clarence told Joe to bend over and grab his ankles, and with Maddox standing by, Uncle Clarence began whaling Joe's butt with the belt.

At the first blow, I felt the urge to rush over and grab Uncle Clarence's arm. Aunt Al seemed to sense this, because she clutched me even tighter. Uncle Clarence whaled Joe over and over again. Joe never said a word, and when Uncle Clarence finally stopped, Joe stood up. He didn't look at anyone or say anything. Instead, he walked off into the woods, along the trail that led to the chestnut tree.

Maddox clapped Uncle Clarence on the back and put an arm around him. "Just to show there's no hard feelings," he said, "let's go have a beer."

CHAPTER FORTY-TWO

Uncle Clarence didn't much feel like having a beer with Maddox, so Maddox left. Uncle Clarence had a racking fit of coughing, then when it was over, he put on his army cap and headed off to the veterans' hall. I sat with Aunt Al and Earl in the kitchen. I had the sense that Aunt Al wanted me there.

No one said anything for a minute, and then Aunt Al spoke up. "What in tarnation did you two think you were doing?"

So she knew.

"It was all my fault," I said. I explained how, ever since Liz filed the charges, Maddox had been throwing garbage on our yard and trying to mow us down with his car, and Liz was hearing voices, so I felt we had to do something to fight back, and Joe was the only one who could help me.

"Honey, I understand the urge to get even," she said, "but you all was throwing rocks at an angry bull."

Aunt Al and I sat at the kitchen table for a while. I asked her about Liz's voices, and Aunt Al said that she sometimes heard God talking to her and at other times the devil. When her family lived in the mountains, all sorts of folk went around speaking in tongues, so maybe it was nothing more than that.

Then Ruth came home from teaching Sunday school. "Why all the long faces?" she asked.

"Your pa had to give Joe a hiding," Aunt Al said.

"Maddox made him do it," I added.

"Dad beat Joe because Mr. Maddox told him to?"

"Right out back," I said.

"Mr. Maddox was here?" Ruth asked. "In our house?" She sat down at the table.

"Just a little while ago," I said. I started explaining what had happened and when I finished, Ruth looked down and ran her fingers through her hair, like her head hurt.

"You know, I never told anyone why I stopped working for Maddox," she said.

Aunt Al gave Ruth a startled look.

"He put the moves on me," Ruth said. "He didn't do what he did to Liz, but he cornered me and started pawing like crazy. I got away, but I sure was scared."

"Honey," Aunt Al said, "I asked you if anything had happened, and you told me no."

Ruth had taken off her cat's-eye glasses and was fidgeting with them. "I never wanted anyone to know."

CHAPTER FORTY-THREE

By then, it was clear that Mom had pulled another one of her disappearing acts. Ever since we'd filed the charges, I'd been calling her in New York, but the phone just rang and rang. I'd call early in the morning, in the middle of the afternoon, and late at night, but there was never an answer.

Finally, after four weeks passed, Mom called. She'd been at a spiritual retreat in the Catskills, she explained. The trip had been spur-of-the-moment with some new friends. She'd tried to call before she left, but she couldn't get through, probably because Tin had unplugged the phone. She'd stayed at the retreat longer than anticipated, and since the Buddhists had no telephone, she hadn't been able to call.

"It was all so good for my head," she said. "I feel very balanced." She started going on about how the Buddhists had taught her about her chi and how to center it, but I cut her off.

"Mom, there's been trouble," I said. "This man attacked Liz. There's going to be a trial."

Mom let out a shriek. She demanded to know the details, and as I filled her in, she kept yelling things like "What?" "How dare he?" "My girls! My babies!" and "I'll kill him!" She was leaving immediately, she said, and would drive all night to get to Mayfield in the morning, adding, "This has shot my chi all to hell."

Mom didn't reach Byler by the time we left for school in the morning, but she had arrived when we returned, which was good because Uncle Tinsley had been able to explain the legal details and Liz didn't have to go through it all again. Mom hugged her. Liz didn't want to let go, so Mom kept hugging her, stroking her hair, and saying, "Everything's going to be all right, baby. Momma's here."

Then Mom turned to hug me. I was surprised by how angry I felt at her. "Where have you been all this time?" I wanted to say. But I said nothing and hugged her back. Mom started rubbing her face against my shoulder. I felt a little wetness, and I realized she was crying and trying to hide it. I wondered if Mom was really going to help us get through all this or if she was just going to be one more person who needed reassurance.

When Liz told Mom how the other kids at school were treating her, Mom said Liz didn't have to go anymore, at least until the trial was over. Mom would homeschool her.

She offered to homeschool me, too, but I took a pass. Most of the kids had stopped giving me a hard time, and besides, the last thing I wanted to do was sit around Mayfield all day, brooding about Maddox, listening to Mom explain the world as she saw it, and reading a bunch of depressing poetry by Edgar Allan Poe, who had replaced Lewis Carroll as Liz's favorite writer. I needed to be out and about.

Since Liz and I had gone back to sharing a bedroom, Mom moved into the other room in the bird wing, the one that had been her playroom when she was growing up. When she told the Byler

High authorities that she would take over Liz's education for the time being, they were happy to oblige, since the upcoming trial had caused nothing but tension at school. Mom avoided getting into arguments with Uncle Tinsley and spent the days with Liz, the two of them writing in journals and talking about survival, transcendence, and life energy, all the subjects Mom had been exploring during her spiritual retreat. Liz clung to Mom and to her words, and Mom clearly enjoyed being clung to. They composed poetry together and finished each other's sentences. Mom had brought her two favorite guitars with her—the Zemaitis and the honey-colored Martin—and she gave the Martin to Liz, promising her she would never criticize her playing no matter what rules Liz broke.

I had been ticked off at Mom when she first showed up, but she seemed to be rising to the occasion. Liz told her about the voices she kept hearing. She was hearing them more often and they were getting scarier. "If the voices are real, I'm in trouble," Liz said. "If they're not real, I'm in bigger trouble." I was afraid Mom would drag her off to a psychiatrist, who would send her to a nut house, but instead Mom said Liz shouldn't fear the voices. That was how the mind and the soul talked to each other, she said. When you argued with yourself, those were voices. When your conscience told you something was a bad idea, that was a voice. When the muse whispered lyrics in your ear, it was a voice. Everyone heard voices, Mom said. Some of us just heard those voices more clearly than others. Liz should listen to the voices, channel them, and turn them into art, poetry, and music. "Don't be afraid of your dark places," Mom told her. "If you can shine a light on them, you'll find treasure there."

CHAPTER FORTY-FOUR

Mom had never made a big deal out of Christmas, telling us every year that it was a pagan holiday the Christians had co-opted, that Christ was actually born in the spring. Uncle Tinsley said he had ignored it ever since Martha died, but when school let out for Christmas break, he told us that because this was the first family gathering at Mayfield in years, we should do something to acknowledge the holiday. Uncle Tinsley and I found a small, perfectly shaped cedar in the hedgerow along the upper pasture. We chopped it down, dragged it back to the house, and decorated it with the Holladay family collection of fragile antique ornaments, some of them, Uncle Tinsley said, dating back to the 1880s.

We avoided talking about the trial, Mom and Uncle Tinsley made a point of getting along, and on Christmas Day, instead of giving each other presents, Mom decided we should all put on performances. She sang several numbers from "Finding the Magic"—and, in fact, she didn't want to stop, saying, "Okay, if you insist, I'll do one more." Liz recited Poe's poem "The Bells," which, despite its title, wasn't very Christmasy and, in fact, was really dark. I read my Negrophobia Essay, this time remembering to use Uncle Tinsley's pregnant pauses. That prompted Mom to joke that Uncle Tinsley should dig out the old Confederate sword that the Holladays had been handing down for generations and give it to me because I was really getting in touch with my Southern roots.

"All the Confederate stuff around this town gives me the heebie-jeebies," Liz said. "One of the houses on the hill actually flies that flag."

"It's not about slavery," Uncle Tinsley said. "It's about tradition and pride."

"Not if you're a black person," Mom said.

"Hey, Uncle Tinsley," I said, "maybe, for your performance, you can play the piano."

He shook his head. "Martha and I used to play together," he said. "But I don't play anymore." He stood up. "My performance will be in the kitchen." For dinner, he was going to make squash casserole, from the old Holladay family recipe, and roast loin of venison with mushrooms, onions, turnips, and apples.

It was dark by the time dinner was ready. While Liz and I set the table, Mom found a bottle of wine in the basement. She poured glasses for herself and Uncle Tinsley, half a glass for Liz, and a quarter for me. Back in California, Mom liked to drink a little wine in the evening. She'd let me have sips before, but this was the first time she'd given me my own glass.

Uncle Tinsley said his short prayer, thanking God for the bountiful feast before us, then raised his glass. "To the Holladays."

Mom gave her little smile, and I thought she was going to say something sarcastic, but then her face softened. "It's funny," she said. "The Holladays used to be such a big deal." She raised her glass. "To the four of us," she said. "We're all that's left."

Liz stayed home all winter with Mom, who took her job as a teacher pretty seriously. Mom and Liz read Hermann Hesse and e. e. cummings and some guy called Gurdjieff she'd heard about on her spiritual retreat. Mom made up an entire course about Edgar Allan Poe. Liz was particularly drawn to poems like "Annabel Lee," "The Raven," and "The Bells," with lines such as "And the silken sad uncertain rustling of each purple curtain" and "To the tintinnabulation that so musically wells / From the bells, bells, bells, bells." She got such a charge out of the word "tintinnabulation" that she wrote an entire paper on its Latin roots and its place in music.

Uncle Tinsley was working on his geology papers and genealogical charts, as well as making the occasional hunting trip, coming home a couple of times with a dead doe strapped to the hood of the Woody. He also pitched in on Liz's schooling, giving her lectures about calculus, the geology of the Culpeper Basin, and the composition of Virginia's orange clay, explaining C. Vann Woodward and why in point of fact the Civil War should not be called the Civil War—"There was nothing civil about it, for one thing"—and should instead be called the War Between the States.

Maddox kept trying to mow me down with the Le Mans and its new whitewall tires, but since Liz was never with me, I stopped worrying about him as much and started to enjoy school a little more. Miss Jarvis, who was the yearbook adviser as well as my English teacher, talked me into joining the yearbook staff, which was more fun than I expected it to be—more fun than the pep squad. It was also a lot of work. We had to take photos, write captions and sell advertising, come up with the memorial page for the senior who got killed in a car crash—Miss Jarvis said it happened pretty much every year—and create themes for the candid shots, like "Caught Off Guard" and "Silly Dance Moves."

Meanwhile, the kids were getting used to the idea of integration. The football team had a terrible year, and there were still occasional fights between black and white students, but the basketball team was doing better thanks to a couple of really tall black players. One guy was so big that he was called Tyrone "The Tower" Perry, or sometimes just Tower, and he was such a good player that we gave him an entire page in the yearbook. The cheerleaders were also looking more like a team, the black girls doing a little less dancing and the white girls doing a little more. Vanessa's mother, who owned a beauty parlor for black women and sold Avon cosmetics, had a powder-blue Cadillac, and she started driving a group of black and white cheerleaders, including Ruth, to the away games.

With Liz and Mom wrapped up in their homeschooling, I ended up spending a lot of time at the Wyatts' house. That beating had really changed Joe. He pulled into himself and talked even less than before. But then Dog came along.

Joe had always wanted a dog. Uncle Clarence thought a dog that didn't hunt or herd sheep and just sat around scarfing down dog food was a waste of money. After the beating, however, Aunt Al talked him into letting her get one for Joe, saying the dog could live off table scraps. We all went to the pound, where Joe picked out a black-and-white dog that was a mix of a bunch of breeds, Aunt Al said, some border collie, probably some hound, maybe a little terrier. Joe called him a purebred mutt and named him Dog.

"You're lucky," I told Joe. "I wish I had a dog."

"We can share him," Joe said.

Dog was a smart, saucy little guy who followed Joe everywhere. He went with Joe to the bus stop every morning, and when Joe got off the bus in the afternoon, Dog was sitting there waiting for him, regardless of the weather. That mutt really lifted Joe's spirits.

It actually snowed a couple of times that winter, and Joe and I got into some fierce snowball fights with the other mill hill kids, the whole gang of us interrupting the fight to pelt passing cars and everyone, including Dog, running for the woods when the drivers got out to try and chase us down, shouting, "Come back here, you lintheads!"

When all was said and done, except for the Maddox mess, I was having a great time in Byler.

CHAPTER FORTY-FIVE

I had a pretty good feeling about the trial. We met a couple of times with Dickey Bryson, the prosecuting attorney. He was a bulky man and although his ties always seemed too tight, he smiled a lot and loved to tell jokes. He'd been a star linebacker on the Byler Bulldogs, his picture hung on the wall of the Bulldog Diner, and some people still called him by his high school nickname, Blitz.

The case was pretty simple, Dickey Bryson told us, and the trial would be, too. He'd start with the deputy who took Liz's statement and the photos, then he'd put me and Uncle Tinsley on the stand to testify about Liz's beat-up condition when she came home, then he'd put Wayne on to testify as to what he'd witnessed when he drove Liz and Maddox around, and finally, he'd put Liz on to give her version of events.

It seemed to me like a slam-dunk case. Maddox did what he did. He knew it, we knew it, and once the jurors heard the truth, they'd know it, too. After all, we had an eyewitness, and he wasn't biased, he wasn't a relative or a friend. He was completely impartial. How could we not win?

I kept repeating this to Liz, but as the trial date got nearer, she became a nervous wreck and sometimes would gag like she was going to throw up.

The morning of the trial, the sky was clear, but it was so wickedly cold that the rhododendron leaves were curled up like skinny cigars. Liz, Mom, and I were getting dressed in the bird wing when Liz put her hand to her mouth and rushed into the bathroom. Her stomach was empty, but I could hear her retching and heaving over the toilet. When Liz came out, wiping her mouth with the back of her hand, Mom handed her a box of mints. "Nerves aren't necessarily a bad thing," she said. "Most performers have anxiety at showtime. Katharine Hepburn used to throw up every night before going onstage."

I put on the lime-green pants I hadn't worn since the first day of school, and Liz got out her orange-and-purple skirt. We wanted to look respectable, and these were the only dressy clothes we had—I mostly wore jeans, and Liz had gypsy-like outfits she'd put together from Mom's old stuff in the attic. We'd burned all the clothes Maddox had bought us. I was afraid Mom was going to wear one of her hippie dresses or, even worse, one that showed off her cleavage. Instead, she pulled out a pair of black pants and her red velvet jacket, like she was the one going onstage.

"Mom, you sure that's the right thing to wear?" I asked.

"You two can dress for the judge if you want," she said. "I'm dressing for the jury."

Uncle Tinsley was waiting for us at the foot of the stairs. He had on a pin-striped suit with a vest and a little gold chain hanging from the watch pocket. No one felt like eating breakfast, so we piled into the Woody. During the trip into town, we all kept trying to buck Liz up.

"Don't let Maddox scare you," I said. "He's just a bully."

"You've got the facts and the law on your side," Uncle Tinsley said. "You'll do fine."

"Keep eye contact," Mom said, "take deep breaths, and channel your chi."

"Just what I need—platitudes from the pep squad," Liz said. "You're all so excruciating."

That ended the bucking up. We rode along in silence for a couple of minutes, then Liz said, "I'm sorry. I know you're all trying to help. I just want this to be over."

The courthouse, on Holladay Avenue, was a big stone building with turrets and tall windows and a statue of a Confederate soldier in front. We pushed through the revolving brass door and found just about everyone involved in the whole mess milling about in the lobby. Maddox was there, wearing a shiny dark blue suit, and so were Doris and the Maddox kids. Doris was carrying the new baby, with Jerry Jr. hanging on her skirt. Cindy held Randy, who by then was two. When Maddox saw us, he glared. I glared right back. If it was a staring contest he wanted, I'd give him one.

Dickey Bryson was talking to another man in a suit and said something that made the other man laugh. The man turned around and started talking to Maddox while Dickey Bryson came over to us carrying an accordion file under one arm. He told us that the man talking to Maddox was his attorney, Leland Hayes. He'd be cross-examining us.

"Are you supposed to be joking around with Maddox's lawyer like that?" I asked.

"Byler's a small place," he said. "It pays to be friendly to everyone."

Just before nine o'clock, Joe and Aunt Al pushed through the revolving glass doors, followed by Wayne Clemmons, who took a final drag from a cigarette and stubbed it out in the lobby ash-tray. Before I could catch his eye, the bailiff opened the doors to the courtroom and ushered us in.

The courtroom had a high ceiling with a row of heavy brass chandeliers, and the tall windows let in the pale March light. It all had a solemn feel, and the benches and wooden jury chairs looked hard, as if they were designed to make sure no one got too comfortable.

"All rise," the bailiff called, and the noise we made standing in unison reminded me of church. The judge came in, an unsmiling man whose black reading glasses, perched on the end of his nose, matched his black robe. He took a seat at his big elevated desk and looked through the papers on it without once glancing up at all the people in the courtroom.

"Judge Bradley," Uncle Tinsley whispered. "He was at Washington and Lee when I was there."

So far, so good, I thought. The whole trial—with the uniformed deputies, the judge in his robe, the stenographer seated at her strange little typewriter—seemed like it was going to be a very serious and official proceeding, and I took that as a positive sign.

"Mr. Maddox," the judge said, "stand and be arraigned."

Maddox stood up and straightened his shoulders. A woman at a small desk in front of the judge also stood and read the charges against him: attempted rape, aggravated sexual assault, and assault and battery.

"What is your plea, guilty or not guilty?" the judge asked after each charge.

"Not guilty!" Maddox said each time, his loud voice echoing off the high ceiling.

"You may be seated."

Maddox sat back down. He and his lawyer were at a table on the far side of the gallery railing. At the table next to them, Dickey

Bryson was busily scribbling on a yellow legal pad. I hoped Maddox could feel my eyes boring into the back of his head. I hadn't given up on the staring contest.

A uniformed deputy ushered in a group of men and women who sat down on one side of the courtroom. "Jury pool," Uncle Tinsley whispered. I'd seen a number of them around town, on the hill, at the football games, or in the grocery store. One of them was Tammy Elbert, the woman who'd driven us to Mayfield when we first arrived in Byler, the one who said she'd have given anything in high school to be Charlotte Holladay. That seemed like another good sign.

The judge talked for a few minutes about the beauty of our legal system and the duties of jurors and the responsibilities of citizens. Then he asked the witnesses to come up to the front. After we came forward, he asked the people in the jury pool if any of them knew any of us or any of the attorneys.

One man in a plaid jacket stood up. "I know just about everybody here," he said. "Reckon we all do."

"I reckon you do," the judge said. "Would that prevent any of you from delivering an impartial verdict?"

They looked at one another and shook their heads.

"No one, then? Is there any other reason any of you cannot be impartial or should not serve?"

They shook their heads again.

"Let the record show that no juror believes he cannot be impartial."

The two lawyers stood up and started reading off names from their legal pads. The people who were called climbed into the jury box. Tammy Elbert was one of them. Within about ten minutes, the jury box was filled, and the rest of the pool left the courtroom. At that point, the judge asked the witnesses to step outside, so we all followed the deputy through the doors, leaving Mom sitting on the bench in her red velvet jacket next to Joe and Aunt Al.

Wayne lit a cigarette and headed down the hall toward the ash-tray while the deputy led the rest of us into a small room. A percolator of burnt-smelling coffee sat next to a plate of glazed donuts, but they didn't whet anyone's appetite. In less than half an hour the deputy came back, beckoning Uncle Tinsley to follow him. About twenty minutes later, the deputy came back again and this time he beckoned me. As I closed the door, I gave Liz a thumbs-up.

CHAPTER FORTY-SIX

The clerk swore me in, and I sat down in the witness chair. Maddox was leaning back with his arms crossed, as if challenging me to pull this off. In the gallery behind him, Uncle Tinsley had taken a seat next to Mom and was giving me encouraging nods. The jurors in the jury box were studying me like I was some sort of curiosity.

Sitting in the witness chair, all those people staring at me with cocked heads, made my mouth dry and my throat tight. When Dickey Bryson got up and asked me to state my name, my voice came out in a little squeak. Yikes, I thought, and glanced at the jury. The man in the plaid jacket grinned like he thought it was funny.

"Take your time," Dickey Bryson said.

In answer to his questions, I explained how Liz and I had started working for the Maddoxes, how I mostly did stuff for Mrs. Maddox, how Liz was more like Mr. Maddox's personal assistant, and how he had set up the passbook savings accounts. Dickey Bryson then asked what happened the night Liz came back with Wayne, and I told the jury everything I could remember. The more I talked, the more comfortable I felt, and by the time Dickey Bryson said "No further questions," I thought I had done a fairly good job.

Leland Hayes stood up and buttoned his jacket. He had short

graying hair and a long sunburned nose. When he smiled, crow's-feet formed at the corners of his slate-colored eyes, which twinkled in a way that made you think he enjoyed doing what he did.

"Good morning, young lady," he began. "How are you today?"

"Fine. Thank you."

"Good. Glad to hear it." He walked up to the witness box, carrying his legal pad. "I know it's not easy, coming in here and testifying, and I admire you for doing it."

"Thank you," I said again.

"So you worked for Jerry Maddox here?" Leland Hayes pointed at him.

"Yes, sir." Dickey Bryson had told me to keep my answers short.

"It was mighty generous of him to give you a job, wasn't it?"

"I suppose. But we worked for our money. It wasn't charity."

"Did anyone else offer you a job?"

"No. But we worked hard."

"Just answer yes or no. Now, why did you go to work for Mr. Maddox?"

"We needed the money."

"Why did you girls need money? Didn't your parents provide for you?"

"Lots of kids work," I said.

"Answer the question, please. Do your parents provide for you?"

"I only have one. My mom. My dad died."

"My sympathies. That must be tough, growing up without a dad. How did he die?"

Dickey Bryson stood up. "Objection," he said. "Irrelevant."

"Sustained," the judge said.

I looked over at the jury. Tammy Elbert had a tiny smile. She knew how my dad had been killed. They all did. They also knew he wasn't married to Mom.

"Now you're living with your uncle, isn't that correct?"

"Yes, sir."

"Why is that? Is it because your momma can't take care of you?"

"Objection," Dickey Bryson said again. "Irrelevant."

"I'll proffer that it is relevant, Your Honor," Leland Hayes said. "It goes to the question of motive and character. Which is the heart of our defense."

"I'll allow it," the judge said.

"So why aren't you living with your momma?"

I looked over at Mom. She was sitting very erect with her lips pressed together. "It's sort of complicated," I said.

"You strike me as a very smart young lady. I'm sure you can explain to the jury something that's sort of complicated."

"Mom had some stuff she needed to do, so we decided to visit Uncle Tinsley."

"Stuff? What stuff?"

"Personal stuff."

"Can you be more specific?"

I glanced at Mom again. She looked like she was about to explode. I turned to the judge. "Do I have to answer that?" I asked.

"I'm afraid so," the judge said.

"But it's personal."

"Personal matters often come out in a court of law."

"Well"—I took a deep breath—"Mom had sort of a meltdown, and she needed some time to herself to figure things out, so we decided to come visit Uncle Tinsley."

"So you two girls came to Virginia on your own. All the way from California. Did your momma even know you were coming?"

"Not exactly."

"Brave girls. Has your momma ever done that before? Left you on your own?"

"Just for short periods. And she always made sure there were plenty of chicken potpies for us to eat."

"Well, that was real responsible of her." Leland Hayes glanced at the jury. Tammy Elbert had swiveled around to look at Mom, whose face was almost as red as her velvet jacket.

"So your mother is a performer?"

"A singer and a songwriter."

"And performance is a form of make-believe, right?"

"I guess."

"Does your mother engage in a lot of make-believe?"

"What do you mean?"

"Has she ever, say, made up a boyfriend who didn't really exist?"

"Objection!" Dickey Bryson shouted. "Irrelevant."

Mom was looking over at the jury and violently shaking her head.

"I'll withdraw the question." Leland Hayes cleared his throat. "When your mother had her meltdown, she left you to survive on your own. That's tough. It meant you had to do whatever it took to get by. Even tell lies if you felt you had to."

"Objection. Argumentative."

"Sustained."

"I'll rephrase. Have you ever needed to lie to get by?"

"Nope," I said emphatically.

"Did you or did you not lie to your Uncle Tinsley about working for Mr. Maddox?"

"That wasn't exactly a lie," I said. "We just decided not to mention it."

"So you didn't lie to your uncle, who had let you into his house and was feeding you and taking care of you. You just misled him?"

"I guess."

"You like your Uncle Tinsley, don't you?"

"He's great."

"He's looking after you because your mother wasn't. So you want to make him happy, and you want to try to please him. When you're not misleading him. Isn't that correct?"

"I guess," I said again. I could see another setup coming, but there was nothing I could do about it.

"Has your uncle ever told you that he dislikes Mr. Maddox?"

"He had a good reason to."

"Because Mr. Maddox recommended that the owners of Holladay Textiles terminate your uncle's relationship with the mill?"

"Other things, too. Uncle Tinsley thought he treated the workers bad—"

The judge cut me off. "Just answer yes or no."

"So would you ever lie about Mr. Maddox if you thought it would make your uncle happy?"

"Objection!" Dickey Bryson shouted.

"Sustained," the judge said.

Leland Hayes looked at his legal pad again. "Just a couple more things," he said. "Did you eat food from the Maddoxes' refrigerator without their permission?"

"If I was making the kids sandwiches, I'd sometimes make myself one, too."

"So you did eat the Maddoxes' food without their permission?"

"I didn't think I needed it."

"Did you also drink Mr. Maddox's vodka without his permission, which was one reason he had to fire you?"

"What?"

"Yes or no."

"No!" I shouted.

"Did you steal money from his dresser drawer, which was the other reason he had to fire you?"

"No!"

"Do you have a vendetta against Mr. Maddox?"

"No."

"Is Joe Wyatt your cousin?"

"Yes."

"Did you and Joe Wyatt slash the tires of Mr. Maddox's car?"

I looked down at my hands. "I didn't do it," I said.

"So Joe Wyatt did it?"

I shrugged. "How would I know?"

"Maybe because you were there. Remember, Miss Holladay, that you're under oath. Did you help Joe Wyatt plan or carry out this crime?"

"It's because Maddox was trying to kill us!" I shouted. "He was all the time trying to run us over with that Le Mans. We had to protect ourselves. It was self-defense—"

"I think we get the picture," Leland Hayes said. "A nasty little feud. No further questions."

"But I need to explain—"

"I said no further questions."

"You're not giving me a chance to explain!"

"Young lady, that will be all," the judge said.

Once Leland Hayes sat down, Dickey Bryson stood up again. He asked me to tell the jury what I'd meant by saying Maddox tried to run us down, and I told them how, when we were walking to the bus stop, he'd come barreling down the road in his Le Mans and swerve at us and we had to jump into the ditch to get out of his way.

Then Leland Hayes had another turn. "Did you ever report these alleged incidents to the police?" he asked.

"No," I said.

"So there's no record of these alleged incidents ever taking place."

"But they did."

"The jury can decide that. What you are admitting is that you and Mr. Maddox were feuding?"

"I guess you could call it that. But it all started because he—"

"No further questions."

The judge told me to step down, but I could hardly move. I had just betrayed Mom. I had ratted out Joe. And I had admitted lying to Uncle Tinsley. How did that happen? I believed I was in the right. In fact, I knew I was in the right. All I wanted to do was get up and tell the truth about what Maddox did to Liz, and I ended up looking like a lying, stealing, feuding tire-slitter. Part of me was outraged, but part of me just wanted to slink out of the courtroom and crawl down some deep, dark hole and stay there.

I finally stepped down from the witness stand. Dickey Bryson told me that since I'd finished testifying, I could sit in the gallery. As I walked by Maddox, he shook his head and looked at the jury as if to say, Now you see the kind of kid I've had to deal with.

I took a seat between Mom and Uncle Tinsley. He patted my arm, but Mom just sat there, rigid as stone.

Dickey Bryson asked the bailiff to bring in Wayne Clemmons, who'd been pacing up and down in the hallway, smoking cigarettes. He was wearing a gray windbreaker, and he hadn't bothered to shave. After he swore his oath and took a seat, he mumbled his name, keeping his head down like he was studying the laces of his work boots.

Dickey Bryson asked him to describe what he had witnessed on the night in question.

"Nothing much," Wayne said. "All's I know is Maddox and the girl was in the back of my car, arguing about money. She wanted money from him. But I didn't really witness nothing."

Dickey Bryson looked up, startled. "Are you certain?"

"I was driving the car. My eyes was on the road."

The lawyer riffled through his accordion file and held up a piece of paper. "Mr. Clemmons, did you or did you not give a statement to the police saying that you had observed Jerry Maddox physically and sexually assaulting Liz Holladay in the back of your taxi?"

"I don't recollect what I told the police," Wayne said. "I was drinking at the time, and my memory's been all shot to hell since I came back from 'Nam. I forget things that did happen and remember things that didn't happen."

"Mr. Clemmons, let me remind you that you're under oath here."

"Like I said, my eyes was on the road. How was I supposed to know what was going on in the backseat of the car?"

Before I even realized what I was doing, I was on my feet. "That's a pack of lies!" I shouted.

The judge banged his gavel down hard and said, "I'll have order in this court."

"But he can't sit there and lie—"

The judge banged his gavel again and roared, "Order!"

Then he motioned to the bailiff, whispered in his ear, and the bailiff left through the side door. A few moments later, I felt a hand clutch my shoulder hard. I swiveled around, and there was the bailiff. He beckoned me with his finger. I stood up and glared at Wayne Clemmons, who was still looking down at his boot laces. The bailiff led me out of the courtroom, and after he closed the door, he said, "Judge don't want you back inside for the duration."

Almost immediately, the door to the courtroom opened, and Wayne walked out.

"Why'd you lie?" I blurted out.

"Enough, young lady," the bailiff said.

Wayne just shook his head and lit a cigarette as he walked down the hallway and out the revolving door.

"Don't go back into the witness room," the bailiff said, "and no talking to the other witnesses."

I sat down on a bench in the hallway. After a couple of minutes, the bailiff came back out and opened the door to the witness room. "You're up, miss," he said. Liz walked out and followed him into the courtroom, not once looking my way.

It was past one o'clock by the time the doors to the courtroom opened and everyone filed out. Liz came through the doors flanked by Mom and Uncle Tinsley, like they were guarding her. She had her arms crossed and her head down. Joe and Aunt Al were behind them.

"How did it go?" I asked Liz, but she walked right past me without saying anything.

"Just hunky-dory," Mom said.

"That attorney was pretty hard on her," Uncle Tinsley said. "Then Maddox took the stand. He basically said he fired you for stealing, and the two of you made this all up to get back at him."

"Dirtbag liar!" I said. "They couldn't possibly believe that."

"I think they don't know what to believe," Uncle Tinsley said. "But we really shouldn't be talking about it until the trial's over."

We went over to the Bulldog Diner and took a table in the back, under the photographs of Bulldog players, including the one of Dickey "Blitz" Bryson. The lawyers and the judge came in and took a table in the middle, followed by some of the jurors, who sat at the counter. Just as we were getting our menus, the Maddoxes came in and took a table in the front.

"There's the dirtbag!" I said.

"Hush," Uncle Tinsley said. "Don't talk about the case. You want to cause a mistrial?"

"How can we eat in the same room as him? I'm going to spew this time."

"Everyone from the courthouse always eats here," Uncle Tinsley said.

"It's one of the joys of small-town life," Mom said.

The waitress came over and asked what we wanted.

"We should all be ordering baloney," I said loudly.

After lunch, we went back to the courthouse and sat on the uncomfortable benches in the hallway as the jury began deliberating. I figured they'd be there for the long haul, sorting through the evidence and debating legal issues, but in less than an hour, the bailiff called everyone back into the courtroom. He told me that, since the testimony was over and the jury had reached a verdict, the judge was allowing me to return to the courtroom.

The jurors filed in. When I looked at Tammy Elbert, she kept her eyes on the judge. The clerk passed the judge a piece of paper. He unfolded it, read it, and refolded it. "The verdict is not guilty on all charges," he said.

Aunt Al gasped and Mom shouted, "No!"

The judge banged his gavel. "Court dismissed."

Maddox slapped Leland Hayes on the back and went over and started shaking the jurors' hands. Liz and I sat there in silence. I felt completely confused, like the world had turned upside down, and we were living in a place where the guilty were innocent and the innocent were guilty. I didn't know what to do. How were you supposed to behave in a world like that?

Dickey Bryson stuffed his papers back into his accordion file and came over to where we were sitting. "These he-said-she-said cases are tough to prove," he said.

"But we had a witness," I said.

"Not today you didn't."

CHAPTER FORTY-SEVEN

We got into the Woody. Uncle Tinsley headed down Holladay Avenue saying nothing. I took Liz's hand, but she pulled it away and leaned against the door. Mom was so agitated that she could hardly contain herself. Her fingers trembled as she lit a cigarette. That defense attorney was a monster, she told us. All those outrageous, untrue things he had said about her. And the way he had behaved toward her girls was hideous. He had treated Liz even worse than he had me, she went on. He had taken Liz's imagination and creativity and used them against her. He accused her of constantly making things up—for example, changing the endings of the stories she read to Maddox's daughter, Cindy. He said Liz's banged-up face in the police photos could have been caused by Tinsley Holladay smacking her for coming home late. He asked Liz about the perv we'd ditched in New Orleans, then told the jury that this was evidence she called men "perverts" without any proof and that she considered outsmarting them a game and a challenge. The lawyer actually said that Liz's two favorite authors, Lewis Carroll and Edgar Allan Poe, were themselves perverts. He declared that Liz was essentially a habitual liar with an overactive imagination and an obsession with the idea of perverts—and that in itself, he told the jurors, was more than a little perverted.

Mom started going on about how much she hated Byler. The town was full of hicks, rubes, crackers, and lintheads. It was small-minded and mean-spirited, backward and prejudiced. Sitting in that courtroom was the most humiliating experience of her life. We were really the ones on trial, not Maddox, put on trial for our values and our lifestyle, for our willingness to go out in the world and do something different and creative with our lives instead of wasting away in this stifling, dying, claustrophobic mill town.

"Shut up, Charlotte," Uncle Tinsley said.

"That's the problem with this town," she said. "Everyone's supposed to just shut up and pretend nothing's wrong. Little Bean was the only one with the guts to stand up and say it was all a pack of lies."

"The jury thought what I said was all a pack of lies," Liz said in a quiet voice. "Nothing happened. You heard the verdict. Nothing happened." I was sitting next to her in the back of the Woody. She looked out the window. "Was it a pack of lies," she said, "or a lack of pies?" She pulled up her legs and wrapped her arms around her knees. "Pack of lies. Lack of pies. Plaque of eyes, arranged by size. Or black-eyed lies?" Liz was speaking in a distant monotone, almost to herself. "Plucked-out eyes. Lucked-out lies. Synthesize. Between my thighs." She paused. "To no surprise, to our demise." She was still staring out the window. "All the liars told their lies." There was another pause. "Who denies the lies? Who will scrutinize the lies? The size of lies? Who will pluck the liars' eyes? Who cries, who spies, who sighs, who dies?"

"Please stop it," I said.

"I can't."

The day seemed to have gone on forever, but it was only midafternoon by the time we got back to the house. While the morning had been clear, the sky had clouded over, and a cold, foggy drizzle had started up. Liz said she was going up to the bird wing to spend a little time by herself and maybe take a nap. Uncle Tinsley decided to build a fire in the living room and sent me out to fetch kindling from the woodshed. I couldn't find any good kindling, so I chopped some from a couple of small logs, using the little hatchet that hung on the wall.

After the trial, it felt good to be doing something simple and physical. You set up the wood on the chopping block, brought the hatchet down hard, and the wood split cleanly into two pieces. Then you stacked it and set up another piece of wood. Everything went the way it was supposed to. No tricks, no surprises.

When I had enough kindling, I laid it in the canvas tote, added some twigs from the old tack box Uncle Tinsley stored them in while they dried out, then carried it all back to the house, covering the tote with my arm so the wood wouldn't get rained on.

Uncle Tinsley was on his knees in front of the fireplace, wadding up newspaper and tearing cardboard into strips. Mom was sitting in a brocade wing chair next to the hearth. She and Uncle Tinsley seemed to have decided that they were tired of fighting. Instead, Uncle Tinsley was going on about the importance, in getting a good blaze going, of the right amount of starting material—paper, cardboard, twigs, kindling, small seasoned pieces—and not until that was burning in a lively way did you add your logs. Otherwise, all it did was smoke.

"Bean, why don't you go see if Liz wants to come down," Mom said. "She could probably use a little primal heat."

I climbed the stairs to the second floor. Uncle Tinsley always kept the radiators off except when the temperature fell below freezing, and the hall was chilly. The rain had gotten heavier, and you could hear it drumming on the metal roof. When I opened the door to our room, I saw Liz lying on the bed with her clothes still on. I was going to turn around and let her sleep, but she suddenly made this groggy, gurgling noise that scared me.

"Liz?" I said. "Liz, are you okay?"

I sat down next to her, shaking her arm and calling her name, and when she looked up, her eyes were blurry and unfocused. She said a few words in a slurred voice, but I couldn't understand them. I ran back downstairs. "Something's wrong with Liz!" I screamed.

Mom jumped out of her chair, and Uncle Tinsley dropped the log he was holding. We all ran up the stairs. Uncle Tinsley shook Liz hard, and she responded with the same sort of slurry and incomprehensible noises.

"Did you take anything?" Uncle Tinsley shouted at her.

"Pills," she mumbled.

"Pills? What pills?"

"Mom's pills."

Uncle Tinsley looked over at Mom. "What kind of pills is she talking about?"

"She must mean the sleeping pills," Mom said.

"You've got sleeping pills?"

"So?"

"Jesus, Charlotte. Go check the bottle."

Uncle Tinsley started slapping Liz's face and dragged her off the bed. Liz stumbled and fell to the floor. Uncle Tinsley said that we needed to get Liz woken up.

Mom came back and said the bottle was empty but there had been only a few pills left, maybe six or eight at the most. Uncle Tinsley half-carried Liz into the bathroom while Mom followed, explaining that as the trial got nearer, she'd given Liz a pill from time to time to help with her nerves. At the sink, Uncle Tinsley forced Liz to drink several glasses of water and then kneel over the toilet while he stuck his fingers down her throat. She vomited all over his hand, but Uncle Tinsley kept at it until all he got from her was dry heaves. Then he pulled her into the bathtub and turned the shower on cold and they stood there in their clothes, getting soaked. Liz started coughing and flailing around, hitting Uncle Tinsley and asking Mom to make him stop, please stop.

"He's getting the poison out, honey," Mom said.

"It's not supposed to be fun," Uncle Tinsley said.

"Shouldn't we call an ambulance?" I asked.

Mom and Uncle Tinsley said no at exactly the same time. Tripping over each other's words, Uncle Tinsley said, "We've got it under control," and Mom said, "She'll be all right." After a moment, Mom added, "We've had enough dealings with people in uniform for one day."

Once it seemed like the drugs were out of Liz's system, Uncle Tinsley brought her one of his big flannel shirts. Mom and I helped her into it, then wrapped her in a blanket and took her down to sit by the fire while Uncle Tinsley changed into dry clothes. Mom made Liz hot coffee, and I toweled and combed her hair.

"Did you try to kill yourself?" I asked Liz.

"I just wanted to go to sleep," Liz said. "I just wanted everything to go away."

"That's really stupid," I said. I knew it wasn't a nice thing to say, but I couldn't help myself. "That's what Maddox has been doing, trying to kill us, and you're going to do it for him?"

"Leave me alone," Liz said. "I feel like crap."

"Bean's right," Mom said. "He'd love to hear you came home and OD'd. Don't give him that satisfaction."

Liz just sipped her coffee and stared at the fire.

CHAPTER FORTY-EIGHT

Liz was still deep asleep when I woke up the next morning. I nudged her to see if she was okay, and she muttered that she was alive but wanted to be left alone. Since it was Saturday, I let her stay in bed.

I went down to the kitchen, where Uncle Tinsley was drinking coffee and reading his latest geological newsletter. I fixed myself a poached egg on toast and was sitting next to him eating it when Mom came in carrying a book.

"I've got a terrific idea for a road trip," she said, and held up the book. It was a guide to the famous trees of Virginia. Mom said Liz and I were always going on about the special trees around Byler, the big poplars by the high school and the chestnut in the woods behind the Wyatts' house. But those trees were nothing compared to some of the truly spectacular trees in this book—the bald cypress in the Nottoway River Swamp that was the biggest tree in the entire state, the three-hundred-year-old red spruces in the Jefferson National Forest, the enormous live oak in Hampton under whose branches a Union soldier read the Emancipation Proclamation to a group of slaves, the first time it was ever read in the South. There were dozens, Mom went on, each of them fascinating and potentially life-changing, and what the three of us girls could do was drive around visiting the trees, communing with their spirits. "They'll inspire us," Mom said. "It's exactly what we need right now."

"A road trip, Charlotte?" Uncle Tinsley asked. "Seems a little half-baked."

"You're always so negative, Tin," Mom said. "Whenever I come up with ideas, you always want to shoot them down."

"What about school?" I asked.

"I'll homeschool you," she said.

"We're just going to leave?" I asked.

"We can't stay here," Mom said. "That's out of the question." She looked at me strangely. "I mean, you're not saying you want to stay here, are you?"

I had been so overwhelmed by the trial and the verdict and Liz's taking those dumb sleeping pills that I hadn't even thought about what we were going to do next. "Mom, I don't know what I want to do," I said. "But we can't just leave."

"Why not?" Mom asked.

"Every time we run into a problem, we just leave," I said. "But we always run into a new problem in the new place, and then we have to leave there, too. We're always just leaving. Can't we for once just stay somewhere and solve the problem?"

"I agree," Uncle Tinsley said.

"You tried to solve a problem by bringing those charges against Maddox," Mom said, "and see where it got you."

"What should we have done? Run away?" Suddenly, I was furious. "You're pretty good at that, aren't you?"

"How dare you speak to me like that? I'm your mother."

"Then act like one for a change. We wouldn't be in this whole mess if you had been acting like a mom all along."

I had never talked to Mom like that before. As soon as I said it,

I realized I had gone too far, but it was too late. Mom sat down at the table and started sobbing. She tried to be a good mother, she said, but it was so hard. She didn't know what to do or where to go. We couldn't all fit into the crummy little one-room apartment she'd rented in New York, and she couldn't afford anything better. If we didn't want to go on the road trip, maybe we could find a house in the Catskills near her spiritual retreat, but there was no way she was staying in Byler. There was just no way.

Uncle Tinsley put his arm around Mom, and she leaned into his shoulder. "I'm not a bad person," she said.

"I know you're not," Uncle Tinsley said. "This has been difficult for all of us."

I almost apologized for what I'd said, but I stopped myself. I felt I was right and Mom needed to face facts. So I let Uncle Tinsley comfort her, poured a glass of orange juice for Liz, and went upstairs to see how she was doing.

Liz was still asleep, but I kept nudging her until she finally rolled onto her back and looked up at the ceiling.

"How do you feel?" I asked.

"How do you think I feel?"

"Pretty awful," I said. "Here, drink this."

Liz sat up and took a sip of orange juice. I told her about Mom's idea for the road trip and the possibility of moving to the Catskills near that spiritual retreat of hers. Liz didn't say anything. In any event, I went on, Mom said she had to get out of Byler, so we had to decide what we were going to do.

"You're the older one, but here's how I see it," I said. Mom's road-trip idea was just as cockamamie as all her other ideas. And the Catskills plan was downright wacky. I didn't want to go off to some spiritual retreat and live with a bunch of Buddhist monks. And what if Mom took off or had another one of her meltdowns when we got there? Were the monks going to take care of us? Also, there were only three months of school left. We should at least finish out the school year in Byler. It wasn't such a bad place. We had Uncle Tinsley and we had the Wyatts. They weren't going to take off. Finally, the business with Maddox was over. We might not like how it ended, but it had ended.

"I don't know," Liz said. "This all makes my brain hurt." She set her orange juice down on the nightstand. "I just want to sleep."

I went back downstairs. Uncle Tinsley was building another fire in the living room, and Mom was sitting in the wing chair. Her eyes were a little puffy from that crying jag. She seemed unusually calm but also sad, and I realized I was no longer angry. "Mom, I'm sorry about some of those things I said. I know it hurt."

"It wouldn't hurt if weren't all so true," Mom said.

"I can be a jerk sometimes," I said.

"Don't apologize for who you are," she said. "And don't ever be afraid to tell the truth."

"Miss Clay at school says I got myself one ugly mouth."

"She's right," Mom said. "And if you can make it work for you, that ugly mouth will get you far."

CHAPTER FORTY-NINE

Liz stayed in bed all that day and slept through the night. The next morning, she still refused to get up. After breakfast, Uncle Tinsley asked me to help him clean the gutters. We were walking back from the barn, each carrying one end of the aluminum extension ladder, when all of a sudden those two emus came wandering up the driveway. The birds didn't seem afraid at all, cocking their heads and looking around with their enormous caramel-colored eyes.

"They must have gotten loose from Scruggs's field," Uncle Tinsley said. "Scruggs never did tend his fences."

We set the ladder on the ground, the emus studied it warily, and I ran inside to get Liz, who pulled on a pair of jeans and rushed down the stairs. By then, the emus were moseying up toward the barn, making that gurgly drumming noise deep in their throats. They took those long, deliberate steps, bobbing their heads each time they raised a leg. The smaller emu had one foot that turned to the side and dragged slightly when it walked, as if the foot had once been injured. Their movements were somehow both awkward and graceful, and they kept glancing back and forth as if to reassure each other that it was safe.

Uncle Tinsley decided he'd better get in touch with Scruggs, who needed to know about any loose livestock, and he went inside to make the call. When he came back out, he said he'd spoken with Scruggs and the emus actually belonged to Scruggs's son-in-law, Tater, who was working a job over in the valley and wouldn't be back until the day after tomorrow. Tater was the only one who knew how to catch the birds, so Scruggs had asked if it wouldn't be too much of an imposition for us to keep them until Tater returned.

"I reckon that's the neighborly thing to do," Uncle Tinsley said. "But we'll need to get them into the pasture."

The emus had meandered past the barn into the orchard. They were a few feet from the gate that led into the main pasture, which was surrounded by old three-board fencing. Walking slowly behind the emus, our arms stretched out, we were able to herd them the short distance to the open gate. Once they had gone through, Liz quickly shut the gate and latched it.

Later that morning, we brought Mom up to the field to show her the emus, but when she got a good look at them up close, the size of their talons unnerved her, and she said she wanted nothing to do with them. Liz, however, found them captivating. While Uncle Tinsley and I got back to the business of cleaning the gutters, which were so clogged that little green sprouts were growing out of them, Liz spent the whole afternoon leaning on the fence, watching the emus. She couldn't believe anything so strange-looking as those two emus would just show up. They seemed not of this world, she said, like creatures from a prehistoric era, or aliens from another planet, or maybe even angels. She decided that the bigger one was a male and the smaller was a female, and she named them Eugene and Eunice.

Not only did Liz love the emus, she also fell in love with the word "emu." She pronounced it "emyou" and also "emooo," drawing out the sound like a mooing cow. She pointed out that "emu" was "you-me" backward, and she came up with a whole list of neat words that rhymed with "emus," everything from "refuse" to "snooze" to "blues" to "choose" and "chews."

That night, she looked up emus in Uncle Tinsley's *Encyclopaedia Britannica* and kept bombarding us with information about them, how they came from Australia, how they could run forty-five miles an hour, how the males sat on the nest, how they had these unique double feathers with two plumes growing from each quill.

"They're so weird and so beautiful," she said.

"Like you," I said.

I meant it as a joke, but Liz nodded. She felt that she was sort of like an emu herself, she said. Maybe that was why she'd had flying dreams ever since she was a little girl—at heart, she was an emu. She was sure the emus also dreamed of flying. It was another thing they had in common. Both she and the emus wanted to fly—they just didn't have the wings they needed.

CHAPTER FIFTY

On Monday morning, I went back to school. The trial had been over for two days, but we still hadn't figured out what we were going to do next. Mom was set on clearing out of Byler. She kept talking about that harebrained road trip and also about going to the Catskills, or maybe Chincoteague Island to see the wild ponies. Liz, meanwhile, kept refusing to go to school. When she wasn't watching the emus, she was in our room, obsessively writing emu poetry. One poem went:

> *Never fight with emus*
> *Because emus never lose.*

Another one went:

> *When they sneeze,*
> *Emus choose*
> *To use*
> *Tissues.*

And then there was:

Emus do peruse
The news,
Sometimes alone,
Sometimes in twos.
But,
Asked what they think,
Emus just blink.
Emus rarely share their views.
They don't refuse.
They use a ruse,
Pretending to be quite confused.

On Wednesday afternoon, Tater and a couple of buddies arrived in a pickup with an empty cattle trailer attached to it. Tater was a small, slope-shouldered guy with sandy hair and a tight, unsmiling mouth. He barely thanked us for keeping his emus, and immediately started complaining about those stupid birds, what a trouble they were, worst deal he ever made. Some guy up in Culpeper County sold them to him as a breeding pair after convincing him that emu meat and emu eggs would be the next big thing, but this pair wouldn't breed or even lay eggs. He'd have barbecued them a long time ago, only he'd learned that the meat was gamier than hell—tasted like shoe leather—so all the damn birds did now was walk around scaring the cattle and shitting those big emu piles everywhere. Good for nothing but bear bait.

With Uncle Tinsley directing, Tater backed the trailer up to the pasture gate. We all trooped into the field, though Mom hung back, complaining that she wasn't wearing the right shoes. Besides, she didn't trust those emus—they could turn on us in an instant.

Liz had brought some bread along and tried luring the emus

into the trailer, but when they got near the ramp, they peered into the dark, confining interior, gave Liz one of their funny cross-eyed looks, and scurried off. We spent over an hour hollering and waving our arms, trying to shoo the emus toward the trailer. It didn't work. Whenever we got them close, the emus screamed and flapped their stunted little wings and dodged away. Once Tater managed to get a hand on Eugene's neck, but the bird kicked out with one of his huge taloned feet, and Tater had to jump back. "Goddamn birds," he said. "They're so stupid. I should just shoot them."

"They're not stupid," Liz told him. "They just don't want to do what you want them to do. And why would they?"

"Well, I hate the ugly buggers," he said.

"You hate them?" Liz asked. "I love them."

Tater stopped and looked at Liz. "You love them?" he asked. "You can have them."

"Oh my God," Liz said. And she actually fell to her knees and held her arms out. "Thank you. Thank you so much."

Tater looked at Liz like she was insane.

"Wait a minute," Uncle Tinsley said. "We can't just take these emus. Who's going to look after them?"

"Me," Liz said.

"I'll help," I said.

"Please," Liz said.

"We're talking about a serious long-term commitment here," Uncle Tinsley said.

"That's right," Mom said. "Anyway, we're not staying in Byler. We're moving. To the Catskills. Or wherever."

"We can't just leave these emus," Liz said.

Mom got a puzzled expression. "You're telling me you want to stay in Byler because you fell in love with a couple of big, disgusting birds that happened to walk up the driveway?"

"They need me. There's no one else to look after them."

"We don't belong here," Mom said.

"The emus don't belong here, either," Liz said, "but they're here." Mom started to say something and then stopped.

"We'll keep the darn birds," Uncle Tinsley told Tater. Then he looked at Liz. "But only if you go back to school."

"All right," Liz said. "I'll go back to school."

"What about you, Mom?" I asked. "What are you going to do?" I watched Mom. She studied the sun setting behind the distant blue mountains.

"I can't stay here," she finally said. "I just can't."

The next day, Liz went back to school and Mom packed to return to New York. Everything was going to turn out for the best, she said. When she got to New York, she would find a publisher for Liz's emu poetry. She was also going to find a rent-controlled apartment on the Upper West Side where we could all live real cheap, and then she would get us into one of those special public schools for gifted kids. She also talked about how maybe we could all spend the summer in the Catskills.

Everyone got up early the following morning. A thunderstorm had passed through right before daybreak and you could still smell the electricity in the clear, wet air. Mom put her suitcase in the trunk of the Dart and hugged us all. She was wearing her red velvet jacket. "The Tribe of Three," she said, "will be together again soon."

We watched as the Dart disappeared around the bend in the driveway.

"She's gone," Liz said.

CHAPTER FIFTY-ONE

When Liz returned to school, it had been a week since the trial, and I hoped the other kids would stop teasing her and move on to something else. They didn't completely, but Liz developed a way of dealing with it. She drifted through the hallways in her own world, as if no one else existed, and after school she played her guitar and worked late into the evening on her emu poetry. She also drew illustrations—emus reading newspapers, emus blowing their noses, emus playing saxophones.

Despite Mom's talk about finding a publisher, Liz was terrified to show her poetry to anyone except family. If someone criticized her writing, she'd be crushed—so I took it on myself to copy a bunch of the poems and slip them to Miss Jarvis, who sought out Liz and told her she had real talent. Liz started spending lunch hour in Miss Jarvis's classroom. A few of the other Byler High outsiders went there as well—Cecil Bailey, who was always talking about Elizabeth Taylor and sometimes got called a queer; Kenneth Daniels, who wore a cape and also wrote poetry; Claire Owens, an albino who said she saw auras around people; and Calvin Sweely, a guy with a head so big that, when his class was studying the solar system, some smart aleck nicknamed him Jupiterhead, and it stuck. No one at Miss Jarvis's lunch hour made fun of anyone else, and she encouraged them and praised their individuality. Liz had felt like such a scorned outsider at Byler that she hadn't realized the school had other outsiders as well. Discovering them was a real revelation.

CHAPTER FIFTY-TWO

I'd been so busy with Liz and the emus that I hadn't seen much of the Wyatts since the trial, but one April afternoon shortly after I turned thirteen, Liz and I came home from school to find Uncle Tinsley and Aunt Al sitting on the front porch.

"Big goings-on down at the mill," Uncle Tinsley said.

"Your Mr. Maddox went and got hisself fired," Aunt Al said.

"What?" Liz said like she couldn't believe what she was hearing. I punched her in the shoulder.

"Al here was an eyewitness," Uncle Tinsley said. "She walked all the way out here to tell you what happened."

"And a fine walk it was, too," Aunt Al said. The verdict acquitting Maddox had really gone to his head, she explained. Wayne Clemmons had left the county the day after testifying, and people were saying Maddox had gotten to him one way or another—bribed him or threatened him. Some even believed that Maddox had attacked Liz in the taxi because he knew that he'd be able to turn Wayne into a witness on his behalf.

Anyway, once the trial was over, Maddox became convinced he could get away with anything, could do whatever he wanted to anyone he wanted, both on the mill floor and around town. He had been a pushy son of a gun before the trial, Aunt Al said, but after he was acquitted, he went completely out of control, cursing and shoving the men and groping the bosoms and bottoms of the women. He caught one girl eating an egg-salad sandwich at her loom when it wasn't lunchtime, and he smashed the sandwich in her face. That was when the slowdowns started. The workers had just had more than they could take from Maddox, and they were going to do whatever they could get away with to cause trouble for him. Thread got tangled. Looms and spindles started breaking, and repairs took forever. Lights went out. Toilets got clogged, and drains backed up.

The mill owners expected the foremen to get results, whatever that took, and if one of them didn't, it was his fault. The owners didn't want excuses. Maddox began riding the workers harder, and they fought back with even more slowdowns.

It started to get to Maddox, Aunt Al went on, and last night he plumb lost it. He got into an argument with Julius Johnson, a beefy black man who was Vanessa's uncle, over Julius taking a long bathroom break. Maddox started yelling at Julius, poking him in the chest. There had been a rumor that Maddox hit on Leticia, the cheerleader—though the coloreds kept those things to themselves, Aunt Al added—and that may have been on Julius's mind. Anyway, Julius, who was almost as big as Maddox, grabbed his hand and told Maddox not to be poking on him, he needed to start showing people a little respect. Maddox slapped Julius across the face, right there in front of the whole shift. That sure brought the place to a halt, but before anyone could even say boo, Julius tackled Maddox, and those two big fellows ended up down on the shop floor trading punches until the security guard pulled them apart.

"Both Maddox and Julius was fired," Aunt Al said. Julius had become an instant hero among the black folk of Byler, and Samuel Morton of Morton Brothers Funeral Home, which serviced the coloreds, had already offered him a job. People were also saying that the mill owners were actually glad to see Maddox go. He'd become more trouble than he was worth.

Aunt Al reached over and tapped Liz on the arm. "If some skinny white girl was willing to stand up to Jerry Maddox," she said, "I reckon Julius Johnson figured he couldn't do any less."

CHAPTER FIFTY-THREE

We fed the emus when we got home from school, with chicken feed Uncle Tinsley bought on the cheap from Mr. Muncie. It got to the point where as soon as they saw us, they'd come running up to the fence, Eugene leading the way and Eunice following, her gimp leg swinging to the side with each step.

I loved those ugly overgrown chickens, but not the way Liz did. She positively doted on them. She brought them treats like cookies and broccoli. She followed them around the field, studying their behavior. Eugene would let her get close enough to stroke him, and he even ate out of her hand, but Eunice was more skittish and didn't want to be touched, ducking away and running off whenever Liz reached out, so Liz left her food on the ground. The emus were her responsibility, she kept saying, she was their protector, and she constantly worried about them. A bobcat might attack them, some boys might shoot them for kicks, they might get loose and end up as roadkill.

One afternoon a couple of weeks after Maddox got the boot, we went up to the pasture to find the gate open and the emus gone. We ran back to the house and Uncle Tinsley told us that a crew from the power company had come through that morning trimming branches back from the wires, and they must have forgotten to close the gate. Liz was so upset, she was shaking. We piled into the Woody and drove around, finally spotting the emus in a hay field beside a country road a mile from Mayfield.

The hay field, which was owned by Mr. Muncie, had barbed-wire fencing and an open gate. Liz got out and shut the gate, so the emus were safe for the moment, but none of us knew how to get them home. We'd been able to herd the emus into the big pasture at Mayfield, but they'd been only a few feet from the gate. There was no way we could herd them along the road all the way back to Mayfield. Or transport them. Even with Tater and his crew, we couldn't get the emus into that cattle trailer. Liz was practically hysterical.

"We need to rope those birds," Uncle Tinsley said.

That night he called Bud Hawkins, a farrier down the road who owned a rodeo horse, to see if he could try lassoing the emus, and Bud said he'd meet us at the hay field the following afternoon. Uncle Tinsley told us to recruit some friends as well. The more hands, the better. The next day at school, I told Joe, who said he'd round up a few buddies. Liz invited her new lunchtime friends, but we didn't know how many we could count on.

When we pulled up to the hay field in the Woody that afternoon, Bud Hawkins was already there, leading a sturdy bay horse off his trailer. The emus were on the other side of the field, watching suspiciously. While Bud was saddling up his horse, a green Rambler drove up and Miss Jarvis got out along with a few of the outsiders, including Kenneth Daniels in his black cape. A couple of minutes later, Aunt Al arrived in a pickup she must have borrowed, with Earl beside her and Joe and his buddies in the bay. Then came the powder-blue Cadillac with Ruth, Vanessa, Leticia, and a couple of the black athletes, including Tower.

With everyone watching, Liz walked over toward Eugene, carrying a bowl of feed and a big, soft piece of rope with a loop in it. She placed the bowl on the ground, and when Eugene started pecking at the feed, she slipped the loop up past his head and around his neck. Joe brought Earl over, and the boy reached out and stroked Eugene's neck.

Meanwhile, Bud trotted his horse toward Eunice. When she took off, he galloped after her, swinging the lariat over his head. Some of the kids were running around trying to help, Kenneth waving his black cape, Tower holding out his long arms, Ruth and Leticia clapping and rooting them on.

Despite her bad leg, Eunice could really cover ground, darting to the side every time Bud threw the lariat. After almost an hour of chasing after her, he trotted back to the fence. His shirt was soaked with sweat, and his horse's chest was covered with lather. "The good news is, the bird's starting to get wore out," he said. "The bad news is, we're completely wore out."

Uncle Tinsley had been leaning against the Woody watching, but now he took charge, telling everyone to go into the field and gather behind Eunice, then form a long line, arms extended. Liz led Eugene through the gate and onto the road. With the kids in the line behind her touching fingertips, Eunice had nowhere to go but forward. She cautiously followed Eugene.

It was all going pretty well until we got to the corner of Mr. Muncie's hay field, where the fence line stopped. That was when Eunice panicked and hurled herself at the barbed-wire fence, trying to get back to the safety of the hay field. She squeezed through but tore a bloody raw spot on her back. When Eugene realized that Eunice had taken off, he panicked as well, lurching and hissing so wildly that Liz pulled the rope off, and, just like Eunice, he scrambled through the fence, skinning his back.

I felt like kicking a rock. After more than an hour of work, we were worse off than when we started. The birds were back in the same darned field, and now they were all dinged up. The strange thing was, while Liz and I were really upset, everyone else seemed to be having the time of their lives. Uncle Tinsley was beaming and slapping people on the back, congratulating them on great team-work, while the kids were hooting and bonking each other and doing head-bobbing, elbow-flapping emu imitations as we all walked back to the cars in the late-afternoon light.

CHAPTER FIFTY-FOUR

Now that the weather was warmer, I had gotten into the habit of biking over to the Wyatts' house on Saturdays to say hello and tuck into a plate of Aunt Al's eggs fried in bacon fat. Liz usually rode out to check on the emus, Mr. Muncie having said it was fine to keep them in his hay field until we figured out how to get them back. After the failed roundup, Liz decided we wouldn't be able to capture the emus—we couldn't outrun them or outsmart them. All we could do was befriend them and try to win their trust, and that was what Liz had started working on.

One Saturday in early May, I walked into the Wyatts' kitchen to find Aunt Al sitting at the table next to Earl, writing a letter. She'd just heard from Truman, she told me. Though he'd tried hard to be optimistic, he said, he had to admit that despite the best efforts of the U.S. military, the war wasn't going the way the generals said it was going. The Americans were trying to turn the war over to the Vietnamese, but the Vietnamese didn't seem to want it, and drugs had become a serious problem on the base. Truman and his girl-friend, Kim-An, who'd been teaching Vietnamese to servicemen at the base, were seriously talking marriage. But Kim-An was worried about her family, since her father also worked for the Americans, and she wanted to know whether, if she and Truman did marry, she could bring her parents and her sister to the States.

"Clarence ain't none too keen on the idea," Aunt Al said, "and I always assumed Truman would marry one of our Byler girls. But I'm telling him that if he does bring this Kim-An back home, I'll move heaven and earth to help get her family over here, because ain't nothing more important than family." She folded the letter and put it in an envelope. "How about some eggs?"

As I was mopping up the drippings with toast, Joe came into the kitchen. "I'm going to the dump," he said to me. "Want to come?" All kinds of neat stuff got left at the dump, and Joe liked to see if he could fix things other people had thrown out. He would find a broken lawn mower or record player or sewing machine, bring it home, take it apart, and put it back together. Sometimes he could even get it to work.

The dump was on the far side of the river, and we walked across the clanking bridge, Dog trotting along behind us. It was a bright but windy spring day, the big flat-bottomed clouds sailing by overhead.

"What do you think about the news from Truman?" I asked.

"About the war or about the Vietnamese girlfriend?"

"Both."

"Truman's real smart," Joe said. "You never win betting against Truman. If he says the war's going bad, then the war's going bad, I don't care what my pa says."

We had come to the far side of the bridge. "Does that mean you're not enlisting?" I asked.

"Don't mean that at all." Joe picked up a flat rock and skipped it across the river. "You don't stop fighting just because you start losing. Truman taught me that." He turned around. "If Truman gets out in one piece," he said, "and he wants to bring that girl and her family with him, well, I never figured I'd have slant-eyes for kin, but those

Oriental women can be right pretty. Roger Bramwell over in Floyd County came back from the service married to a Filipino gal. They got real cute kids."

The dump was surrounded by a chain-link fence and sheets of corrugated tin, with clumps of wild daylilies flowering all happy and orange on the other side. People left appliances and machinery—just about everything potentially salvageable—to the left of the gate and we spent most of the afternoon rummaging through boxes full of broken old stuff, examining eggbeaters, testing typewriters, and spinning the dials on old radios. Dog had a field day chewing on chicken bones and chasing rats. Joe found a neat wind-up clock he thought he could fix, and he brought it with him when we left at the end of the afternoon.

We walked back across the bridge and along Holladay Avenue, Dog at our heels. After passing the courthouse, we turned down a block lined with old buildings and crepe myrtle, crossed the railroad tracks, then took a shortcut through a cobblestone alley between the drugstore and the insurance agency. Behind the drugstore was a small parking area with a wooden staircase leading up to the building's second floor. At the bottom of the stairs, parked next to a metal trash can, was Maddox's Le Mans.

I hadn't seen Maddox since the trial, but I knew I was going to run into him sooner or later, and I dreaded it. There was no sign of him, however, or of anyone else, for that matter. As we came up to the Le Mans, Dog trotted ahead, stopped, lifted his leg, and started peeing on one of the whitewall tires. It was almost like he knew who owned the car. Joe burst out laughing, and so did I. It was just about the funniest thing I'd ever seen in my life.

All of a sudden, the door at the top of the stairs flew open and

Maddox came charging down, bellowing with rage about how dare that damn mutt take a piss on his car, it was vandalism, as bad as the tire-slashing we little delinquents did, and this time he'd caught us red-handed.

Maddox reached down and grabbed Dog by the scruff of the neck, popped the trunk of the Le Mans, and threw Dog in.

"Don't you hurt Dog," I said. "You hurt everything. You hurt my sister and you know it."

"Jury didn't see it that way," he said. "Anyway, I've had enough of you, so shut up. This dog's a menace, running around without a leash." He opened the door of the Le Mans and flipped the seat forward. "Now, you two get in the back," he said. "We're going to see your folks."

Joe and I looked at each other. I'll admit I was pretty scared, but we couldn't just let Maddox drive off with Dog. Joe threw the clock in the trash can, and we climbed into the car.

No one said anything on the drive through town. I stared at the back of Maddox's thick neck, just like I had during the trial, and listened to Dog's muffled barking from inside the trunk. I couldn't believe it. I'd thought we were finished with Maddox, but now it seemed like the whole business was starting up again. Winning in court wasn't enough. He'd always be after us. This feud would go on forever.

Maddox pulled to a stop in front of the Wyatts' house. Dusk was approaching and the lights were on. Maddox opened the glove compartment, pulled out a blunt-nosed revolver, and shoved it in the pocket of that hooded black sweatshirt he sometimes wore. Then he got out and popped the trunk again, grabbed Dog by the scruff of the neck, and held him at arm's length as he marched into the house without bothering to knock. Joe and I followed. Aunt Al was at the kitchen table, cutting the ends off asparagus stalks.

"Call your husband," Maddox said.

Aunt Al looked at Maddox and Dog and then at Joe and me. "What's going on?"

"I said call your husband."

Aunt Al stood up, moving slowly, like she was buying time while she decided what to do. Before she could say anything, Uncle Clarence appeared in the doorway.

"You got a gun, Clarence?" Maddox asked.

"Why you asking?" Uncle Clarence said.

"Because we need to put this dog down. He's out of control. He's a danger."

"Did he attack someone?" Aunt Al asked.

"All he did was pee on Mr. Maddox's car," I said. "On the tire."

"That's all?" Aunt Al said. "That's what dogs do."

"Damaged my personal property, is what he did," Maddox said. "He's got to go down. I'm not here to discuss it. I'm here to see this dog put down."

"You're not the boss anymore," Uncle Clarence said.

"But I can still kick your ass. You don't got a gun, Clarence, I got my revolver."

"I got a gun," Uncle Clarence said.

"Go get it," Maddox said. "Bring it out back."

Dog had been growling and squirming in Maddox's hand the whole time. Maddox barged through the living room and out the back door into the little yard between the house and the woods. Uncle Clarence disappeared and came back a moment later, carrying a rifle.

"Dad, you can't kill Dog," Joe said.

Uncle Clarence ignored him. "You all stay in here," he said, and went through the back door after Maddox.

We all stood there paralyzed. I was half in shock. I knew Uncle

Clarence hadn't wanted Joe to get Dog, but I couldn't believe he'd shoot the little guy. I looked over at Joe. He said nothing, but his face was ash-colored.

We heard an incredibly loud shot that echoed up in the hills behind the house.

And then Dog started barking. We ran to the back door. The sun had set, but in the fading light, we could see Uncle Clarence standing there with the rifle in his hands. Maddox was lying faceup in Uncle Clarence's freshly planted vegetable garden. His leg was twisted awkwardly to the side, and I could tell he was dead.

"Good Lord, Clarence," Aunt Al said.

"Thought he was a bear," Uncle Clarence said. "Heard a noise out back and went to investigate. You all were inside. You didn't see nothing."

He looked down at his rifle. "Thought he was a bear," he said again.

CHAPTER FIFTY-FIVE

And that was what Uncle Clarence told the policemen who came to the house. Thought he was a bear. It was dark. Maddox was big as a bear and was wearing that black sweatshirt. When the police asked Uncle Clarence what Maddox had been doing in the backyard, Uncle Clarence said he didn't know because he hadn't asked him because he thought he was a bear.

Aunt Al, who had Earl in her lap, said we'd all been inside and hadn't seen anything. Joe and I nodded in agreement. No one mentioned the business about Dog. The police roped off the backyard, sent for an ambulance to pick up the body, and brought Uncle Clarence down to the station for questioning. Aunt Al called Uncle Tinsley to come and get me. When he arrived, she briefly told him the same story we told the police. Uncle Tinsley listened quietly. "I see," he said.

We were both silent most of the way home, then Uncle Tinsley finally said, "Thought he was a bear, did he?"

"Yep," I said.

Uncle Tinsley had his eyes on the road. "Well, that's an explanation people around here can live with," he said. "I know I can."

We drove a little farther in silence, and then he looked over at me. "You seem to be holding up pretty well," he said. "You feeling okay?"

"Yep," I said.

I'd never seen a dead person before. I thought it might be upsetting, but it just wasn't. Maddox getting killed didn't make me what I would call happy, even though I'd wanted to kill him myself. Maybe I was numb. What I did feel was extremely focused, like I was going through a tunnel and couldn't afford to look to either side, but instead had to pay complete attention to what was in front of me and keep moving forward.

Uncle Tinsley rolled down his window and took a deep breath. "Smell that honeysuckle," he said.

By the time we got home, the moon was out, skinny and silver. The porch lights were on, and Liz was standing at the top of the steps waiting for us.

"What happened?" she called out.

"Maddox is dead!" I shouted.

Uncle Tinsley and I climbed the front steps. "It was getting dark, and Clarence Wyatt heard a noise behind the house," Uncle Tinsley said. "He says he thought it was a bear and shot it. Turned out to be Maddox."

Liz stared at us a moment. "I feel dizzy," she said. "I feel sick. I need to lie down."

She ran into the house. I followed her up to the second floor and down the hall to the bird wing. She threw herself on the bed, but after a moment, she sat up and started rocking back and forth.

"Uncle Clarence didn't think Maddox was a bear," Liz said. "What really happened?"

I sat down next to her and started explaining, and Liz burst into tears. "It's okay," I said.

"No, it's not," Liz sobbed. "What about Doris and the kids? What about that new baby?"

"He had money and all those houses he rented out," I said. "She's better off without him."

"But those kids don't have a dad anymore."

"We don't have a dad," I said. "We got by."

"No, we didn't. Look at what's happened. And it's all my fault."

Liz's sobs got even louder. She was working herself into a state, heaving and gasping for air, and I worried that she might have a complete breakdown and maybe take sleeping pills again or do something just as bad. Then she started shaking her head and going on about how she'd killed Maddox, killed Maddox, killed the mad ox, willed it, killed it, she made the mad ox die, she made the bad bear lie, trapped in a dark box, the mad ox, the bad bear, the bad ox, the mad bear, the dark box, the big trap, the backseat, the black car—she made it halt, and it was all her fault, all her fault, all her fault.

"It's not your fault," I said. "He started it all. But now it's over." I began stroking her hair and repeating, "It's not your fault. It's over, it's all over," and after a while she stopped crying and nodded off.

I sat with her, listening to her even breathing, then got up to turn off the light and leave when Liz suddenly said, "Beware the bear."

I looked back down at her. Liz was talking in her sleep.

CHAPTER FIFTY-SIX

Truth be told, I worried that it might not be over. What if someone had seen us getting into Maddox's car in the alley? What if a neighbor on the hill had seen the three of us drive up? At the very least, the police must wonder what the heck Maddox was doing in the Wyatts' backyard.

The next day was Sunday. When I woke up, morning light filled the bedroom, and the birds outside our window were making their usual racket. Next to me, Liz was sleeping right through it, and I took that as a good sign. Downstairs, Uncle Tinsley was dressed in a seersucker suit and a striped tie. He said he'd decided to go into town and, as he put it, show his face and take the pulse of the people. And the places to do that were the Baptist church and the Bulldog Diner.

Liz woke up a little while later and she seemed better, but she still looked pale and fragile. She spent the morning playing the guitar while I worked in the garden, weeding around the irises and thinking about my sister. Liz deserved a medal for what she'd gone through, I told myself.

I put down the trowel and went up to the bird wing, where I took my dad's Silver Star out of the cigar box in the cradle. I had never actually put it on. I felt you had to earn the right to do that. Liz certainly had, not just for everything she'd gone through but for protecting her kid sister from their mother's wackiness until I was old enough to handle it. So had Uncle Clarence, not just for shooting Maddox but for taking on the work of a man when he was only a boy so that my dad would have a home. So had Aunt Al, for breathing in lint every night at the mill and then going home to care for her sick husband and her special little Earl. So had Uncle Tinsley, for taking in his two wayward nieces, and Mom, for coming back to a place she hated, to be there for Liz. All I'd done was get into a fight with Lisa Saunders and backtalk Miss Clay.

I took the Silver Star downstairs. Liz was sitting on the piano bench with her guitar.

"This is for you," I said, and held out the medal. "You deserve it."

Liz put down the guitar and took the medal. She looked at it for a minute. "I can't take this," she said. "It was your dad's." She handed it back. "But I'll never forget that you wanted to give it to me."

Uncle Tinsley returned after lunch. We followed him into the living room, where he sat down in the brocade wing chair and loosened his tie.

Everyone in Byler knew about the shooting, of course, he told us. That was all anyone was talking about. What no one could figure out was what Maddox had been doing behind the Wyatt house. The police had asked Doris. She didn't know, but she was demanding an investigation. They'd also talked to the Wyatts' neighbors, but people on the mill hill hated Maddox and didn't much like the cops, either. So no one saw anything and no one heard anything—except the gunshot. Everyone heard that.

The town was full of speculation. Maddox couldn't have been

up to any good. People suspected it had something to do with the feud. Was he just lurking? Spying on the family? Maybe he was planning an ambush. But if that was what he was up to, why was his car parked out front? Still, he had that revolver on him. At the very least, he was trespassing, and a man had the right to protect his family and his property. That was why, after questioning Uncle Clarence, the police hadn't arrested him. His story was simple and made sense. People in these parts were always getting into hunting accidents. Over in the next county, some bird-watcher from up north who was wearing a white shirt was killed on opening day of deer season.

And Maddox was a troublemaker even for the police, filing lawsuits and complaints, evicting tenants, riding the men at the mill, and putting moves on women all over town. The cops knew that just about everyone in Byler except Doris was glad Maddox was gone, and so, despite a few unanswered questions, they were more than willing to shrug the whole thing off.

"Accidents happen." Uncle Tinsley held up his hands. " 'Thought he was a bear.' "

He sat in the wing chair for a minute, then he said, "I believe I'll play the piano."

He opened the French doors in the ballroom and took the green velvet cover off the grand piano. He propped up the lid, sat down on the bench, ran his hands over the keys, hit a few chords, and then started playing some classical stuff. It sounded pretty good for classical stuff, even to someone tone-deaf like me, and Liz and I listened for a little while. Then she said, "We need to go get the emus."

Uncle Tinsley was still playing when we left the house. We got ropes from the barn and walked along the road to the hay field. It was near feeding time, and the emus were standing at the gate waiting for us, like they usually did.

After three weeks of trying, Liz had finally gotten Eunice to eat out of the bowl while she held it. It had taken another week for Eunice to let Liz stroke her back while she was eating. That afternoon, as Eunice pecked away, Liz stroked her with the rope, getting her used to it, then slipped it around her neck. Eunice paused, gave Liz a puzzled look, then went back to eating. I quickly put my rope over Eugene.

Liz and I both knew this whole emu-rescue business could turn out to be a big waste of time. Or worse. Now that we'd caught them, the emus might kick us with their talons or peck out our eyes or run into the road and cause a traffic accident. And once we got them back to Mayfield, those darned emus might just escape again. Even so, they were in our care now and we were doing what we had to do.

We led the emus out onto the road. They were a little frantic at first, but then they seemed to find something almost calming about the rope, like it was a relief to give up the fight. Eugene and I were in the lead. He was actually ahead of me, pulling on the rope as if he knew where we were going and wanted to get there. Every now and then a car passed and the driver slowed and the kids inside rolled down the windows and waved wildly at the sight of Liz and me bringing those big crazy birds back home.

ACKNOWLEDGMENTS

A number of books provided useful background information, including *Hard Times Cotton Mill Girls* by Victoria Byerly, *Mighty Giants: An American Chestnut Anthology*, and *Remarkable Trees of Virginia* by Nancy Ross Hugo and Jeff Kirwan.

I'd like to thank Laurie Taylor Rice, an extraordinary woman who happens to be my sister-in-law, friend, and trusted first reader. My gratitude also goes to her husband, Joel Rice, a great guy whose family owned a mill and who generously shared his mill-town memories with me.

My deep thanks and admiration to V. R. "Shack" Shackelford, the quintessential country lawyer, for confirming points of legal procedure, and Thomas C. "Bucky" Waddy, who shared his law enforcement expertise. Cheryl Jarvis brought music and so much more into my life. Adrianna Cowan-Waddy, Cathy Inskeep Marco, and Mike and Betty Long have all made this displaced West Virginian feel truly at home.

My magnificent editor, Nan Graham, lavished all her passion and intelligence on these pages. Brian Belfiglio gave wise counsel. Jennifer Rudolph Walsh is a dear friend, an amazing advocate, and a superb agent.

Thanks to my brother, Brian, who is my North Star.

And of course, John, who helps me shine light on dark places.

ABOUT THE AUTHOR

Jeannette Walls was born in Phoenix, Arizona, and grew up in the Southwest and Welch, West Virginia. She graduated from Barnard College and was a journalist in New York City. Her memoir, *The Glass Castle,* is one of the bestselling memoirs of all time and has been translated into thirty languages. She is the author of a novel, *Half Broke Horses,* named one of the ten best books of 2009 by the editors of *The New York Times Book Review.* Walls lives in rural Virginia with her husband, the writer John Taylor.

A Guide for Reading Groups

1. It takes a certain amount of courage for two young girls to make their way cross-country from California to Virginia without their mother. Why are Liz and Bean able to take on such a journey?

2. Discuss Bean and Liz's mother. What do her disappearances say about her ability to raise her children?

3. At the Byler Independence Day parade, Bean says, "Mom . . . had been telling us for years about everything wrong with America—the war, the pollution, the discrimination, the violence—but here were all these people, including Uncle Clarence, showing real pride in the flag and the country. Who was right?" (pg 86). This idea of opposing cultural viewpoints comes up numerous times during the girls' stay in Virginia. How do Liz and Bean's views differ from the more provincial townsfolk of Byler? Do the sisters stop seeing eye to eye? Is there a "right" way to look at things, or is much of opinion and belief based on context?

4. Can we trust Bean's assessment of Jerry Maddox? Is there some truth to Maddox's later accusation that Liz and Bean are wont to make up fantasies in a big game of "What's Their Story?"

5. A number of adults advise Bean against seeing a lawyer after

Maddox assaults Liz. What does this say about the adults of Byler? Are there ever grounds to let injustice stand? Would Liz and Bean have been better off forgetting the ordeal, or were they right to challenge Maddox's abuse of power?

6. Discuss the Wyatt family and their involvement in the Holladays' lives. What do Aunt Al, cousins Joe and Ruth, and Uncle Clarence offer Bean that she might not otherwise have? Consider especially Bean and Joe's tire outing, as well as Clarence's handling of Maddox's demands at the house.

7. After Bean's English class reads *To Kill a Mockingbird*, she notes, "For all of Miss Jarvis's singing its praises as great literature, a lot of the kids in the class had real problems with the book . . . (pg. 151). How do the students' reactions reflect the racial tensions in Byler?

8. What changes do you see in Bean over the course of the story? Does she take Liz's place as the strong, centered Holladay sister?

9. After Maddox is cleared of all charges, Bean says, "I felt completely confused, like the world had turned upside down, and we were living in a place where the guilty were innocent and the innocent were guilty. How are you supposed to behave in a world like that?" (pg 229). What do you think Bean and Liz learned about the adult world from the trial? How does one behave in a place where terrible things are allowed to happen without reprisal?

10. What do you think the emus represent for Liz?

11. When Bean starts waving at strangers, Liz notes, "You've gone native." (pg 60). Have the girls become true Byler residents by the end of the novel? Is there still a bit of California in them? Or a bit of their mother?

12 Is there justice in the way Maddox is ultimately dealt with?

Turn the page for an extract from
Half Broke Horses
Jeannette Wall's debut novel

PB ISBN: 978-1-84739-831-4

THOSE OLD COWS KNEW trouble was coming before we did.

It was late on an August afternoon, the air hot and heavy like it usually was in the rainy season. Earlier we'd seen some thunderheads near the Burnt Spring Hills, but they'd passed way up to the north. I'd mostly finished my chores for the day and was heading down to the pasture with my brother, Buster, and my sister, Helen, to bring the cows in for their milking. But when we got there, those girls were acting all bothered. Instead of milling around at the gate, like they usually did at milking time, they were standing stiff-legged and straight-tailed, twitching their heads around, listening.

Buster and Helen looked up at me, and without a word, I knelt down and pressed my ear to the hard-packed dirt. There was a rumbling, so faint and low that you felt it more than you heard it. Then I knew what the cows knew—a flash flood was coming.

As I stood up, the cows bolted, heading for the southern fence line, and when they reached the barbed wire, they jumped over it—higher and cleaner than I'd ever seen cows jump—and then they thundered off toward higher ground.

I figured we best bolt, too, so I grabbed Helen and Buster by the hand. By then I could feel the ground rumbling through my shoes. I saw the first water sluicing through the lowest part of the pasture, and I knew we didn't have time to make it to higher ground ourselves. In the middle of the field was an old cottonwood tree, broad-branched and gnarled, and we ran for that.

Helen stumbled, so Buster grabbed her other hand, and we lifted her off the ground and carried her between us as we ran. When we reached the cottonwood, I pushed Buster up to the lowest branch, and he pulled Helen into the tree behind him. I shimmied up and wrapped my arms around Helen just as a wall of water, about six feet high and pushing rocks and tree limbs in front of it, slammed into the cottonwood, dousing all three of us. The tree shuddered and bent over so far that you could hear wood cracking, and some lower branches were torn off. I feared it might be uprooted, but the cottonwood held fast and so did we, our arms locked as a great rush of caramel-colored water, filled with bits of wood and the occasional matted gopher and tangle of snakes, surged beneath us, spreading out across the lowland and seeking its level.

We just sat there in that cottonwood tree watching for about an hour. The sun started to set over the Burnt Spring Hills, turning the high clouds crimson and sending long purple shadows eastward. The water was still flowing beneath us, and Helen said her arms were getting tired. She was only seven and was afraid she couldn't hold on much longer.

Buster, who was nine, was perched up in the big fork of the tree. I was ten, the oldest, and I took charge, telling Buster to trade places with Helen so she could sit upright without having to cling too hard. A little while later, it got dark, but a bright moon came out and we could see just fine. From time to time we all switched places so no one's arms would wear out. The bark was chafing my thighs, and Helen's, too, and when we needed to pee, we had to just wet ourselves. About halfway through the night, Helen's voice started getting weak.

"I can't hold on any longer," she said.

"Yes, you can," I told her. "You can because you have to." We were going to make it, I told them. I knew we would make it because I could see it in my mind. I could see us walking up the hill to the house tomorrow morning, and I could see Mom and Dad running out. It would happen—but it was up to us to make it happen.

To keep Helen and Buster from drifting off to sleep and falling out of the cottonwood, I grilled them on their multiplication tables. When we'd run through those, I went on to presidents and state capitals, then word definitions, word rhymes, and whatever else I could come up with, snapping at them if their voices faltered, and that was how I kept Helen and Buster awake through the night.

By first light, you could see that the water still covered the ground. In most places, a flash flood drained away after a couple of hours, but the pasture was in bottomland near the river, and sometimes the water remained for days. But it had stopped moving and had begun seeping down through the sinkholes and mudflats.

"We made it," I said.

I figured it would be safe to wade through the water, so we

scrambled out of the cottonwood tree. We were so stiff from holding on all night that our joints could scarcely move, and the mud kept sucking at our shoes, but we got to dry land as the sun was coming up and climbed the hill to the house just the way I had seen it.

Dad was on the porch, pacing back and forth in that uneven stride he had on account of his gimp leg. When he saw us, he let out a yelp of delight and started hobbling down the steps toward us. Mom came running out of the house. She sank to her knees, clasped her hands in front of her, and started praying up to the heavens, thanking the Lord for delivering her children from the flood.

It was she who had saved us, she declared, by staying up all night praying. "You get down on your knees and thank your guardian angel," she said. "And you thank me, too."

Helen and Buster got down and started praying with Mom, but I just stood there looking at them. The way I saw it, I was the one who'd saved us all, not Mom and not some guardian angel. No one was up in that cottonwood tree except the three of us. Dad came alongside me and put his arm around my shoulders.

"There weren't no guardian angel, Dad," I said. I started explaining how I'd gotten us to the cottonwood tree in time, figuring out how to switch places when our arms got tired and keeping Buster and Helen awake through the long night by quizzing them.

Dad squeezed my shoulder. "Well, darling," he said, "maybe the angel was you."

WE HAD A HOMESTEAD on Salt Draw, which flowed into the Pecos River, in the rolling gritty grassland of west Texas. The sky was high and pale, the land low and washed out, gray and every color of sand. Sometimes the wind blew for days on end, but sometimes it was so still you could hear the dog barking on the Dingler ranch two miles upriver, and when a wagon came down the road, the dust it trailed hung in the air for a long time before drifting back to the ground.

When you looked out across the land, most everything you could see—the horizon, the river, the fence lines, the gullies, the scrub cedar—was spread out and flat, and the people, cattle, horses, lizards, and water all moved slowly, conserving themselves.

It was hard country. The ground was like rock—save for when a flood turned everything to mud—the animals were bony and tough, and even the plants were prickly and sparse, though from time to time the thunderstorms brought out startling bursts of wildflowers. Dad said High Lonesome, as the area was known, wasn't a place for the soft of head or the weak of heart, and he said that was why he and I made out just fine there, because we were both tough nuts.

Our homestead was only 160 acres, which was not a whole lot of land in that part of Texas, where it was so dry you needed at least five acres to raise a single head of cattle. But our spread bordered the draw, so it was ten times more valuable than land without water, and we were able to keep the carriage horses Dad trained, the milking cows, dozens of chickens, some hogs, and the peacocks.

The peacocks were one of Dad's moneymaking schemes that didn't quite pan out. Dad had paid a lot of money to import breeding peacocks from a farm back east. He was convinced that peacocks were a sure-fire sign of elegance and style, and that folks who bought carriage horses from him would also be willing to shell out fifty bucks for one of those classy birds. He planned to sell only the male birds so we'd be the sole peacock breeders this side of the Pecos.

Unfortunately, Dad overestimated the demand for ornamental birds in west Texas—even among the carriage set—and within a few years, our ranch was overrun with peacocks. They strutted around screeching and squawking, pecking our knees, scaring the horses, killing chicks, and attacking the hogs, though I have to admit it was a glorious sight when, from time to time, those peacocks paused in their campaign of terror to spread their plumes and preen.

The peacocks were just a sideline. Dad's primary occupation was the carriage horses, breeding them and training them. He loved horses despite the accident. When Dad was a boy of three, he was running through the stable and a horse kicked him in the head, practically staving in his skull. Dad was in a coma for days, and no one thought he'd pull through. He eventually did, but the right side of his body had gone a little gimp. His right leg sort of dragged behind him, and his arm was cocked like a chicken wing. Also, when he was young, he'd spent long hours working in the noisy gristmill on his family's ranch, which made him hard of hearing. As such, he talked a little funny, and until you spent time around him, you had trouble understanding what he said.

Dad never blamed the horse for kicking him. All the horse knew, he liked to say, was that some creature about the size of a mountain lion was darting by his flanks. Horses were never wrong. They always did what they did for a reason, and it was up to you to figure it out. And even though it was a horse that almost stove in Dad's skull, he loved horses because, unlike people, they always understood him and never pitied him. So, even though Dad was unable to sit in a saddle on account of the accident, he became an expert at training carriage horses. If he couldn't ride them, he could drive them.

I WAS BORN IN a dugout on the banks of Salt Draw in 1901, the year after Dad got out of prison, where he'd been serving time on that trumped-up murder charge.

Dad had grown up on a ranch in the Hondo Valley in New Mexico. His pa, who'd homesteaded the land, was one of the first Anglos in the valley, arriving there in 1868, but by the time Dad was a young man, more settlers had moved into the area than the river could support, and there were constant arguments over property lines and, especially, water rights—people claiming their upstream neighbors were using more than their fair share of water, while downstream neighbors made the same claim against them. These disputes often led to brawls, lawsuits, and shootings. Dad's pa, Robert Casey, was murdered in one such dispute when Dad was fourteen. Dad stayed on to run the ranch with his ma, but those disputes kept erupting, and twenty years later, when a settler was killed after yet another argument, Dad was convicted of murdering him.

Dad insisted he'd been framed, writing long letters to legislators and newspaper editors protesting his innocence, and after serving three years in prison, he was set free. Shortly after he was released, he met and married my mom. The prosecutor was looking into retrying the case, and Dad thought that would be less likely if he made himself scarce, so he and my mom left the Hondo Valley for High Lonesome, where they claimed our land along Salt Draw.

Lots of the folks homesteading in High Lonesome lived in dugouts because timber was so scarce in that part of Texas. Dad had made our home by shoveling out what was more or less a big hole on the side of the riverbank, using cedar branches as rafters and covering them over with sod. The dugout had one room, a packed earth floor, a wooden door, a waxed-paper window, and a cast-iron stove with a flue that jutted up through the sod roof.

The best thing about living in the dugout was that it was cool in the summer and not too cold in the winter. The worst thing about it was that, from time to time, scorpions, lizards, snakes, gophers, centipedes, and moles wormed their way out of our walls and ceilings. Once, in the middle of an Easter dinner, a rattler dropped onto the table. Dad, who was carving the ham, brought the knife right down behind that snake's head.

Also, whenever it rained, the ceilings and walls in the dugout turned to mud. Sometimes clumps of that mud dropped from the ceiling and you had to pat it back in place. And every now and then, the goats grazing on the roof would stick a hoof clear through and we'd have to pull them out.

Another problem with living in the dugout was the mosquitoes. They were so thick that sometimes you felt like you were swimming through them. Mom was particularly susceptible to them—

her bite marks sometimes stayed swollen for days—but I was the one who came down with yellow jack fever.

I was seven at the time, and after the first day, I was writhing on the bed, shivering and vomiting. Mom was afraid that everyone else might catch the disease, so even though Dad insisted that you got it from mosquitoes, he rigged up a quilt to quarantine me off. Dad was the only one who was allowed behind it, and he sat with me for days, splashing me with spirit lotions, trying to bring the fever down. While I was delirious, I visited bright white places in another world and saw green and purple beasts that grew and shrank with every beat of my heart.

When the fever finally broke, I weighed some ten pounds less than I had before, and my skin was all yellow. Dad joked that my forehead had been so hot he almost burned his hand when he touched it. Mom poked her head behind the quilt to see me. "A fever that high can boil your brain and cause permanent damage," Mom said. "So don't ever tell anyone you had it. You do, you might have trouble catching a husband."

MOM WORRIED ABOUT THINGS like her daughters catching the right husband. She was concerned with what she called "proprieties." Mom had furnished our dugout with some real finery, including an Oriental rug, a chaise longue with a lace doily, velvet curtains that we hung on the walls to make it look like we had more windows, a silver serving set, and a carved walnut headboard that her parents had brought with them from back east when they moved to California. Mom treasured that headboard and said it was the only thing that allowed her to sleep at night because it reminded her of the civilized world.

Mom's father was a miner who had struck gold north of San Francisco and became fairly prosperous. Although her family lived in mining boom towns, Mom—whose maiden name was Daisy Mae Peacock—was raised in an atmosphere of gentility. She had soft white skin that was easily sunburned and bruised. When she was a child, her mother made her wear a linen mask if she had to spend any time in the sun, tying it to the yellow curls on the side of her face. In west Texas, Mom always wore a hat and gloves and a veil over her face when she went outdoors, which she did as seldom as possible.

Mom kept up the dugout, but she refused to do chores like toting water or carrying firewood. "Your mother's a lady," Dad would say by way of explaining her disdain for manual labor. Dad did most of the outdoor work with the help of our hand, Apache. Apache wasn't really an Indian, but he'd been captured by the Apaches when he was six, and they kept him until he was a young man, when the U.S. Cavalry—with Dad's pa serving as a scout—raided the camp and Apache ran out yelling, "*Soy blanco! Soy blanco!*"

Apache had gone home with Dad's pa and lived with the family ever since. By now Apache was an old man, with a white beard so long that he tucked it in his pants. Apache was a loner and sometimes spent hours staring at the horizon or the barn wall, and he'd also disappear into the range now and then for days at a time, but he always came back. Folks considered Apache a little peculiar, but that's what they also thought of Dad, and the two of them got along just fine.

To cook and wash, Mom had the help of our servant girl, Lupe, who had gotten pregnant and was forced to leave her village outside Juárez after the baby was born because she had brought shame on the family and no one would marry her. She was small and a little barrel-shaped and even more devoutly Catholic than Mom. Buster called her "Loopy," but I liked Lupe. Although her parents had taken her baby from her and she slept on a Navajo blanket on the dugout floor, Lupe never felt sorry for herself, and that was something I decided I admired most in people.

Even with Lupe helping her out, Mom didn't really care for life on Salt Draw. She hadn't bargained for it. Mom thought she'd married well when she took Adam Casey as her husband, despite his limp and speech impediment. Dad's pa had come over from Ireland during a potato blight, joined the Second Dragoons—one of the first cavalry units of the U.S. Army—where he served under Colonel Robert E. Lee, and was stationed on the Texas frontier, fighting Comanches, Apaches, and Kiowa. After leaving the army, he took up ranching, first in Texas, then in the Hondo Valley, and by the time he was killed, he had one of the biggest herds in the area.

Robert Casey was shot down as he walked along the main street of Lincoln, New Mexico. One version of the story held that he and the man who killed him had disagreed over an eight-dollar debt. The murderer's hanging was talked about for years in the valley because, once he'd been hanged, declared dead, cut down, and put in his pine box, people heard him moving around, so they took him out and strung him up again.

After Robert Casey's death, his children started arguing over how to split up the herd, which fostered bad blood that lasted for the rest of Dad's life. Dad inherited the Hondo Valley spread, but he felt his elder brother, who'd taken the herd to Texas, had cheated him out of his share, and he was constantly filing lawsuits and appeals. He continued the campaign even after moving to west Texas, and he was also battling away with the other ranchers in the Hondo Valley, traveling back to New Mexico to lodge an endless stream of claims and counterclaims.

One thing about Dad was that he had a terrible temper, and he usually returned from these trips trembling with rage. Part of it was his Irish blood, and part of it was his impatience with folks who had trouble understanding what he said. He felt those people thought he was a lamebrain and were always trying to cheat him, whether it was his brothers and their lawyers, traveling merchants, or half-breed-horse traders. He'd start sputtering and cursing, and from time to time, he'd become so incensed that he'd pull out his pistol and plug away at things, aiming to miss people—most of the time.

Once he got into an argument with a tinker who overcharged to repair the kettle. When the tinker started to mock the way he talked, Dad ran inside to get his guns, but Lupe had seen what was coming and hidden them in her Navajo blanket. Dad worked himself into a lather, hollering about his missing guns, but I was convinced Lupe saved that tinker's life. And probably Dad's as well, since if he'd killed the tinker, he might have ended up swinging, hanged like the man who'd shot his pa.